THE LISTENERS

THE LISTENERS

JORDAN TANNAHILL

HARPER**AVENUE**
an imprint of HarperCollins*Publishers*Ltd

Published by Harper Avenue, an imprint of HarperCollins Publishers Ltd

First edition

HarperCollins Publishers Ltd
Bay Adelaide Centre, East Tower
22 Adelaide Street West, 41st Floor
Toronto, Ontario, Canada
M5H 4E3

www.harpercollins.ca

Library and Archives Canada Cataloguing in Publication
Title: The listeners / Jordan Tannahill
Names: Tannahill, Jordan, author.
Identifiers: Canadiana (print) 20210173297 | Canadiana (ebook) 20210173300 |
ISBN 9781443465342 (hardcover) | ISBN 9781443464130 (softcover) |
ISBN 9781443464147 (ebook)
Classification: LCC PS8639.A577 L57 2021 | DDC C813/.6—dc23

Printed and bound in the United States of America

LSC/H 9 8 7 6 5 4 3 2 1

For James

THE LISTENERS

1

THE CHANCES ARE THAT YOU HAVE, AT SOME POINT, stumbled upon the viral meme of me screaming naked in front of a bank of news cameras; a moment of sheer abandon forever rendered as a GIF, pasted in comment threads and text messages the world over. The chances are that you have also seen the coverage of the tragic events that unfolded thereafter on Sequoia Crescent. And the chances are that you probably think of me as some brainwashed cultist, or conspiracy theorist. I wouldn't blame you for believing these things, or any of the other wildly sensationalized stories that have circulated in the days, weeks, and months since.

The truth is that I am a mother, and a wife, and a former high school English teacher who now teaches ESL night classes at the library near my house. I love my family fiercely. My daughter, Ashley, is the most important person in my life. You read about parents disowning their transgender sons, or refusing to speak to their daughters for marrying a Jew, or not marrying a Jew, and I think—well that's just barbarism. Faith is basically a mental illness if it makes you do something so divorced from your natural instincts as a parent. I remember holding Ashley when she was about forty-five seconds old, before she had even opened her eyes, when she was just this slimy little mole-thing, nearly a month premature, and I remember thinking I would literally commit murder for this creature. As I held her I imagined all of the joy and pleasure she would feel, all of the pain that I would not and could not protect her from, and it completely overwhelmed me. I imagined the men who would hurt her one day, and I imagined castrating them one by one with my bare hands. All of this before she was a minute old! So no, I have never understood how anyone could ever put any creed or ideology before their love of their child—and yet, this is precisely what Ashley accused me of doing in the year leading up to the events on Sequoia Crescent.

I have attempted to recreate the events in this book as faithfully as my subjective experience of them will allow. I wrote these words myself. I did not have a ghost writer. I did not write this book to cash in on whatever minor and temporary notoriety I might have accrued, or to somehow exonerate myself. I wrote it as a way of making sense of my circumstances.

I have always turned to books for this. I've been a voracious reader since I was a girl. I was raised by a single mother and a television. There were no books in our apartment growing up, so I would take out as many as I was allowed from the library, and sometimes a few more which weren't returned. I've always been drawn to stories of women pushed to the brink, living through extraordinary times, and enduring remarkable hardship. I have no time for stories about people mired in self-pity or self-destruction, who flounder around helplessly and hopelessly, I mean who cares, just get on with it. Even though my life really goes down the shitter in this one, I hope that you'll take me at my word when I say that I truly fought every second of the way, and I did not, and still do not, see myself as a victim. In fact, I'm sure many people see me as a villain in this story, but I try not to see myself as that either.

In high school, I was an aspiring essayist in the mould of Joan Didion. I had visions of postgraduate nomadism, smoking half a pack a day and driving my way across America, stumbling into the eye of the zeitgeist with my notebook and pen in hand. I used to wear a big army jacket with deep pockets stuffed with dog-eared copies of Rimbaud and Pound. All I wanted back then was to see my name in print. That was before I got pregnant at twenty-two, married Paul, and enrolled in teacher's college. I never harboured regrets, though. I enjoyed being a young mom. When Ashley was growing up, we used to finish each other's sentences. People would joke we were telepathic, and sometimes I half believed we were. I'd be thirsty and she'd bring me a glass of juice. Or I'd wake up knowing that she'd had a nightmare and walk into her bedroom before she even cried out for me.

All that to say, I never expected I would wind up writing a book after all these years, and certainly not under these circumstances. It just got to the point where I couldn't bear to hear another person's take on my story, another pundit or talk-show host weighing in on the events of Sequoia Crescent like they knew a damn thing about it, or making light of the tragedy for a late-night-show laugh. And trust me, I can take a joke. I'm sure I laughed harder than most of you at my frazzled hair and flopping boobs in that meme. But if you want to know the full truth, that requires digging deeper than an easy punchline.

The thing I still struggle to wrap my head around is how did something so small, so innocuous precipitate the complete unravelling of my life. How all of this soul-searching, transcendence, and devastation could begin with a low and barely perceptible sound.

Do you hear that?

I was lying beside Paul in bed. He was reading the *New York Times* on his tablet, and I was marking student essays on *Twelfth Night*.

Hear what? he asked, still reading his article.

I put the essay down on the comforter. It's like a—humming, I said. Paul looked up, and we both listened for a moment.

A humming?

Like a very low hum, I said. He frowned, shrugged, and returned to his tablet.

I don't hear it.

I picked up the essay and tried to get back into it. After a minute or so, Paul asked me if I enjoyed myself at dinner. I nodded, non-committally. The evening was supposed to be just another monthly meeting of my all-women's dystopia book club, but it turned into me cooking an overly involved tagine to celebrate Nadia's birthday—and then husbands were invited. Paul pointed out, rightly, that this was just my way. He was drafted into the role of sous-chef for the evening, bless him. The nine of us spent most of the dinner talking about Trump, and the Mueller report, which then mutated into an intense and wide-ranging discussion about ethics and faith which had half the table speaking animatedly, and the other half in silence.

Paul turned his head on the pillow, and said, You know, I wasn't totally comfortable with you calling us atheists.

It took me a moment to realize what he was talking about. I looked up from my essay. I'm sorry?

At dinner. You said we didn't believe in God.

What else could I've said? Tara asked me point-blank.

Well I would say that, maybe, I actually do, he replied. Paul held my gaze until I laughed.

Which god?

What do you mean—?

Like Jesus Christ?

Paul looked at me like I was an idiot. Yes, he said.

And his dad?

I studied Paul's face, wondering if this was all a set-up for one of his laboured jokes. He then told me that ever since his father died in the fall, he had found himself thinking about faith.

Well not just thinking about it, but—

But—?

Praying.

Praying? When?

In my head, in the car sometimes.

He told me that he found being back in the church for the funeral strangely comforting, and that it stirred something in him. He said he knew I would diminish it, which was exactly why he hadn't told me, and I said no, I wasn't diminishing it, as I tried to compose my face. He said that he'd been considering trying to find a church in our area that he could try visiting, even just once a month or something. That's when I figured this was probably a test and that he was baiting me, perhaps because he was still a bit drunk and wanted to square some argument from earlier in the evening, but I certainly wasn't going to bite. I just opened my eyes wide and nodded. He then reminded me, as if I need reminding, that Cass and Aldo are Evangelical.

So?

So, you were quite rude about it.

I wasn't.

Yes, you were. You were being forceful and dismissive.

Well I certainly didn't mean to be, and if Cass thought so, she can tell me herself tomorrow.

I was hoping that was the end of it, but I could tell it was still working on Paul as he lay there, staring up at the ceiling. For such a giant man, he could be like a little boy when he stewed on something.

I actually think I've buried this part of myself for years because of you, and now I—

Oh please.

—no I do, because of your atheism, but I think if left to my own devices my tendency might actually be towards faith.

Left to your own devices your tendency is also towards microwave dinners and *The Wire* on Netflix.

He turned his head towards me again and smiled, then reached over and gently pushed my face with his big paw.

If you want to start going to church, you can knock yourself out, I said. But leave me out of it.

I never suggested otherwise, he replied.

Paul knew better than to talk to me about God. I had invested twenty long years in un-fucking his head with that stuff. I'd seen what the church had done to people like his mother, and there was no way I was going to live a small, mean life under the thumb of the patriarchy. My feeling on the matter was: I had my shit together, I didn't need God. That's pretty much how I've felt since I was sixteen, when it suddenly struck me that God was no different than every other guy in my high school; he wasn't interested in me unless I was down on my knees.

Paul and I had actually done a pretty good job at synchronizing our belief systems for two people who were only together because one inseminated the other when they were both just a couple of years above the legal drinking age. When we met, I was a polyamorous riot grrl teaching English to Latin American refugees, and he was an unskilled labourer building the kind of tract housing we're living in now. He was a hulking six feet four. Shy and polite, who danced purposefully with his shoulders. Not the kind of guy who'd normally finger a young woman on public transit, or join her at migrants' rights protests. Acid, avocados, personal grooming, Tarkovsky—I kicked open a lot of doors for him, quickly. He was always a bit dazzled by how I carried myself socially; how I always seemed to be the linchpin in my group of friends. He once told me I made being important look like making a sandwich.

In those days, even his absence in the room could turn me on; his underwear on the floor, his sweat on the bedsheets, his smell on the pillow. We were full of the unreasonable happiness of a new couple. Sometimes I would be in the shower behind him and think, Remember what water looks like on his neck, with his thin gold chain and freckles, remember always, because maybe I knew these communal showers were a temporary thing, a chapter in our love, and they were, of course. But thankfully I did remember. I still remember what the water looked like on Paul's young neck.

Paul had a beauty that begged to be remarked upon on a regular basis, and to not do so, to treat his beauty as something I could take for granted, felt luxurious and extravagant. What's more, he had no idea he was beautiful, and no idea that I thought so, and I got an almost erogenous thrill at withholding those facts from him. I once told him he had a face like a cornflake—open and sunny, with dimples. This wasn't received with the spirit in which it was intended. He looked his best when frustrated or concentrating intently. Whenever he bit his lip, I thought of a little toy train I used to have as a girl. The train had a face on it, and I used to pull it around on a rope.

We'd been seeing each other about six months when the pregnancy happened. It was my decision to keep the baby, but we needed Paul's family's help, which came with the proviso that we get married. Paul was poor but secretly harboured dreams of being rich, whereas I was poor and secretly harboured dreams of being glamorously poor. Poor with taste. Jean Genet poor. Paul ended up starting his own contracting business when Ashley was twelve, and

it took off, and ever since then we've found ourselves in a totally
different stratum of life. But when you grow up with nothing, it
becomes a pathology. Paul teases me that I wear out my underwear
so much I need a belt for them. I'm perfectly content to repair a
snapped-off rear-view mirror with duct tape, or use a hair dryer
that sparks. I'm clumsy and break things all the time, which I
sometimes think is because I'm still not used to having many *things*,
things not made of plastic, things like delicate vases perched on
bookshelves and lamps on end tables.

I grew up urban poor, but Paul was a proper redneck, sharing
a bedroom in a plywood-floored bungalow with three brothers a
half-hour outside of Amarillo, where you could write your name
in dust on the windshield of a car if you left it un-driven for more
than three days; a gentle and earnest redneck who's happy to fall
asleep to a woman reading poetry to him. Everything about Paul
is oversized. Hands, ears, face, heart. If I had to describe him in
a word, it would be 'concerned.' Concerned about me, my happiness, if I'm too cold, too hot, too quiet, concerned about Ashley,
about her grades, her friends, her haircuts, concerned about the
future, our finances, global warming, concerned about what his
neighbours think of him, about his mother getting older, sick,
dying, his alcoholic brother, concerned about being good, being
right, being on time. I am decidedly unconcerned.

As Paul climbed out of bed and padded over to the ensuite to
pee, I picked the turgid essay back up, but before I could find my
place in it, I stopped. It was still there. I could still hear the sound.
It wasn't my imagination. There was a very low, reverberating tone,
only just perceptible below the echoing of Paul's urine in the toilet
bowl, the soft din of the air conditioning, and the muffled Face-
Time conversation coming from Ashley's room down the hall. It
was quite possible that the sound had been there all along and I
had just never noticed. But now that I had, it struck me as peculiar.

Paul flushed and walked back into the room. What's wrong? he asked.

I pointed into the air. It's still there, I said. He sighed and shook his head, but we both listened, this time for ten whole seconds, scanning the room with our eyes.

I don't hear anything, he said eventually.

It's almost like a vibration, I said.

Paul asked if I left the hood vent on in the kitchen. I couldn't rule it out. I groaned, peeled myself from bed, and pulled on the nightgown I'd left bunched on the floor. I trundled out into the hall, passed Ashley's room, and descended the stairs into the darkness of the ground floor, where a constellation of red and green LED lights signified security alarms, fire detectors, carbon monoxide detectors, Wi-Fi, thermostat controls, all of the systems animating the body of our house, unnoticed and unappreciated like breathing or circulation. I entered the kitchen and listened. The hood vent was off. The fridge sounded normal. But the hum was still there, just as loud as it had been in the bedroom.

I walked into the dining room, and again, the sound remained unchanged, which I found unnerving. I wondered if I was suffering from some sort of tinnitus. I raised my hands and pressed them over my ears, and the sound was dampened. It wasn't in my head. The sound was coming from somewhere. I stood in the dark beside the table, where the plates from dinner were still piled, abandoned until the sobriety of morning, and I began to turn my head slowly, hoping to detect some variation in volume or direction. I then began to pace around the room. The moment I felt certain the sound was coming from one direction, and moved towards it, it suddenly seemed like it was coming from directly the opposite direction, behind me. I wondered if it might be our neighbour Farhad working with a power tool in his garage; he's been known to mow his grass at ten o'clock at night. But that noise would have a clear direction. Whatever this was seemed completely diffuse.

Ashley? I called upstairs. I waited for a reply, then walked into the front hall, to the foot of the staircase. *Ashley?*

Yeah, she shouted down from her room.

Can you check—? Did someone leave the bathroom fan on up there?

There was a pause, and then the sound of her door opening. She appeared at the top of the stairs in plaid boxer shorts and a baggy white t-shirt, scratching her scalp through her post-gender haircut. Ashley once said her spirit animal was Sinéad O'Connor, circa ripping up the photo of the Pope on *Saturday Night Live*.

What? she asked.

The bathroom fan. Did you leave it on up there?

She disappeared for a moment and then returned, shaking her head. I described the sound to her. She listened for a moment, and then shook her head again. Guess I'm just losing my mind, I said, shrugging.

Perimenopause, she replied.

What?

It happens.

You're such a little wench. I'm forty.

Old wench.

Wench betch.

Feigned cruelty was our preferred mode of address. I can't remember how the wench thing began; just another inside joke that kept transmogrifying over the years. Other nicknames included Momma Wench, Momma Claire, Claire Danes, and Dame Wench. My top names for her included Ash Wednesday, Ashton Kutcher, and Ashscratcher. Paul joked only the NSA could decipher the encryption on our communication.

Ashley looked down and brushed her shoulders. Or maybe it's the solar storms, she said. Apparently they're the largest ever. Did you hear about this?

No.

They're going to mess with our electronics, and some scientists said maybe even with our moods and basic cognitive functions, so . . . She widened her eyes and then slipped from view, like an imp returning to her bottle.

I wandered back into the dining room. There was something about the noise that seemed almost atmospheric. I looked up at the vent in the ceiling, walked over to the thermostat and turned off the air conditioner, but the hum persisted, all the more clearly. It occurred to me that it could be a vibration in the walls, or in the foundations of the house, perhaps from a micro-tremor. We've been known to get small earthquakes in the area from time to time. I walked over and touched the nearest wall but felt nothing. I put my ear up to it, and the sound didn't change. I then knelt down and pressed my ear against the cool hardwood—again, nothing.

Bear? Paul called from upstairs.

I should have just left it then. I should have stood up, fixed my hair, and walked back up to bed. I should have folded myself into Paul's warmth, closed my eyes, and put it out of my mind. That would have been the end of it, and my life would have stayed as it always had. But it was already too late. It had gotten under my skin. And believe me when I say that I'm not an obsessive person. I don't fuss about details. I'm not a perfectionist. I couldn't give a shit if the house is spotless, even for company. I'm usually very laid-back, in fact too much so sometimes for Paul's liking (or the liking of his parents). But for some reason I just couldn't let it go. A part of me was probably thinking that the sound indicated some issue with the house, which was still relatively new, and slapped-up quickly like all tract housing, and Paul was constantly finding problems with the pipes, or the air ducts, or the seals around the windows, which drove him crazy as he was always fastidious with his own work. But, if I'm honest, it went much deeper than that. The sound unnerved me. There was just something about it that wasn't right, that wasn't like any other bit of white noise I'd heard before, and I knew it would keep me up until I figured out what it was.

I'll be up in a minute, I called back.

But I wasn't. I stalked around the house for another two hours, long after Paul had given up on me and fallen asleep. I moved around in the dark, navigating furniture through muscle memory, stopping every so often to hold my breath and make myself as quiet as possible. The noise persisted, low and droning, with very little variation or modulation. Sometimes I thought I detected a slight bend in pitch, but then I think I was simply focusing on it too intently. I searched the living room, the basement, the garage, unplugging every appliance, the Wi-Fi router, the microwave, the TV, the hot water heater, gutting the smoke detectors of their batteries. At one point I even flipped the breaker. As I did, I suddenly remembered being six, and losing power in a lightning storm. There was something revelatory about the silence that followed. I never considered that our apartment had a nervous system, or that it whined so loudly. I marvelled that there were sounds we could only perceive in their absence, and found it unsettling to realize how much I had managed to condition myself not to hear. How much I had to tune out just to get by.

Eventually I took two Ambien and crawled into bed, my heart pounding out of frustration. I stuffed a pillow over my head. After half an hour I fished a set of earplugs out of the drawer below the sink in the ensuite—but they did nothing. I lay there trying to meditate. I did some stuff with my chakras. I opened my eyes and saw the clock turn three. Then four. The noise wasn't at all loud, in fact I'm sure most people would have had to strain to hear it, but to me, in the silence of the house, it began to feel all-consuming. It was a bit like overhearing a couple's whispered conversation behind you at a restaurant and then being completely unable, for the life of you, to focus on anything else—not the noise of the other diners, not the waiter, not the person sitting right in front of you.

By half past four, I couldn't lie still a moment longer. I took out my earplugs, walked back downstairs, and out the front door. The night was warm. There wasn't a breath of movement on the street. No wind disturbing the leaves, or planes tracing the sky. Just the smell of creosote and ionized air; of rain amassing somewhere in the distance. The stillness lent everything the uncanny feeling of a film set. Perhaps one of those horror films where some infernal force kills off the teenagers of the neighbourhood one by one. Those always seem to be set in suburbs like these—catalogue homes, young trees, driveways lined with SUVs. My eyes were scratchy. Raw. I felt cloudy from the Ambien. I crossed the front yard, walked out onto the street, and listened. It wasn't in my head, or the house—it was there. It was coming from somewhere outside, maybe from next door or down the street, or maybe somewhere beyond our neighbourhood altogether; it was impossible to gauge its distance.

Just then I noticed a shadow moving almost imperceptibly down the street towards me. I strained my eyes against the dark and watched as it drew closer. It slinked into the glow of a nearby streetlight and I realized it was a coyote. White-tipped ears and a white triangle of fur on his neck. He seemed too slight to be adult. He looked more like a teenager or a tween coyote, if there's such a thing. It made me smile to see him. I often hear the coyotes as I lie in bed, barking and yipping out there in the night. But this one made no noise as he slipped back into darkness. I waited for him to reappear in the pool of light nearest me—but he didn't. He was gone.

I felt sorry for the coyotes. My neighbours hated them, because they dragged dogs and cats out of backyards and ate them. But that was just their nature. I had always felt a certain kinship with them; mangy interlopers in middle-class suburbia. My neighbours somehow forgot that the wilderness was just a block away. At the end of our street, the city gave way to badlands. The bottom of an ancient, inland sea where a vertical mile's worth of sea creatures settled atop one another over millions of years, condensed, and liquefied into crude—which explained some of the three-car garages and grotesque McMansions in neighbouring subdivisions. If you looked at our city at night, from space, our suburb was like a little finger of light, poking out into the dark. We were at the far northern edge of the sprawl; of civilization. And the edge wasn't sharp. In fact, it seemed to be getting blurrier. Sometimes the wild crept in and overturned garbage cans after sunset, or shat on your front step. Other times it was the neighbourhood boys going feral. Howling and smashing beer bottles against garage doors or firing Roman candles down the street.

Claire?

I startled and turned. Paul emerged from the shadows holding a golf club. What the hell is going on? he asked. I was standing in the middle of the street, barefoot and in my nightdress. I couldn't imagine any neighbours were up at this hour, but we would've been quite the sight—me standing there below the streetlight, and my husband advancing towards me with a long iron.

Bear, we've been tearing the house apart looking for you.

Ashley's up too?

Yeah, we've been beside ourselves. The power's out.

I apologized and rubbed my face. I hadn't meant to turn this into some big production. It was nothing, really, just a barely audible noise, and now all of us were awake at four in the morning, and Paul was holding a golf club, a golf club? I finally registered this and started laughing.

I woke up and couldn't turn on the lights, he said, drawing closer. I couldn't find you anywhere. I thought someone was in the house. The front door was open, the furniture was all—It's not funny, why are you laughing?

So you thought you'd grab—

It was what was at hand!

Paul wore his emotions large and naked on his face; it's something I've always found endearing, and sometimes teased him about when we watched movies. I laughed at the sheer panic on his face, but I also found it very touching. Paul had a rather rare heart condition for a man his age called compassion. He looked like 'a big bruiser,' as he would say, but when it came to his emotional intelligence, I would've put him in the upper one or two percentile of men I've encountered in my life. I'm sure his brothers characterized him as whipped and put upon, but then I would rather be waterboarded for eternity than married to any of them. I liked that my husband took up a nine-iron when he found me missing from bed. I recommend everyone find themselves a partner who picks up a nine-iron when they're missing.

What the hell is going on?

I composed myself and shook my head wearily. I couldn't sleep, I said.

So you thought you'd wander outside at four o'clock in the morning in your nightgown, he replied.

I didn't know what facial expression I should be wearing, and I was too tired to even tell which one I currently had on, so I rubbed my hand over my face like an eraser. I'm trying to figure out where it's coming from, I said. I told you—twelve, one, two o'clock I couldn't sleep, I told you.

Paul closed his eyes, stuck his thumb and index finger into the sockets, and said, I can't believe you're still talking about this fucking hum.

And I can't believe you can't just shut up and listen.

Did he seriously not hear it, even now that we were standing outside in the quiet of the night? He said I could use his earplugs, and I pulled them out of my nightgown pocket and tossed them on the ground.

So what, you've just been out creeping around in the dark?

I chuckled again at the absurdity of it all, I couldn't help it. A bit sinister, isn't it? I asked.

Uh yeah, like a lot sinister, he said, softening.

He was standing right beside me now, his eyes glistening in the streetlight. I realized, in the surprise of his approach, that I had forgotten about the coyote. I considered telling him about it, but decided to keep it as a private revelation. He wasn't in the right headspace. I looked down at the ground for a moment, and then back up at him; his face was still a big, sweet drawing of concern.

My hands were shaking, and I suddenly wished I had pockets to hide them in. I crossed my arms instead. Don't dismiss this, I said.

I'm not.

Or think I'm exaggerating.

No, I just—

Then what?

I don't know what you're talking about.

I'm telling you.

Okay.

I'm more sensitive to these things.

He made to rebut but swallowed and closed his eyes. I know, he said.

You didn't believe me before about the gas leak.

That was a smell.

Which I smelled and you didn't and could've blown us up. I've felt earthquakes you haven't felt. Twice I've heard when the radiator in the car was broken before you.

Those things exist, Claire. This isn't a thing.

The shadows from the streetlight fell harsh on Paul's face and made him look haggard. Old. He was standing an arm's length away, but I felt very far from him. I told him I was sorry about the power. I didn't mean to keep it off for long, I said, I just flipped the breaker for a moment to check.

Wait, what? You cut the power?

I told him I hadn't intended to leave it off, I just needed to know, I needed the silence.

You cut the power? Paul repeated, his disbelief giving way to anger.

I just had to know it wasn't in my head, and now I know it's not, it's—I gestured down the street—it's out there.

Where? Over there? The Campaneles' yard? he said, pivoting around and pointing at our neighbours' house. I knew he was being facetious, but the thought had actually occurred to me that the sound might be coming from the Campaneles' pool pump, and I told him as much. He said no, there was nothing coming from their yard, stop being ridiculous, and I informed him that their new pool was, in fact, absolutely huge, as in practically a lake, and that I bet they needed a massive pump for it that probably ran throughout the night. I was always shocked, when I flew out of the city, just how many people had pools. In the desert! This landscape was never meant to sustain cities, let alone personal swimming amenities.

Paul put the head of the golf club down on the asphalt and leaned against it like a jaunty cane. And what, are you going to pole-vault over their fence to investigate? he asked. I suggested walking over to their yard and at least seeing if I could hear it getting louder. I knew I was pushing it. Paul had a long fuse, but it wasn't endless.

And what if they see someone snooping around their backyard? he asked. They'll call the police.

Then when else am I going to?

Leave it.

I could just go over to their gate.

No.

I can't afford to lose sleep over this.

Paul looked astounded and replied that neither could he. The truth was the sound could have been coming from any of the houses or yards around us. I turned on the spot, taking in the street.

Claire, it's four-thirty in the morning, why're you doing this to me?

I'm not doing anything to you, I'm trying to figure this out.

This? This is you doing something to me. Look at where we are. You're not even wearing any goddamn shoes.

As he continued to talk, I became aware of a slight pressure in my head. It wasn't particularly painful; it wasn't a headache, per se. It was more like a thickness. A fullness. As I focused on it, I realized I could feel it in my chest as well. It took me several moments to connect it to the sound. I realized that I was actually feeling the sound. Like waves of pressure. I felt it resonating in the cavities of my body; my skull. Permeating my empty spaces. As I thought this, I felt a tingling in my nose. I wiped it with my hand, and when I looked down, I noticed my hand was glistening with blood.

Oh my god.

What?

My nose—

I saw Paul see the blood. Jesus Christ, he murmured, and I told him to leave Jesus out of it. What's wrong with you? he asked.

Maybe you should try an exorcism.

I think a Kleenex will do for now. Just hold your head back and let's—

Don't—touch me. I took an unsteady step back. You're just completely dismissing this, *this*, I said, holding out the bloodied back of my hand.

The sound is giving you a nosebleed?

Don't say it like that.

How am I supposed to say it?

And what if it is, what if it's pulverizing my brain, Paul, and you're offering me earplugs and Kleenex.

Just come inside. Please.

Do you believe me?

I—

Look, I said, wiping a fresh smear onto my hand, as if that were proof enough. The nosebleed, the pressure, the sound, they did feel connected, and at least the blood was something tangible Paul could see. Say you believe me, I said.

He bucked his head back, as if he was worried I was going to touch him with it. Frankly, I would've loved to have smacked a big red handprint on his face like a cave painting in Lascaux. He just couldn't bring himself to say it. He insisted it was all stress induced, as in made up, as in stop being hysterical, and I said wow, shaking my head and smiling without joy. Wow.

Okay, he said, defeated. I believe you.

That I hear something?

Yes.

And you believe that thing, that sound, really exists?

He raised and dropped his arms, and asked, How can I possibly know whether the sound only you can hear—?

Because I'm telling you, and that should be enough.

He just looked at me like a dumb dog, and I turned and started walking away.

Hey. C'mon. Where're you—? What do you want me to say? You're being completely insane.

I stopped walking and yelped in frustration. It just burst out of me. I was shaking, with adrenalin. Am I throwing a little tantrum, I thought, yes, I think I am, right here in the middle of the street.

I laughed at myself. Christ on a cracker. I was beyond the reach of even Paul's compassion. Was that really it? Was that all he was capable of? I wanted to tell him I know what I fucking hear and it's your deficiency, Paul, not mine, that you don't believe me. I turned around to shout, but found him already beside me, reaching out, and enfolding me in his arms. I let him hold me for a long, still moment, until he said, with tenderness, I believe you.

I wiped my nose. No, you don't.

I do. He whispered it into my ear and held me tighter. I do, I believe you. I believe you, and I love you. He pulled away, and I turned around to look at him. I love you, he said again.

That's when I noticed the sky beginning to lighten. A moment later, I heard the first trill of birdsong.

Did you hear that? I asked.

He sighed and shook his head. No.

It's morning.

2

I USED TO THINK JOGGERS WERE THE LOWEST FORM OF life on Earth. I vowed never to debase myself like that. And yet, within two years of moving to this area, I had a thirty-minute morning route. Even I was startled by the speed with which my conviction collapsed. On my morning runs I liked watching cars parked along the street emerge from the dawn mist. They seemed like armoured dinosaurs, or giant, prehistoric armadillos. Houses became the fog-cloaked cliff faces of some Mesozoic canyon. In this netherworld, I liked to imagine that all time existed on top of itself; ancient creatures living alongside those of the future. I was just as likely to happen upon a startled deer as I was a drone, piloted by some neighbour's antisocial son. But most mornings I didn't encounter a single other soul. It was usually the one time of day I could be alone with my body. When I could become pure motion.

When it came to jogging, I was a creature of habit. I wore the same pair of leggings, the same top, the same sunglasses. I always set out at six, on the dot. If I set out a few minutes later, I felt behind the entire day. I called that feeling 'dragging my ass.' I liked to avoid it. I stuck to the same route because I knew better—I was hopeless with directions, and the streets in my neighbourhood twist and loop back on themselves, such that even after six years I still found myself getting turned around.

Ashley and I made shared, customized Spotify playlists and gave them names like Death to Incels (Bikini Kill, Hole, M.I.A.), Hold My Drink (Lizzo, Nicki Minaj, Megan Thee Stallion), Sad White Boys Anonymous (Sufjan Stevens, Sam Smith, Bob Dylan). The morning after the first sleepless night, I put on Ashley's playlist masterwork, Impeach President Krump, turned up the volume a notch higher than usual, and set out at a pace. It felt good to move, even if I was exhausted. I passed all the familiar homes on my route, a copy-and-paste combination of bungalows and two-storey houses of tan-painted stucco with faux shutters and red clay roof tiles, pebbled front yards filled with yucca, chubby succulents, and curving stone walkways that led to front doors hiding below blocky archways. A few streets over, I began to pass the upper-income homes aspiring towards a kind of Disney-esque royalty with medieval turrets, New England dormers, and Edwardian gables, an architecture unmoored from time and taste.

I'm still not quite sure how I let myself become suburbanized. It had always been a goal of Paul's to own a 'proper' house, the kind of house that he had spent years building. I guess there was a sort of poetry to that. We each wanted things for Ashley that we never had as kids. He wanted her to have quiet, space, bike paths. I got her a vibrator for her fourteenth birthday. I allowed Paul to persuade me that I'd reached the age where I required proximity to nature. Small birds disembowelling rodents in my backyard. Large expanses of sky. I told myself—life is more vivid out here than in the city. I've come to realize that isn't the case. It's more like how even a whisper sounds loud in a silent room.

As I rounded the corner back onto Cascadia Drive, I came across a crew of workmen in high-vis vests. They were standing around and assessing a forty-foot black pole they had just installed, a few paces back from the road. I found something about the tall pole disquieting. Unearthly, even. Like an alien monolith. As I stood there, my neighbour Linda appeared, walking her ghost dog. I'm not sure what breed of dog it was, but it was very stark and very grey. In the morning mist, it seemed almost spectral. I don't know what would possess someone to buy such a haunted-looking animal. Linda wandered over to me, arms crossed, and eyes fixed on the pole. She groaned and shook her head.

Well there she is.

I assumed she was referring to the pole, and not to me. What is it? I asked.

That's the cell tower they were telling us about, she said, turning to me. She widened her eyes, as if the tower was a friend of ours who'd just shown up in a particularly ugly dress, and we didn't have the heart to tell her.

Who was telling us about it? I asked.

They stuck those notices about it in our mailboxes last week, remember? I told her I didn't. Linda explained how the tower was supposed to improve cell and data service in the neighbourhood. I guess we'll see, she said.

They must've started installing last night, I said.

What is it? She addressed this question to the dog, who was whimpering.

I debated for a moment whether to bring up the hum, and decided I had nothing to lose. I asked Linda if she had noticed it. A kind of droning sound, I said, that started sometime last night.

She looked back up at me, cocking her head to the side. You mean from the tower? she asked.

Well I don't know, that's what I'm wondering, I replied.

She glanced around and shrugged. I doubt they've turned it on yet, she said. They've only just installed it. Her dog pulled on its leash and began to lead her onward. But then what do I know about these things, she called back.

I'm sure what Linda didn't know about these things could fill a book.

Over the next few days I managed to speak with a few other neighbours, as they were tending to their yards, or putting out the trash, but no one else seemed to hear the sound. Paul continued to insist that he believed me. I knew he didn't, but I appreciated his support. Every passing day he grew more and more worried. I wasn't sleeping at night. I started developing migraines, which I had never really had before. Whether they were from the sound itself or the lack of sleep, it's hard to say, but holy mother of god were they intense. The nosebleeds continued, periodically. The thing was, the sound wasn't at all loud or abrasive. It was just there, all the time, constantly wearing me down, eroding me. And yet, at times, even I began to doubt whether it existed.

I kept going into school because that's me—I power through. In class, I popped Tylenol and kept the blinds drawn. One afternoon, during a lesson on *Beloved*, I had to devolve things into a class discussion just so I could sit down and gather myself for a few moments. While I was doing so, a student asked me a question which I didn't hear; I only realized when I looked up and noticed the entire class staring at me. Another student asked if I was all right. At that point I thought it was probably more alarming to pretend that I was than to simply address the problem, so I asked the class if they could hear it as well.

Like a deep, vibrating . . . hum, I said. Just somewhere there, in the background. I searched their puzzled faces. No one said a word. Or is it . . . Or is it just in my head? I stammered. I suddenly felt ridiculous. I noticed two boys smirking and whispering in the back row. I probably should have avoided the word 'vibrating.' I heard more whispers, followed by titters, followed by uncomfortable, muffled laughter. Never mind, I said, and apologized. I assigned some reading and ended class early. I'm sure that gave them plenty to talk about that lunch hour.

Generally I couldn't care less what students thought of me, though I sensed I was well-liked. They laughed at my jokes. They knew they could speak their minds in my class. I was always encouraging them to question received wisdom and authority. There was a certain group of boys who referred to me as 'Miss,' even though I was 'Ms. Devon' to all the other staff and students. Miss, can I open the window? Miss, can I use the washroom? I noticed these boys didn't use this epithet for other teachers. It used to affront my feminism, but I grew to find it vaguely endearing, as if it communicated a kind of familiarity. I suspected it also signalled some unconscious, or perhaps conscious, sexualization of me amongst these boys that I felt ambivalent but probably not altogether unhappy about. If I ever gave any serious thought to my currency among my students it was for Ashley's sake. I couldn't imagine it was easy to go to the same school where your mother taught.

Over the lunch hour, after my little episode, I ate leftover curry out of a Tupperware container in the staff lounge as Cass recapped last night's episode of *Drag Race* for me. I didn't watch the show but I followed it closely through her enthusiastic and detailed retellings. Like an ancient bard, she could hold the entire mythology of the series in her head, referencing the exploits of drag queens from past seasons as if they were demigods in a grand, cosmic pantheon.

At some point she noticed that I wasn't following her monologue with my usual focus.

Hun, are you all right?

Yeah, I'm . . . Sorry.

You still not sleeping?

I was really not on my usual form. I apologized again, and she told me cut it out with the sorrys. She leaned over, placed a hand on my knee, and told me I looked like crap. I told her I felt like it. I always trusted Cass to tell me how it was. A lot of the other staff found her loud and abrasive, and she was, but I was drawn to women who took up space; I came from a prodigious line of them. Cass lived bigger. Why wear two colours when you can wear five; why smile when you can laugh; why diet when you're going to die. We first met working together on a production of *Into the Woods* in my second year at the school. I was the director, and she, being the school's music teacher, was the musical director. It almost killed us. We had big blowouts, even in front of the students. We had creative differences over everything—casting, blocking, costumes, lighting; things that had nothing to do with her remit. She had seen the show 'done in New York' and wanted to remain 'faithful to its original spirit,' whereas I wanted to gender-swap some of the roles, and have a very minimal set, which she claimed was 'too arty by half.' But I simply refused to give all the juicy roles to half-committed, tone-deaf boys when there were a legion of more capable girls, and I sure as hell wasn't going to fill the stage with a papier-mâché forest, or whatever aesthetic horror she was advocating, I can't even remember now. At any rate, we survived the collaboration and emerged out of it as friends, and have proceeded to subject ourselves to staging four more musicals since then including one that Cass herself wrote about Amelia Earhart, which we do not speak of.

Together with our friend Nadia, we were each other's emotional pit crew. Nadia worked in the special education department at our school before she moved across town. When Cass was going through chemo, Nadia and I kept her fridge stocked with casseroles, soups, pies. After Nadia's mother died, Cass and I took her to a Janelle Monáe concert on edibles. They were my big sisters, both a decade older. They had survived abusive childhoods, abusive first marriages, remarried Christian guys with goatees, and now drew a lot of strength from their faith, especially Cass.

Listen, she told me, as we walked out of the staff lounge at the end of the lunch hour, I'll cover your afternoon class.

No, what?

I have a spare now. Go home. Sleep. I'm serious.

That's—

Shush. Woman. Get your little Fjällräven Kånken and go.

You just wanted to say that.

I'll walk you to your class; you can fill me in on the lesson plan.

No, no, it's fine. Really, love. Ashley has a game after school anyway.

Oh come on, you're not staying for that.

I am, I want to.

She gripped my shoulder and looked into my eyes as the afternoon bell rang. Don't be a martyr, yeah? If you need to take a couple of days, just talk to Valeria.

After school, I found a quiet place in the bleachers on the back field. It was just a friendly match with the nearby Catholic school, not part of the regional tournament or anything, but I still tried to catch as many of Ashley's games as I could. It was usually when I did my marking, and when I didn't have marking, I brought a book. I got through all of *Anna Karenina* last season. I liked the cadences of a game: the shouting, the whistle trills, the colliding storm fronts of colour. I couldn't care less about sports. It still confounded me that my daughter, who shared a part of my soul, somehow ended up a jock—and yet with none of the compensatory pleasures of being a lesbian.

I was pretty sure she saw me sitting in the stands, but she didn't acknowledge me. She usually waved or stuck out her tongue. I wondered if word had reached her about my little episode in class. Surely she wouldn't hold that against me. As the game went on, I really did get the sense that she was ignoring me. I began to get in my head about it. I was probably just exhausted and out of sorts. I stayed a little longer until I decided not to make her any more awkward by lingering around, looking so haggard, and I slipped out. I had never left a game of hers early before. As I walked to my car, I wasn't sure if she would be hurt or relieved when she noticed, and I wasn't sure which pained me more.

Paul and Ashley basically took opposite approaches to dealing with my 'condition,' as they started calling it. Paul became increasingly doting and protective, cooking meals, arranging medical appointments, buying noise-cancelling headphones. Ashley pulled right away. Her selective acknowledgement of my existence continued days after the game until the point where she began completely blanking me as she passed in the school halls. The first time she did it, it felt like she'd stabbed me with a steak knife. My behaviour in class and around the school was evidently becoming a topic of conversation, and she was punishing me. I began going to significant lengths to engineer my movements through the building to avoid encounters with her. It became completely untenable.

I finally walked into her room one night to confront her about it. She was lying on her bed watching a video on her phone. I lay down beside her, our hair touching. She was watching a documentary about whale hunting in Japan. I lay there beside her, looking up at the ceiling, listening to the video. After a couple of minutes she reached out and laid the top of her hand across my forehead.

You're like fuckin' *Night of the Walking Dead*, Mom.

I exhaled. I know.

You look hollowed out.

Hmm. Thanks.

She turned her head to look at me, her eyes right beside mine. Honest, she said. Have you even looked at yourself in the mirror?

I own one, yes.

Well it's a bad scene, wench.

I'm aware.

You're burnt out.

I nodded, and she lightly gripped the top of my head while still looking into my eyes. Stop coming to school, she said. Please. I'm literally begging you.

I'm embarrassing you.

Yes. You are. I'm sorry, but yes.

My eyes stung and I closed them. I remembered my mother once showing up smelling of liquor to a parent-teacher meeting and wishing I could evaporate into thin air. I remembered feeling how desperately I never wanted my daughter to be embarrassed by me. I swallowed and mumbled a promise to Ashley that I would speak to Valeria in the morning about taking some stress leave.

Valeria Moreno, my school's principal, allowed me to use the entire allotment of my year's paid sick leave. I hadn't intended to be off for so long, but it soon became clear that I was not getting better. On my GP's advice, I took an additional two weeks of unpaid leave, but even then, I wasn't sleeping. I spent my days home alone, medicating, meditating, masturbating. I'm not sure you realize just how unhinged you can get if you haven't really slept for weeks on end. Your brain is not nearly as robust as you'd like to think it is. Throughout this time, Paul accompanied me to my appointments with the audiologist, Dr. Sandra Heard (I kid you not), who ran a gamut of tests and ruled out tinnitus, spontaneous otoacoustic emissions, and basically all other medical explanations. She believed I might be hypersensitive to white noise in my environment, and that I was becoming fixated on a tone that would normally go unnoticed; something she had occasionally seen in patients who were dealing with acute stress. I told her I hadn't felt particularly stressed before all of this began. I wasn't directing the school musical that year, I liked my students, I had good colleagues, things were fine with Paul, we had some debt but who didn't? Dr. Heard said that was all beyond her pay grade but encouraged me to consider speaking to a therapist.

So I started seeing Dr. Humberto Gompf, who proposed using cognitive behavioural therapy to train my brain to essentially just relax and ignore the noise. He didn't seem to place much stock in my suggestion that the sound might have had a real-life origin in my neighbourhood—like the electromagnetic waves from the new cell tower, for instance, or perhaps a rumble from the industrial park over in Ranchlands. Was I supposed to take medication and do therapy just so I could cope with noise pollution? Was I supposed to train myself to be less sensitive? When did being too perceptive become a liability, a deficit, and who did it serve for that to be the case?

When trying to describe the sound to my doctors, or my neighbours, or to Paul, I came to realize that I could only ever talk about it through analogy. How else could you articulate a sensation that another couldn't perceive? It was like describing a colour to a blind person; it could only ever be like another sense. Grey like the smell of streets after a rainstorm. Yellow like the heat of bedsheets in morning sunlight. At night, as I lay in bed, it sounded like someone was idling their engine in the driveway. Or like an airplane flying overhead, that low atmospheric roar; except it never got further away, it just kept going for hours and hours. Or like being in a tenth-floor apartment and hearing jackhammering in the basement, reverberating up through the concrete walls. Or the deep rumble of a bass note at a concert, sustained for days.

One night, I couldn't lie still a second longer. The hum was peeling my skin like a potato. I imagined Paul waking up to find just one long skin-curl beside him. I slipped out of bed and went for a walk. It was a clear night. The hum was the only sound. I had never heard it so intensely. I walked with no particular destination in mind, and yet it felt purposeful. Was I in a dissociative state? It's quite probable. I began imagining I was in a movie. In the movie, I got to the end of the street, rounded the corner, and I saw it. A tall, dark shadow, like a scar on the night. The cell tower. A shiver ricocheted through me. I stared at the tower for a long while, and then started walking towards it. As I walked towards it, I asked it, in my mind: Is it you? Are you doing this to me? I stopped at the curb, bent down, picked up a palm-sized stone—and chucked it at the tower. At first I missed, so I picked up two more stones, and I threw one, then the other, and the third one hit the tower bang on, and made a loud, metallic *clang*. It was shockingly loud. It surprised me. I mean, I was surprised at myself—a grown woman, a high school teacher, a mother—throwing stones at a tower like some preteen neighbourhood delinquent. But I think I was most surprised by the tangibility of everything. The tower was really there. It existed. And my body existed. They weren't just things that I had also imagined.

3

PAUL'S GOODWILL AND PATIENCE RAN OUT. AFTER THE
first month, he moved me into the guest room, saying he couldn't
afford nights of insomnia either, which was fair enough, though
it still felt a bit like I was being put in some kind of quarantine,
or asylum. Paul called the guest room The Gym, because that's
where his exercise equipment was; whereas a more appropriate
name would have been The Storage Closet, or perhaps The Room
of Failed Resolution. It had bare white walls that we never bothered decorating. Needless to say, it didn't help my sleep.

After two months, I had to make a decision whether to return
to work or go on extended disability, which would have seen a
major reduction in my pay—something we really couldn't afford.
So I returned to class, no more rested than before, still hearing the
noise, but much better at pretending that I didn't.

At lunch on Thursday of my first week back, as I was packing
up papers at my desk, I looked up and noticed a student of mine,

Kyle Francis, standing in the doorway. He was wearing an over-sized sweatshirt, and an earbud in his left ear. His hair was so blond it seemed almost white. It had the effect of making him look at once like a baby and an old man. One had to really study his face to find his eyebrows. He had always been something of a phantom in class. He never spoke unless I called on him, though the few times I had, his insights were genuinely disarming: a specific inter-pretation of a Ray Bradbury short story, for instance, or a reading of a Langston Hughes poem, that I had truly never considered in all my years of teaching those texts. His mind worked differently, when it was working—he was becoming increasingly checked-out in class.

Sorry. Do you, uh—have a second?

Hi, Kyle. What can I do for you?

He canted his head down. I'm not really sure how to talk about it, he said.

Well let's not do it across the room, I replied.

He made to close the door, but I told him to keep it open. It was school policy; no teacher can be alone with a student behind a closed door. I proffered a chair, he crossed to me and sat down. I leaned back against the edge of my desk and crossed my arms.

So.

He cleared his throat and stared down at his hands. I know I've been uh—pretty distracted in class recently, he said.

Yeah. You have.

And I just wanted to let you know I'm sorry. And I want to try harder.

Okay. I appreciate that.

I'm not trying to disrespect you. When I was sleeping . . . I didn't mean to like . . . He trailed off, looking pained as he glanced towards the door.

I know, I said, pulling the chair out from behind my desk, and sitting down beside him. I'm just frustrated because I know what you're capable of, I said, and he nodded. What're you listening to? I asked. He apologized and pulled out his earbud.

What was it?

Just some old school stuff.

Mozart?

A smile flickered across his face. Exactly, he replied.

Knowing you, I wouldn't be surprised, I said.

Kyle put on a bit of a brooding, tough guy act, but I always suspected in another life he could just as easily have been a band geek. He handed me one of his earbuds. I listened for a moment, before pulling it out with incredulity—Missy Elliott is not old school!

Get Ur Freak On?

It's like—

From 2001! That's the year I was born, he said.

This gave me a feeling akin to vertigo. I still hadn't quite wrapped my head around students having no memory of the Twin Towers falling. I told him that I thought he was talking about Public Enemy.

Miss, that's Smithsonian, he replied.

I handed the earbud back to him. But seriously, I said, I don't want any Secret Service in my classroom, okay? It makes me feel like you don't give a damn about what I'm saying, and that you don't care. And I know that's not the case. Or maybe it is.

He looked slightly pained, and said no.

And it makes it impossible for you to concentrate, and then you fall asleep.

I know.

So what's going on? I still don't have your proposal. The essay's due Monday.

I'm stuck, he said.

What's your book?

He reached into his bag and pulled out a massive, dog-eared tome. He flipped it over to reveal the cover—*The Magic Mountain*, by Thomas Mann. I laughed.

He shifted his body under his sweatshirt, self-conscious. I know it's a little ambitious, he said.

Uh . . . yeah. No wonder you're tired, walking around with this brick in your bag.

I took the book from his hands and started to leaf through it. The font was minuscule. It's set in a hotel in the Alps or something, right?

Hmm. So, this young engineer named Hans travels to Davos—

Hans? I said, affecting a German accent.

Yes, *Hans*, Kyle replied, smirking, with a yet-thicker accent, goes to visit his cousin in this, like, secluded sanatorium in the mountains for people with tuberculosis, but then he ends up getting this fever and becomes convinced, well the doctors convince him that it's the early signs of tuberculosis, and what was supposed to be a short visit turns into him living there for seven years. But it's probably all psychosomatic.

And you're going to write a thousand-word essay on this—I flipped to the back—seven-hundred-and-twenty-page book?

I'm trying.

You were assigned *The Catcher in the Rye* and *Of Mice and Men*—

Or a book of your own choosing, he interjected.

Right, but, lemme just—I placed *The Magic Mountain* down on my desk and retrieved copies of both *The Catcher in the Rye* and *Of Mice and Men* from my top drawer. I proceeded to stack them beside the Mann. Combined, they barely made up a third of the height of *The Magic Mountain*'s spine. I asked him whether he saw my point.

Kyle shrugged and leaned back in his chair. Most people are illiterate, he said.

Or you're a bit of a show-off, I said, and he cracked a half smile. But really, I think you've bitten off way more than you can chew here. What's your thesis?

He pinch-wiped his mouth with his thumb and index finger. I wanna write about the dualism in the book between, like, a skepticism towards both belief and disbelief, he said.

Okay.

I could tell he was trying to impress me, and I didn't want to give him the satisfaction of showing him that I was. Do you have that written down somewhere on paper? I asked.

Not yet.

Do you have anything written down yet?

He shook his head. I was irritated, but I also couldn't help feeling a bit charmed. He knew he was bright, and he knew that I knew he was bright. Perhaps he had psyched himself out about actually following through and delivering on that promise, lest it turned out not to be quite so impressive as we had imagined his squandered genius to be.

Okay, I replied. Remember, I'm not looking for a PhD here. One thousand words. It's really not that much.

He looked back down into his hands and nodded. I told him that I wanted him to show me what he had by next Monday and handed him back his book. And no more Rip Van Winkle in class, okay?

I know, I'm sorry.

As he packed away his book, I noted the dark circles under his eyes. You really do look tired, Kyle. He ignored this comment for a few seconds as he zipped up his bag, then looked up at me.

I'm not sleeping, he said. He was about to say something else but stopped himself.

Why's that? I asked. He shrugged. I asked him if he was having problems with friends, and he said no.

Luke and Mohammed?

No, those guys are cool.

You sure?

It's not that.

He was bouncing his leg nervously. He saw me notice and stopped.

Because you could tell me if it was, I said. I'm always here. But you gotta give me a chance. I pointed to the earbuds sticking out of his sweatshirt pocket. None of this, okay?

It's just sometimes I feel like I need it to block out the noise.

Oh thanks.

I don't mean you.

Seems a bit of a contradiction, no? Needing music to block out the noise.

He wiped his hand across his face. I know, I'm messed up, he said.

I didn't say that.

I can't sleep because of it. The noise keeps me up.

He gave me a pointed look, and my heart started to beat a little faster. What was he saying, exactly? Does your family stay up late? I asked.

No.

Your neighbours?

I'm saying the noise is all the time. Everywhere. It's like—He twirled his finger above his head. We stared at one another, not breathing. At least I wasn't breathing. I didn't realize you could forget how. He then said that, ever since I had asked about the sound in class a couple of months back, he realized that he could hear it too. His eyes darted about my face, searching for some reaction. Do you still hear it? he asked.

I swallowed and nodded. All the time, I replied.

Almost like . . . a kind of rumble.

Yes.

Almost like—

He tried to imitate the sound in his throat. Like a man groaning, after being stabbed. There was no human voice low enough to mimic the hum. It was an impossible sound. But I was strangely moved by his desire to try. I recognized the desire, viscerally. To give voice to the noise no one else heard. And yet someone finally did. Someone sitting a few feet away from me. It was hard to put into words what it felt like; to resign oneself to living invisibly, and then to realize you actually could be seen, by one person alone in the world. The intimacy of that. The relief. And for this person to be a seventeen-year-old boy, a student, and not just any student but Kyle Francis of all people, with his sullen precociousness. And though Kyle fell far short of imitating the hum, he somehow captured the feeling of being haunted by it. I could tell his sound was mine. I recognized it immediately. It made every hair on my body stand on end. He fell quiet, and then asked me what it was. I shook my head and told him that I wished I knew.

At first I thought it was a concussion, he said. I was playing ball and this guy hit me in the head with his elbow and I started hearing it. And it just never went away. But I went to the doctors and like—no concussion or anything.

He glanced towards the door of the classroom again, and then back down at his hands. You're the first person I've told, he said.

Nobody else can hear it, I said. My family, my neighbours, they have no idea what I'm talking about. None of the teachers here.

Yeah, all my teachers are like *hello wake up*, he said, snapping his fingers. My friends think I'm high. I can't concentrate. I'm getting in trouble.

I felt my face flush. I reached out and squeezed his shoulder, which I hoped he read as some kind of apology.

At night it's worse, he added.

Oh my god.

Right?

So much worse.

Between, like, midnight and six in the morning, he said, rubbing his eyes, leaving them red. He was tearing up. I became aware that I was wiping mine with the back of my hand. When it's quiet, he continued. No traffic or planes passing over. If it wakes me up that's it, I can't get back to sleep. I've tried earplugs.

Sure.

They help a bit.

Not me.

No. Because you can still feel it.

Exactly.

He glanced over to the steady flow of students passing in the hallway outside the classroom and asked if he could close the door. I pursed my lips, but didn't say no, so he stood up, crossed the room, and shut it. When he sat back down we started talking about the migraines. The brain fog. I mentioned the nosebleeds. I conceded that it was hard to imagine a sound causing nosebleeds, but he said he didn't think it was at all.

Sounds can cause damage, he said. Those sound cannons they use in protests? And there was that stuff at the American embassy in Cuba, did you read about that?

I shook my head. I was stirred to see this side of Kyle; passionate and invested.

There were these sonic attacks against the embassy workers, he continued. They started hearing these strange, high-pitched sounds at night and started having all these symptoms and eventually had to be sent home. Some of them had permanent brain damage.

God.

It can mess you up.

Maybe we're being attacked by the government, I said, sitting back, eyebrow arched.

Right, he deadpanned. The Cubans are after us.

I chuckled, though I was still tearing up. I exhaled slowly, trying to gather myself. And then I just began to tell Kyle things. I confided in him about my struggles with Paul and Ashley. My confusion and isolation. I don't know why I felt I could be so open with him. It wasn't appropriate, and yet, it felt profoundly comforting.

Paul's your husband?

Yeah.

What's he like?

Like?

What's he look like? I laughed, caught off guard. Never mind, don't answer that, he said. Was just trying to make a mental picture. I told him that Paul was a good man, though thought I was probably crazy.

Kyle looked at me with intent—And are you?

Sometimes I think I am, I said.

He nodded and leaned forward—Well I don't think you're crazy.

And for the first time in weeks, I didn't feel like I was. And it didn't feel crazy for me to lean in and hug him. In fact, in that moment, it felt like the only reasonable thing left to do. I felt his body release ever so slightly into mine. And something passed between us. A secret. A synchronicity. A silence, which communicated everything that we could not yet know or say.

Just then there was a knock on the door, and Cass walked into the room holding two boxed salads, in the midst of saying something about her cat Ricardo, but stopped short as she saw Kyle and me pull away from one another. I left a hand on Kyle's shoulder to indicate to everyone that I was comfortable with what just happened, but he was flustered, and stood up, out of my touch.

Sorry, I said, to Cass. We were just having a difficult conversation.

Of course, sorry, I didn't mean to barge in.

We—

Rain check on lunch?

No, no, we're finished here.

Okay. I can—why don't I just wait for you in the hall. Cass smiled, and walked back out of the room, keeping the door open.

Kyle was looking down at the floor. He seemed angry, or perhaps embarrassed; it was difficult to read his face. I expected him to walk out, but he lingered.

Maybe we can talk about it some more sometime, he said.

Of course. Yes.

When?

I'll be staying after school to mark some papers.

Here?

Yes.

He looked up at me and nodded. He then slung his backpack over his shoulder and made to leave.

Kyle, I said, and he turned back around. His jaw was set; his face neutral. He was already returning to a world beyond my reach. A world far from unguarded vulnerability.

I want to see something for next Monday, okay?

4

YOU MIGHT NOT BE AWARE OF THIS, BUT THE WORLD IS full of untraceable hums and drones afflicting thousands every day, driving people to madness and despair. I wasn't. I had no idea. Not before I became one of the legions affected, and found the chat rooms and message boards filled with people pouring out their plight, long having lost hope in doctors or science or the media to help make sense of their suffering. Hundreds of neighbourhoods around the world seem to suffer from various local sources of noise pollution. Irresponsible industry, lack of government oversight, sloppy urban planning. Except, as much as I searched, I never found anyone living in my area who described my sound. I was sure a few sensitive souls in Auckland or Bristol weren't being kept awake by the same hum that I was, and yet, I still found solace in reading their posts. Yes, I began to take comfort in the company of anonymous lunatics. But then why else was the Internet invented? Cat videos, and the comfort of anonymous lunatics. I found myself spending hours getting lost in different theories of possible sources. The electric grid, wind turbines, submarines, insect noise, meteors, wind passing through underground caverns, the vibrations of waves slamming into the continental shelf, the mating calls of midshipman fish, government mind-control technology, alien transmissions, distant volcanic eruptions—the eruption of Krakatoa in 1883 left the Earth vibrating for days on end. The US military, of course, was a favourite culprit, and many posts talked at length about the very low frequency radio signals used to track vessels deep under the ocean; sonar from which nothing could hide, which turned the ocean inside out like a pocket. And of course there were those who bypassed geology and meteorology altogether and headed straight to God. In the end times the stars will sing, and the great horns of heaven will sound! We were the harbingers of revelation.

Before this, I had never considered all of the unknowable sounds in the world. Sounds we could only see graphed or measured. The deep sounds of the Earth that no one hears. The eruption of volcanic vents thousands of metres below the water. The scraping of icebergs along the ocean floor. The mysterious bursts and burbles of the Earth that even science couldn't fully explain. The skyquakes that boom like cannons on calm summer days over the Bay of Fundy, or cause kitchen plates to rattle on Lough Neagh in Ireland. Or the gas escaping from vents, from vegetation rotting at the bottom of lakes or released from limestone decaying in underwater caves; the explosive and volatile digestive system of the Earth, bubbling, burping, expelling. The concussing of continental shelf fragments calving off into the Atlantic abyss. The roars from solar winds. From magnetic activity. From avalanches. From distant thunder that, through some anomaly in the upper atmosphere, managed to throw its voice across valleys, across mountain ranges to different cities and different states.

Before this, sound was something I took for granted. It was always there, providing pleasant texture and useful information to my day-to-day life. I liked music, but I have never been an aficionado like Paul. I could never tell the difference between the sound quality of a CD and a record. But once this all began, all I could think about was sound. And not just my sound—for I came to think of it as 'my sound,' as if I owned it, or it owned me—but the mysterious dimensions of sound more generally.

One night, after Paul had already gone upstairs to bed, I was sitting with my laptop in the dark of the living room. I googled 'most beautiful sound in the world,' and spent an hour listening to frogs singing in a Malaysian swamp, the cascades of the Neretva River, the chirruping of thrushes at dawn, the wind whipping itself against an ocean cliffside in Sonoma. But when I thought of it, the most beautiful sound I had probably ever heard was a lawn mower. When I was a girl, lying in the hot summer grass of my grandma's bungalow, listening to the sound of her neighbour cutting his lawn in the distance, I remember feeling like I would live forever. The purr of that lawn mower, three or four houses over, was like the sound of eternity itself. Sitting there in the living room, it occurred to me— the entire story of my life could be told through the sounds that have surrounded it. A continuous forty-year playback. A biography of room tones, bird calls, pop songs, voice messages, laughter, train whistles, dog barks, and wind moving through innumerable leaves.

Once I returned to work, I pretended to no longer hear the hum. It was a convincing performance. Paul let me sleep in our bed again, like a dog being let back into the house if it didn't piss on the carpet. Ashley stuck her tongue out at me at her games and poked my bum as I passed her in the halls. I got through my lessons, cracked jokes in the staff lounge, and colleagues resumed sharing the minutiae of their marital dysfunction with me. In other words, things were back on track.

Fast-forward two weeks. About forty-five minutes after the final school bell of the day one evening, I locked my classroom door, walked through the halls nodding goodbye to the cleaning staff, and stepped out into the staff parking lot, which was all but empty. The yellow school buses were gone. A few kids were still waiting across the street for the city bus, smoking. I got into my silver Toyota, drove three blocks, rounded the corner, and pulled over beside a small, shady park. The park was connected, by way of an overgrown path, and the adjacent elementary school's playground, to the back field of the high school. I pretended to be looking for something in the glove compartment so as not to seem suspicious, even though there was no one around. After about five minutes, Kyle appeared in the small park with his hood pulled up, crossed to my car, and climbed into the passenger seat. We drove without talking for a few moments, scanning the nearby streets, before he took off his hood, and we eased into our usual dynamic.

Kyle and I had started meeting up after class. At first, it was just to talk and share experiences. And then, we began to share theories. Neither of us was prepared to believe the sound was in our heads. We figured there must be a source, and if there was a source, then it must be possible to find it. We compared articles we found online, combed through comment threads, and drafted up a list of possible culprits, which we plotted on a map of the neighbourhood—nine computer pages of Google Maps satellite views that we printed out, taped together, and laminated. Before long one thing became abundantly clear—if we wanted to track down the source, we would have to leave the classroom.

We pulled off onto the gravel shoulder of Ranchlands Road, alongside the perimeter fence of the industrial park. We were about as close as we could get to the Grenadier factory without having an employee's pass. I checked my mirrors for passing cars or onlookers and gave the all-clear. Stepping out of the car, I was immediately struck by the din coming from the factory; though I wasn't quite sure the sound was low or reverberant enough to be our hum. Between the gravel shoulder and the fence was a shallow ditch choked with scrub grass and wildflowers. The cicadas screamed as we waded through the overgrowth, burrs sticking to our jeans, until we reached the chain-link fence on the other side.

Kyle removed his phone from his pocket and brought up his audio app. We stood quietly for a moment while he took a measurement. He squinted against the evening sun, small beads of sweat clinging to the translucent hairs above his lip. The air was thick and still. I looked out over the badlands that stretched beyond the industrial park, still untouched by developers. A landscape of horizons and subtle gradations of light. A landscape like an Agnes Martin painting, pure form and colour. The purple geometry of mountains in the distance, and lines receding into oblivion.

The cicadas are throwing it off, Kyle muttered. I noticed a car appear in the dancing heat to the south. I turned my body away from the road. Kyle did the same.

The factory had been on our list of possible sound sources from the start. Grenadier was a major defence contractor, manufacturing aerospace and military parts. I wasn't exactly sure what kind of production activity went on there, but Kyle had read that some industrial furnaces can cause low-frequency rumbles and pressure waves. For now, it was as good a lead as any, even if it didn't quite square with our hum, which, if anything, only grew louder at night, when the factory was closed. And it didn't explain why we only began hearing the hum recently, despite the factory operating since before our neighbourhood was built. Nevertheless, we were too early in our mission to rule out any possibilities.

Kyle looked up from his phone. Seventy-eight hertz, he said. And thirty-two decibels, from about two hundred metres away.

That's a pretty low frequency, I replied, recording the measurements in my notebook, beside the words 'Grenadier plant, Ranchlands Industrial Park.' But we both knew, without having to say it, that it was not low enough. Our theory—well Kyle's theory, really—was that the hum must be an extremely low frequency, just on the threshold of human hearing. Most humans could just about register sound at twenty hertz. It seemed possible that we were simply hearing a sound lower than most people are able to perceive.

Lots of animals can hear and make infrasonic sounds. Some are even thought to be able to perceive infrasonic waves travelling through the Earth in the wake of natural disasters and use these waves as a kind of early warning system. Like the rats and snakes deserting the ancient Greek city of Helike, before it was devastated by an earthquake. Or the animals that fled the areas affected by the Indian Ocean tsunami, hours before disaster struck. I once read that some church organs can produce infrasonic bass notes that induce feelings of transcendence by increasing heart rates and releasing endorphins, causing congregants to tear up, shiver, or feel as if they're communing with God. It wasn't far off the effect the hum had on me, to be honest. The crying and shivering at least.

Once back in the car, I pulled out our map of the neighbourhood. Laying it across the dash, I placed a small yellow sticker over the pixelated aerial view of the industrial park and jotted down the measurements with a thin-tipped black marker. Red stickers would indicate sites producing sounds over a hundred hertz, yellow stickers would indicate sounds over fifty hertz, and green stickers would indicate sounds in the sweet spot—sounds which could be our hum. Hopefully a pattern, or hot spot, would slowly emerge. I folded away the map and shifted the car into drive as we set off towards our next site—the electrical substation on San Mateo Road.

I still think we should visit Harding, Kyle said, pulling out his vape from his pocket.

Hey, what did I say? Not in the car.

I thought it was fine if the window was down.

I bit the inside of my cheek. Sometimes he really tested my patience. I couldn't stand the smell of his flavoured vape: a sickly sweet cherry, which reminded me of childhood cough syrup. The windows were automatic, so I turned the key in the ignition.

Who knows what kind of aircraft or low-frequency weapons they're testing over there, he said, blowing a little aromatic cloud out the window.

We're not driving to Harding, I said. He knew this and didn't press it. The military base in Harding was almost a two-hour round trip. Driving around the neighbourhood together was risky enough, though at least I could always concoct some half-viable excuse that I was dropping him off at home, he having missed his bus, and it being on my way, or some such thing. I'm not quite sure how I rationalized it to myself at the time; particularly as our drives grew gradually longer each passing week, as we expanded the radius of our search. Ultimately, it wasn't about reason. I knew there was no defence of it on professional grounds. But on grounds of emotional welfare and mental health, it was essential. We refused to be victims. We refused to believe we were hallucinating. We were too resourceful, and too proactive to sit back and suffer. If you are being tormented, tortured, you don't sit around talking about it forever. You take action.

As we drove towards San Mateo Road, I pulled my sun visor down against the evening light, and Kyle plugged his phone into the car's sound system. It began to play a plaintive, downtempo R&B song I recognized from the radio. It underscored our drive through the neighbourhood like a soundtrack; though what kind of film this was, and what kind of characters we were, didn't feel immediately clear to me. I couldn't help but feel, sometimes, like the antagonist of my own story. Covertly undermining all the goodwill and stability I had worked tirelessly, for decades, to accrue. As we coasted down sleepy residential streets, I began turning the word *predator* over in my mind. Perhaps because there was a seventeen-year-old boy in my car. Perhaps because we were both on a hunt, our senses tuned. Or perhaps because we had both been preyed upon by this noise; torn apart and devoured by it. I was taking a slightly roundabout route through the neighbourhood to avoid passing near the school, or any more heavily trafficked areas like the mall or the arena. The sunset filled the car with warm orange light.

Have you heard the story about the loneliest whale in the world? Kyle asked. I shook my head, smiling. Well it's not a story, he continued, I mean it's a true story, it's not made up. He's been dubbed the fifty-two-hertz whale. He glanced over at me, but I kept my eyes on the road. He told me about how there was a single lone whale, of unknown species, who had been recorded producing a totally unique fifty-two-hertz call. The call had the sonic signature of a whale, but it didn't resemble any known species, being much higher-pitched, shorter, and more frequent.

Blue whales and fin whales, for instance, Kyle said, using his hands to shape a small whale in front of him, they vocalize around twenty hertz.

This, I had come to learn, was classic Kyle: riffing on an obscure factoid he had gleaned from the Internet to simulate a far vaster knowledge than he really possessed on any given topic. He told me the migration of the fifty-two-hertz whale through the Pacific was strange, in that it didn't match the movement of any other known whale species. It was a mystery. But the same, singular fifty-two-hertz call has been recorded every year since first being detected two decades ago. Calling forever into the void of the dark Pacific. Never to find another of its kind.

The loneliest whale in the world, I said, nodding. I looked up into the sky, as if I might find it hiding in the clouds. A moment later, we pulled off onto the gravel shoulder of San Mateo Road, alongside the electrical substation, with its humming transformers and power towers. I checked my mirrors for passing cars or onlookers, and after a deep breath, gave the all-clear.

5

PAUL AND I REPLACED SEX WITH AUDIOBOOKS. IT WAS A gradual process, over four or five years. Occasionally, we still managed both. After I moved back into our bedroom, following my exile in The Gym, we began listening to *The Magic Mountain*. One night, as the plummy British narration played from the Bluetooth speaker, I was standing at the window, struggling to unclasp my bra, lost in the Alpine majesty of the prose, the long sentences, full of switchbacks, when Paul came up behind me and undid my bra clasp with a dexterousness that belied his big hands.

Who is this again? he asked.

Thomas Mann.

Oh man, oh man, he murmured, sliding his hands over my breasts and cupping them, and I laughed, for when Paul played smooth, it was a caricature of smoothness. There has always been something of a joke about sex for Paul, which probably arose from some innate discomfort with his own, ungainly body. One of us tackled the other down onto the bed, and we were both laughing, which we hadn't done together in a while, and honestly it was probably the laughing more than anything that began to turn me on. I reached over and switched off the speaker, and when I turned back to Paul, he had a truly impressive boner sheathed below his underwear, which he sprang free with gusto.

What're you challenging me to a duel?

He swished it around, En garde!

Sir Gawain, and his Walmart boxers.

Prepare to be run through the gauntlet.

I flopped onto my back, chortling. He lay down beside me with a dopey grin. What? he asked.

You can't run someone through the gauntlet, you're putting two things together.

Sure you can, with a sword.

No, you 'run someone through.' You 'run the gauntlet' when you like—

Oh right.

—do something really hard.

Paul gestured to his jaunty member—Well.

I rolled my eyes, and he climbed on top of me, rubbing his cock against my thigh.

Forged in the smithy of desire, he murmured.

Okay Chaucer, get off, I wheezed, you're crushing me.

He relaxed and splayed himself atop me. I'm dead, he said.

I can't breathe.

Your corpse groom.

I'm serious, get off me.

I actually couldn't breathe and grew panicked and told him firmly again to *get off.* His smile disappeared as he slid off of me. I could tell he felt rejected, which wasn't my intention. I felt a heaviness descend between us. I wanted to keep things light, so I turned to him and smiled.

Fatso.

He chuckled, and I rubbed my hand over his belly. It had just the right amount of hair. Not too coarse or thick. My big bear, I said, in a silly voice, my big, pregnant bear.

Don't.

Third trimester.

He sat up and batted my hand away. I'm serious, he said, I'm sensitive about it.

I propped my head up with my hand. Are you really?

Yes. I am.

I'm sorry.

I made to kiss him on his cheek, but this seemed too impersonal, so I moved towards his lips, but in my indecision, ended up somewhere in between. This tiny failure robbed the kiss of any intimacy. In fact, it suddenly seemed to signify some larger misalignment.

I'm always initiating and you're never up for it, he said. I pointed out that we hadn't been sleeping in the same room, and he asked me whose fault was that.

I don't know, why? I asked. Do you blame me?

Well it's not my fault, he said, lying back down and staring up at the ceiling, his erection subsiding. I asked him why it had to be about fault. There was something about his diminishing erection that I found deeply tragic.

Fuck it, let's do it, I said, getting onto all fours above him, and running my hand up his thigh.

It's fine.

No I do, I really want to.

The moment's passed.

No, I'm—look. I grabbed what remained of his boner. I'm seizing the moment, see? Based on his little jolt, perhaps a bit too forcefully.

Wow, you certainly have.

I slackened my grip a little, and leaned down to kiss him, this time confidently on the lips, open mouthed. Tongues darted, probing. It was a choreography at first. A mimicry. But gradually, it became real. Embodied. We lost ourselves in one another like we hadn't for ages, until he pulled his head away and studied my face with a furtive smile.

It's nice to have you back, he said.

I didn't go anywhere.

He nodded, looking at my eyes but also through me, lost in thought. Oh I was meaning to tell you . . . he said with a chuckle, his eyes focusing back on my face. Lucas sent me this crazy article today about this couple in Florida who reported hearing this humming sound in their house. It kept them up for days, and when they investigated they discovered this humongous wasps' nest in a hollow wall and they had to tear down the entire—

Why are you telling me this? I interrupted. My face felt hot.

I just—

Can we just kiss? I asked. We did for a few moments, until I fell back out of it. Why did you tell me that?

Just forget about it.

But I couldn't. I was irritated and distracted now. Did you tell Lucas about me? I asked.

No, he has no idea; he just sent it to me because he thought it was crazy.

It didn't sound like a wasps' nest, I said, overtop of his reply.

I know, I—

I told him it sounded like distant thunder rumbling all the time, it wasn't a wasps' nest, it wasn't just a funny story in some 'crazy' article. I disentangled myself from Paul and lay back on my side of the bed.

I just thought it was funny.

Well it's not.

Nothing much is anymore, is it, he said, sitting up. I lay there for a long moment, looking at the ceiling, fists balled at my side. I could hear him starting to check emails on his phone.

Maybe I shouldn't sleep here tonight, I mumbled.

Oh c'mon.

I don't think we're ready, I said, sliding out of bed. I started towards the door, but he got up and waylaid me in the middle of the room with a hug from behind. He wrapped his arms around my waist and held me there.

Please, he whispered. I let him hold me, and slowly melt me against his big white slice of Wonder Bread chest. We just stood there, breathing together for a long while, until I felt him getting hard against my thigh.

Oh, and we're back, I said.

I'm throwing down the gauntlet.

I turned to face him. He wore a boyish, expectant look. I couldn't help but smile. He leaned down and kissed me on the lips.

I'm sorry, he murmured. I'm trying.

I know, I said. And I kissed him back. He hovered his lips over my neck, as he slid his fingers down below my waistband. We made our way, fumblingly, back towards the bed, and tumbled down onto it, lips locked. He began pulling off my underwear, and I helped him, pushing it down my legs with my left foot. It felt strange to be aware of both the hum and Paul's panting. I tried to tune out the hum, and focus only on our sharp, quaking exhales. Our grunts. On the moisture of our bodies. The smacking of our skin. I let myself get lost in these sounds—until my phone buzzed with a text on the bedside table. I ignored it, and tried focusing again on his breath, focusing on the sound of our bodies, until another buzz followed, and another. I slammed my hand down over my phone.

Paul stopped. For fuck's sake, he muttered, a drop of sweat sliding off his brow onto my cheek.

Sorry.

Can't you turn it off?

I turned over and glanced at the texts. My stomach plunged.

Who's messaging you at eleven at night?

I brought the phone close against my body to block Paul's view of the screen. It's Cass, I lied. She and Aldo are going through a rough patch. Paul asked what the trouble was, and I shook my head as I read through the texts. Sorry, I'll tell you later, I said, I just need to call her. She's in a state.

Well maybe you can tell her we're in a bit of a state ourselves.

I'm sorry, I said, rising from the bed, and pulling on my nightgown.

We're having sex for the first time in a century, and she's making you take a fucking call.

He lay back in bed like a hot dog dropped from a bun.

I know, I'm sorry, I said again, tying the sash around my waist, and making for the door.

You have all goddamn day to talk with each other at school.

I'll be five minutes!

And what, I'm supposed to just sit here and keep the engine running, he said, dolefully stroking his erection.

Five minutes, I repeated, closing the door behind me.

I slipped out of the bedroom, down the stairs, and into the dining room, my phone the only illumination in the darkness, as I sat down on a chair and dialed the number. As the call rang through, I thought of Paul and his penis upstairs, that sorry scene. I heard a click, and then breathing on the other end of the line.

Hello?

Hey. Kyle's voice was clipped and tight.

What's going on, are you okay?

I just needed to talk to you.

I closed my eyes. We agreed you'd only message in an emergency, I said.

I know, but—

You can't be sending me texts at midnight.

—this is an emergency.

I asked him where he was.

I went for a walk, he said.

Where?

Just around the neighbourhood. I couldn't call from home.

I heard the scrape of his shoe kicking a stone along asphalt.

Listen, are you somewhere private? he asked.

Sort of, I replied, under my breath.

We could meet in the park. Near the school.

No, I can't do that.

Just for five minutes.

I knew something must be wrong, but it was hard to gauge the severity of the problem from his voice.

I can't come out, I said. Just tell me what's going on.

He was silent for a long moment. I asked him if he was still there.

There're others, he said quietly.

What do you mean?

Others who can hear it.

I took a moment to process what he was saying. How do you know? I asked.

There's a guy I play basketball with, Julian Delgado?

I know Julian, I said. I had taught Julian two years ago.

We were playing earlier tonight and I told him.

My breath caught in my throat. What?

Just—

About us?

No, no, about the hum, he could tell something was up with me, and then he told me his mom suffers from it too. It gives her headaches. Keeps her up at night.

Lots of things do that, I said, not hiding my anger. Until now, we had been fastidiously discreet.

No, trust me, she really hears it, he insisted.

How do you know it's the same thing?

Because I talked to her, he said, as my heart sank even deeper.

You talked to his mother?

I'm telling you she can hear it. She described it to me exactly. And then she told me she works for this couple on Sequoia Crescent, and apparently they can both hear it. And this couple? They know of others who can too, and they're organizing a meeting.

I struggled to take in everything he was saying. What . . . what kind of meeting? I asked.

To talk about it. To figure out what it is.

It was clear he was dazzled by the news, but I didn't know what to say. I wasn't even sure how I felt about the prospect of there being others. I had grown accustomed to having a single, secret interlocutor. Our meet-ups made me feel awake to the possibility of wonder and mystery in a way that I hadn't in years. I found myself preoccupied throughout the day with thinking about our next mission; about what leads we had not yet followed up on, or clues we might have missed. During class, or the lunch hour, I made little mental notes of things I wanted to share with him, and sometimes even had the impulse to text him to gauge his reaction. But of course I didn't. In class, I made every effort to hide our bond—which resulted in my more or less completely ignoring him. I avoided any eye contact, and no longer called on him like I used to, which effectively meant he never spoke.

Are you still there? he asked.

Yeah.

It's the Saturday after next, 12 Sequoia Crescent, noon. She wrote it down on a piece of paper for me.

I repeated the address, trying to visualize where in the neighbourhood it was, and then asked him what he thought we should do.

Well obviously we have to go.

I told him it didn't feel so obvious to me. What if there're people who recognize us? I asked. Julian's mother, for instance.

It doesn't matter.

Of course it does, I can't be seen with you out of school.

But—

In a stranger's house on a Saturday afternoon, I mean how—

This is what we've been waiting for, he interjected. There might be someone there who actually knows.

As Kyle spoke I considered how, initially, all I had wanted was for others to validate my experience, and offer up answers. But that was before the strange bliss of complicity I had found with him.

Aren't you curious? he asked.

Of course I am, that's not the point.

Then what are we doing? If we can't take the next step, we're just wasting our time.

I knew he was trying to hurt me with this comment, and he succeeded. I told him that he should just go himself; I couldn't stop him.

What if I arrive first? he suggested. And if there's an obvious red flag I can text you not to come. But if the coast is clear, then I'll text you a thumbs-up. You don't have to sit beside me or let on anything about us.

He went quiet for a moment. I heard a car drive past him. I can't go alone, he said. I need you there.

I felt like a branch being carried by the quick black stream of my own life. I made a small circle with the palm of my hand on the smooth darkness of the dining room table, and sighed. Okay.

Thank you.

And you're sure you didn't tell Julian or his mother about us?

No.

I told Kyle that we were navigating dangerous territory, and he said that he was aware. I looked out the picture window at the dark-grey of the front yard, and the faint glow of the street beyond. I tried to imagine what I would do if I saw Kyle standing out there, talking to me on his phone. I honestly wouldn't have put it past him. There was a wild unpredictability about him. He had the soul of a poet, and the brain of a teenager, full of whimsy and bad impulse control.

No more texting me in the middle of the night, okay?

Okay.

Now, try to get some sleep.

You too, he said. And then after a moment, he added—Good night, Claire.

I felt a jolt at the sound of my name. It was the first time he had ever said it. But then for him to call me 'Miss,' now, would have felt ridiculous. I was suddenly struck by the fact that it had never once come up in any of our chats after class. I wondered how long he had been waiting to say it, or whether he had even given it a thought before now. Before I could say good night, I sensed a shift in the room. A presence behind me. I turned and gasped, and jumped up from my chair, dropping the phone. Jesus Christ—

A shadow leaned against the doorway to the kitchen. Wearing an oversized t-shirt, like a nightdress, and holding a glass of water.

I was parched, Ashley said, taking a languid sip. You could cook an egg on her vocal fry. I put my foot over the bright screen of the phone, hiding the name of the caller as fast as I could. But was I fast enough? My mind raced back over the last five minutes.

Were you just standing there, listening to me?

Who was that?

I suddenly felt hot pressure all over, like my skin couldn't contain me. I crouched down to the floor, grabbed the phone out from under my foot, and pressed the red button to end the call.

Why were you listening to my conversation?

Who were you taking to?

Cassandra.

Oh really, she replied, drolly.

She's been going through a hard time, and I've been trying to—

Are you having an affair?

I laughed, though it sounded more like wind being knocked from my lungs. Ashley reached for the dimmable light switch, and turned up the chandelier over the dining table, just enough to see one another's face.

Is it a woman? she pressed.

What?

I heard you say 'I can't come out.'

I forced a chuckle, but I couldn't tell if she was being serious. I've always thought you were a little dyke-y, she said.

That's not funny, I replied, fixing her with a look.

Is it Mr. Gaddis?

What? No. God no.

I can't be seen with you out of school, she said, parroting me.

She had been listening forensically. I really didn't see any other way out of this. I tried to listen for any movement upstairs, or on the stairs. The last thing I needed was Paul overhearing us.

You have to promise you won't tell anyone.

She cocked her head to the side. Why would I make that promise? she asked.

Because I could lose my job.

Jesus Christ, she muttered. So it is a teacher.

I held the back of my chair and bowed my head. It's not an affair, I said, and it's not a teacher.

What, a student? she asked, with a snicker. The smile suddenly dropped from her face. Oh my god it is.

You have to promise me that you'll keep this between us.

She put her glass of water down hard on the table. What the actual hell are you telling me? she asked.

There's nothing inappropriate happening between us.

Oh my god you're having an affair with a student, she said, her mouth dropping open.

No, I'm not.

I bet I can guess who it is.

Ash, this is not a joke.

She crossed her arms, smirking. Is it Luke? she asked.

I lowered my voice to a vicious whisper—I need you to shut up and listen to me, all right? This could destroy me. I need you to promise I can trust you with this. Please.

She fixed me with a stare, like a genie waiting for my third and final calamitous wish. Fine, she said.

Kyle Francis can hear the hum.

Her eyes darted across my face, the hint of any smile now gone. Kyle Francis? she asked.

I told her how he came to me unprompted, how it caused him the same symptoms, how he'd been in a dark place, and had no one to talk to, and how I was worried about him, so I gave him my number.

I know a few girls who would literally kill you for those digits.

What?

Even though he's, like, a stoner and looks vaguely unwell.

Ash—

And a bit white trash.

Enough.

And is maybe a homo, though who knows.

What?

Can you imagine, a sensitive fag who plays basketball, no wonder everyone's obsessed with him.

Don't—don't use that word.

It's fine, I'm one too, I can say it.

You can say you're queer, but don't use—

No I'm a fag, I'm a gay man, Mom, that's literally my sexuality.

I was too tired to unpick that right then, so I just nodded. I was usually the preferred teacher for kids to come out to, probably because I directed the school musicals, though in the last couple of years a new, fluid vanguard of sexuality was emerging that challenged even my finely honed gaydar. Kyle would certainly be a case in point.

Who knows, but he once sent this video of himself jerking off to Pierre-Antoine Defreine, and he um, Pierre-Antoine, sent it to Emma, who sent it to a bunch of us, and honestly, Mom—this video? Like. I mean I'm not going to show you obviously, but it's legendary.

She then asked me what his midnight emergency was about. Did he run out of pot or something?

I made a little disapproving cluck, which made me feel about seventy years old, and it suddenly struck me that, despite the hours we had spent together over the past while, I still knew very little about Kyle or his reputation among other students. I suppose I shouldn't have been surprised to hear him referred to as a stoner, or as white trash, or even as someone over whom adolescent girls might 'literally kill,' though I was, on all accounts. Ashley crossed her arms, and shifted her weight—Well?

He was calling to tell me that . . . there're others who can hear the noise. And they're meeting a couple of Saturdays from now.

She exhaled sharply and shook her head, like an exasperated parent. She asked me if we spoke often, and I confessed that we did sometimes, after class, but then students came to me with problems all of the time. A lot of difficult issues got brought up in class, through the books we studied, and sometimes students were triggered, or a discussion would cause them to open up to me afterwards, in private. Ashley pursed her lips, frog-faced, in rebuke of my weak defence. Of course these students weren't calling me at midnight.

Sounds like you two have a pretty special connection, she said. I affirmed this with silence. I mean he's smart, she added.

Yes, very, I replied. And very perceptive.

She looked at me with a certain understanding. A gentle concern. I felt something thaw between us, and it suddenly seemed that the possibility of a small reopening might exist in which she and I could speak candidly again with one another, without judgement.

Being able to talk to him . . . I can't even tell you. It's true, what we have is very special. He's my confidant, and I'm his. And I know from the outside it looks—

Fucked up, she said flatly.

I nodded, realizing I had misjudged, and proceeded with caution. You can see why I'm nervous, I said.

Yeah it's uh . . . it's pretty fucked up.

I dug my nails into my palm. I shouldn't have let my guard down like that. I suddenly felt stripped by her gaze. This is why I need to trust you with this, I said.

I don't want to be trusted with this! I don't want to have any part of this, and you shouldn't either. This isn't cool, all right? And I don't want you fucking up your life with this. And my life. Have you even thought about—? Kyle is a friend of mine, like a friend of all my friends.

I know, it's complicated.

No, it's not, she said, eyes wide, it's actually totally simple. Stop. Stop seeing Kyle or anyone else who thinks they can hear your fucking hum.

In that moment, for the first time in my life, I felt afraid of Ashley. I felt an almost dizzying loss of status. When had that shift occurred? I suppose it was just another thing the hum had stripped me of. Or maybe it had been a more gradual attrition over the years, perhaps ever since she started high school when I began to feel a certain slackening of our psychic bond, but I had always felt that was natural, even healthy. It had never alarmed me before. But now, suddenly, this distance felt dangerous. A chasm to fall into.

I think it would be a good idea if you didn't mention this to your father, I said.

She took a sip of water. And what makes you think you can ask me that?

I'm just telling you—

I know what you're telling me, and here's what I'm telling you—stop. Her eyes bored into me as she picked up her water glass. Just—stop, she said. And we can forget about everything. The choice is yours, Mom.

And with that, she walked out of the dining room, and up the stairs. I stood there in the half-light, bracing myself against the table, until I heard the door to her bedroom bang shut, like a gun firing a blank.

6

BEING WITH KYLE WAS TO FEEL A LITTLE LESS ALONE, A LITTLE less scared, and a little less like some messed up Lars von Trier heroine. It was to feel proactive about my own condition, and to refuse victimhood. It was to feel believed. But every mother reading this will understand when I say—when your child asks you to stop, you stop. There wasn't a question. Doing something that caused Ashley hurt or distress was basically the single greatest fear I had lived with since I pushed her slimy, screaming body out of mine. Nothing was worth risking our connection, or her wellbeing, even if it meant remaining mired in the headfuck of the hum forever. So I left for school that morning with the plan to pull Kyle aside, at the end of class, and tell him that we couldn't continue—except, he didn't come to class.

At lunch, Cass and I were eating disappointing sandwiches at my desk and diagnosing a persistent sex dream of hers about Alfred Molina, when there was a knock at the door, and Valeria strode into the room, followed by a compact woman with leathered skin and blond hair faded to the colour of dishwater. Kyle had shown me a photo of this woman before. Her name was Brenda, and she was his mother. A bank teller, probably my age. I always felt a kinship for fellow young mothers. We'd all been through the shit in one way or the other. I could always pick one out in a crowd. Too few years stretched over too much living. Kyle trailed behind both women, eyes to the floor.

Hi, Claire, Valeria said, with a curt smile. Do you have a moment?

Yes, hi, I said, rising from my chair. What's going on?

Well that's what we're here to figure out. Valeria's bob cut jostled as she turned to Cass. Do you mind giving us a few minutes, Cassandra?

Of course, Cass said, glancing at Kyle, and then back at me. I saw her read the fear on my face. She frowned as she gathered her things and made towards the door. Valeria pulled two more chairs over to my desk. From out in the hallway I could hear the conversation and laughter of students, completely oblivious to the imminent implosion of my life. As Cass reached the door she gave me an odd look, which I held, as she closed the door behind her.

Claire, this is Kyle's mother, Mrs. Francis, Valeria said. The familial resemblance was uncanny, especially in the eyes.

Very nice to meet you, I replied, extending my hand.

What're you doing with my son? she asked, ignoring my hand. I told her I would be happy to talk to her about it. Oh really, would you be? she replied, vicious.

Yes, I would. Your son came to me a month or so ago after class, I said, holding her gaze. He told me he'd been distracted during my lessons because he wasn't sleeping, and I asked him—

This noise business is your doing, you put this in his head, she said, cutting me off.

Valeria gestured to the chairs she'd assembled. Why don't we all sit down, shall we?

I told Brenda I had never spoken with Kyle about the noise before he approached me, and I looked to him for confirmation about this, but he was staring down at his hands.

He never once talked about this noise before you, she said. He never even mentioned it and then all of a sudden—She splayed her hands towards Kyle, as if his physical being was all the argument she needed to make. She grabbed a chair and sat down, and the rest of us followed suit.

Can you hear this noise right now? Valeria asked me. I told her that I could. She turned to Kyle and asked if he could too. He looked up but seemed unsure what to say.

Brenda motioned to him—No, you see?

I can, he replied.

Brenda turned and leaned in towards Kyle. You can, what? That's not what you said two hours ago. He sighed and shrugged, and Brenda turned to me, eyes wide. Y'see, you're putting this in his head, she said. Look at him. He has no energy, he's tired, he's depressed. His grades are through the floor. He doesn't listen to me when I'm speaking to him, he just—She gestured off into the distance. And then I find out he's been seeing you after class, she continued. Spending time with you in your classroom and in your car, going on drives with you *in your car*, when the whole time he's been telling me he's been at basketball.

My heart sank. She knew about the drives. How much had Kyle told her, and for the love of Christ, why?

Is this true, Claire, Valeria asked, looking pained, that you've been going on drives with Kyle in your car?

Yes. It is. I heard my voice as if it were thrown by a ventriloquist.

Talking about this imaginary noise, and tell her—Brenda said, turning back to Kyle—driving around looking for this sound like they're chasing ghosts. You are insane.

Is this true? Valeria asked again.

We have gone on a couple drives after school to—I began, weakly.

How many?

Five or six.

Valeria's eyes widened, as if I'd just said an impossibly high number. Five or six drives, she said.

I explained that we mostly just talked, about feeling isolated; about how this had made us feel cut off from our friends and family, and then Brenda claimed I was the reason for his withdrawal; that I was the one who had cut him off. And honestly, if she was Ashley's teacher, and it was Ashley in her car, I'd have been saying the same thing, I'd have been breaking down the door wanting answers too. I knew how this must have looked from the outside. I knew how beyond the pale this was, and of course I sympathized with her, mother to mother. But I wanted to tell Brenda—I saved your son. Did he ever tell you about how he wanted to kill himself? How he started to self-harm? You should be thanking me, lady. You should be thanking me your son is still here, sitting in that chair, looking at his hands.

I took a deep breath and, while trying to keep my voice from quavering, I explained how we had been brainstorming possible sources for the noise and told them about the map of all the sites we had visited. I thought perhaps the level of thought and commitment we'd brought to this would help them understand how seriously we took this; how much it had affected us, and the lengths we would go to to help ourselves, when no one else seemed prepared to. I explained our theory about the noise, and the app on Kyle's phone we had been using to measure the sound at each location. I explained why we chose the sites we did. The electrical substation. The construction work up by Saguaro Drive. The wind turbines out by the interstate. I noticed Valeria grimacing. I tried to imagine how she must have seen me in that moment; a trusted and respected colleague of nearly a decade, suddenly unhinged. Unrecognizable. I exhaled and told them that I was aware of how odd all of this must sound.

We've been trying to educate ourselves the best we can, I said.

Valeria turned to Kyle. Is this true, what Ms. Devon's been saying? she asked. He looked up, ran his tongue along his lower lip, and nodded. Can you please use your words? she asked.

Yes.

So you do hear this noise then, Valeria said. If everything Ms. Devon is saying is true, then you—

Brenda slammed her hand down on the top of my desk. *Stop—* playing with his words.

I'm just trying to get the story st—

I hope you realize I am this close to going to the police with this.

Yes, I understand that, but—

So you better stop putting words in his mouth.

If this is going to proceed, I need to hear the rest of his story.

Brenda pointed her finger at Valeria's face. Do not put words in his mouth.

All right.

Or I am calling the police.

Valeria raised her hands, nodding. She then asked Kyle if she could listen to the recordings he had made of the noise on his phone.

The app doesn't make recordings, it's a spectrogram, he replied. It graphs sound in real time.

It's almost impossible to record the hum itself, I said. We've tried, but there's too much ambient noise.

But it does pick up enough to measure, he clarified. It's not in our heads.

He looked straight at Brenda as he said this, for the first time since they arrived. She narrowed her eyes at him, and then, while still holding Kyle's gaze, she asked if I had ever taken her son back to my house.

Mom, no, Kyle replied, exasperated.

I can assure you, Mrs. Francis, that I would never invite a student—

Assured, do you think I'm assured?

Mom, I've told you.

Told me? You didn't tell me about any of this until I forced it out of you. And only thanks to your daughter, Ms. Devon.

I'm sorry?

Brenda's face dropped. You don't—you don't know about my little exchange with Ashley this morning?

I felt like I had been hit in the stomach with a baseball bat. I wasn't sure if I could withstand what I was about to hear.

Well, Brenda continued, clearly relishing this turn, let me tell you then. I was in the kitchen making coffee. Kyle had left his phone on the counter, and I noticed it light up with a WhatsApp message. 'Do you want to ruin her?' Brenda looked at me, and then at Valeria, eyebrows raised in theatrical indignation, before continuing. That's what it said—'Do you want to ruin her?' So, as you can imagine, I made him come downstairs, unlock his phone, and show me the whole conversation because I damn well wanted to know what kind of son I'm raising.

My throat burned, and no amount of swallowing made it better. Oh Ash, I thought. What have you done?

So once I figured out what was going on, Brenda continued, I messaged her back. I said—'This is Brenda Francis. You tell your mother Yes. I sure the hell do.'

And what did she reply? I heard myself ask.

Brenda removed Kyle's phone from her pocket. Nothing yet, she said, and then looked up at me. But she's read the message.

But she's read the message. Those words gutted me more than

any other. Even now, I still wonder why Ashley never came to warn me of the impending shitstorm before it knocked on my classroom door. Did she want to punish me? Or did she stall out of guilt; out of fear of what she'd accidentally set into motion? I've tried not to let it eat away at me.

To this day, I replay in my head the conversation I had with Valeria, after Brenda had stormed out with Kyle in tow. I hear her telling me how she had the greatest respect for me as a teacher, and how worried she was about me, and how, when I was struggling with burnout, she supported me taking the time off that I needed. And I hear myself still trying to salvage what I could, though already knowing it was too late. I hear her telling me that she's cancelling my afternoon classes, and referring my case to the school board with the recommendation that my contract be terminated, and I hear myself pleading please don't do this to me, and her saying I'm afraid you did this to yourself, and me shouting back that she had no idea, no fucking idea what we were living through, and then that was it, once I swore at her, that was really it. I think about how she waited for me as I collected my things.

One of the great abiding joys of my life had been working with young people; introducing them to the power of language, literature, ideas, and helping free them from all of the patriarchal, white-dominant, homophobic, and generally anti-imagination, anti-pleasure, anti-risk-taking frameworks that they'd been corralled into like cattle. More than a joy, it was also my purpose. For that to be stripped from me was one of the great humiliations of my life. Looking back, the collapse of my identity as an educator was a major turning point. Maybe the turning point. The moment I was no longer a respectable person, not even to myself.

I didn't blame Brenda for razing me to the ground. I probably would have done the same. But I vowed that afternoon that I would not let her destroy Kyle, even if out of love. As a teacher, every so often I would come across a student like Kyle who seemed, like a desert oasis, to exist against all odds, who was curious and well-read, or had the desire to be, but came from a home with no books, where curiosity was discouraged, and where intellectuals were viewed at best with skepticism, but mostly with scorn. I was such a student, born into such a home, and I always recognized others when they came along. In most cases, that curiosity dried up by the time the student reached grade twelve. I watched it happen time and again, a little bit every day, until, by graduation, the student was a dry and hardened salt pan. I never blamed the mothers like mine, or Brenda, who were just doing their best with what they had, long ago calcified themselves. But I refused to let it happen to Kyle.

Valeria walked with me to the parking lot as I carried my things, past students and my colleagues, none of them the wiser about what was unfolding. I couldn't bear the thought of driving home so I just drove around and around the neighbourhood aimlessly, until I headed out onto the highway and into the desert, past shuttered motels, the truck stop, all the way out to Harding, to pull my car over at the military base, where I listened in vain, before driving back home after sunset, the desert the colour of a bruise. I still think about the look on Paul's face as I walked in the door, holding the contents of my desk in a banker's box. I think about how I didn't even have the strength left to talk to Ashley, as she walked in the door a half-hour later, still in her muddied soccer gear. How she ran upstairs and slammed the door to the bathroom, and stood under the hot shower for an hour, before going to bed, and how I didn't cry until I was finally alone in the guest room. I still think about waking up in the morning and dreading the unending hours of daytime ahead, with no company but the hum; and then spending the whole day dreading the return of my own husband and daughter. I think about how Cass, and Nadia, and the book club didn't so much as call or email. I think about what rumours must have begun circulating through the school halls; through the staff lounge; through the air in the form of a thousand text messages. I think of Ashley finding me on the couch one night, staring at my laptop. The air charged with her presence, her silence. I feel the weight of her sitting down beside me.

I messaged Kyle because I was fucking scared for you.

I know, I hear myself saying. I know, kiddo.

But, like, do you really have any clue how much this has completely fucked up my life? I'm the one who has to live with— Kaitlynn and Sarah aren't even talking to me! People are posting all kinds of shit about me. The looks I get? When I walk into the girls' bathroom? Like it's all fine for you to hide away here on the couch, but I'm the one who has to go into school every day and face it all.

As I look at her, I remember the feeling I had the moment I first saw her after giving birth, her face contorted in distress like it was now. The feeling had something to do with the realization that, from that moment on, I would never quite be a whole person again. That there would now always be some part of myself living outside of my body that I had only nominal control over, if any. I loved her with an intensity that startled even me at times, startled me in its animal insistence, like a genetic imperative beyond my reason.

Ashley wiped her eyes and leaned into me and I put my arm around her. And I held her tight. I held her like she might slip away from me. I felt us all slipping. Slipping into a household of secrets, and silences, and resentments. And me, slipping fastest of all, into darkness. Into days of never leaving the house. Never leaving myself. Never leaving the hum.

7

YOU ARE NOT A CRIMINAL
You are not a pervert
You are not malicious
You are not stupid
You are not selfish
You are not insane
You are not cancelled
You are not a cuntface
You are not a bad wife
You are not a bad mother
You are not your mother
You are not your own tired reflection in the mirror
You are not a human-shaped flesh sack
You are not being cosmically punished
You are not the wreckage of your own sublimated desires
You are not going to show up at Ashley's game like this

You are not going to cry in front of Paul again
You are not going to touch yourself while crying again
You are not going to throw Paul's clothes out of the closet again
You are not going to move the bottle of pills from the cabinet
You are not going to call the school
You are not going to call Brenda Francis
You are not going to text Kyle
You are not going to go to that meeting on Sequoia Crescent
You are not going to check Facebook
You are not going to check Facebook
You are not going to check Facebook

8

I WENT TO THE MEETING ON SEQUOIA CRESCENT.

I went to the meeting despite knowing Paul and Ashley would be apoplectic if they found out. I went not knowing, really, whether I wanted to go, or whether it would be productive for my mental health, such as it was. I went not knowing whether Kyle would be there or not; we had stopped all contact. Perhaps I only went because I suspected he would be. I guess that says everything you need to know about where my head was at the time. I was able to go because Ashley had a game that Saturday morning which Paul drove her to and stayed to watch; otherwise I would never have been able to slip away.

I realize some readers might be thinking—hold on, what the hell was all that about not wanting to risk your connection with Ashley, or her well-being? What about stopping when your child asks you to stop? It's hard for me to look back and justify it now, but my thinking at the time was consumed with the overwhelming despair that I was failing Ashley as a mother. I felt I needed to *do* something to get myself out of my stupor. I needed information. Even if she might be mad or hurt in the short term, should she find out, I went to the meeting with the intention of making myself better in the long run, so I could be the mother she deserved, and the partner Paul needed.

There was something in Paul that just kind of gave up on me, when everything with Kyle and my termination came to light. The only time we spoke about it, he told me that he felt betrayed. That it made him feel like 'a chump,' after all of the effort and care he had shown.

I'm done, he said, scrunching up his mouth, and shrugging. I'm just . . . I'm done.

Done with my condition, with my insomnia, with talking about it, with talking to me, with caring. And after everything, I didn't blame him. I felt a kind of desperation that I find it difficult to put into words without making myself sound crazy, which of course I was in a sense, I had completely tipped over into some sort of manic state, and I knew I had too, and was just trying everything I could to pull myself out of it. But then, the more you flail around trying to heave yourself out of the quicksand of mania, the more manic you seem, and the more manic you are.

When I pulled up at the house on Sequoia Crescent, my first thought was—these people pay for professional landscaping. Their driveway asphalt looked freshly laid. Their home was large, without being ostentatious. As I walked up the front path, with its ground-level lights embedded in the stone, I thought about how people with money bought large homes, but people with real money bought large homes that somehow didn't look large. I was anxious, and when I get anxious I get gassy, and I let out a truly noxious fart right as I arrived at the door, and had to wait for a full twenty seconds until things had sufficiently abated before I

rang the doorbell, and it was just as well that I did as the door was
opened almost immediately by a large man with tousled white hair,
a tenure-track beard, and a zippered burgundy sweater. His owlish
face broke into a broad, inviting smile.

Hi, I'm Howard, he said, extending a well-lotioned hand, which
I took, and shook, and introduced myself. As I stepped into the
house, I could hear light and easy conversation in the next room.
Howard was wearing these sort of streamlined grey felt slippers,
and told me I was welcome to keep my shoes on, but I removed
them anyway, and followed him through the front hall, with its
wide-plank hardwood floors, earth tones, and Kabuki theatre
masks on the walls. I followed him into the adjoining living room
where six others were standing, chatting around a low coffee table
as if at a cocktail party. Kyle was one of them. He was holding a
glass of Coke with ice cubes in it. Everyone looked up and smiled
in our direction, except Kyle who fixed his gaze on some indeter-
minate point on the ground between us. Howard introduced me,
and then I shook everyone's hand one by one as they introduced
themselves. When I reached Kyle, we introduced ourselves in a
mumbled and, I suspected, unconvincing little pantomime, but no
one seemed to notice.

Along with a somewhat uncomfortable-looking Scandinavian
couch, and two matching, scooped armchairs, there were four
smooth white kitchen chairs arranged in a loose semicircle on the
far side of the coffee table. I took in the rest of the room—the
large abstract oil painting with heavy impasto, the hand-carved
stone vase on the teak end table, the wine-coloured Moroccan rug;
every object felt considered and placed in specific relation to one
another by a discerning eye. Even the subtle but pervasive scent
of sandalwood felt curated. The vaulted ceiling ascended upward
into a large skylight, bathing the room in a soft, late morning glow.
Opposite the bay window was a wall lined with tall bookshelves

and a sliding wood ladder. The bookcase ladder felt like an affectation, but I was into it.

Howard was a bit of a bookshelf ladder himself—a walking, talking intellectual affectation you couldn't help but admire and delight in, somehow fusty and charismatic at the same time. He was a retired geophysicist who spoke with a warm, honeyed baritone, like the narrator of a nature program who betrays no emotion as wild game are eviscerated by apex predators. If I was someone who sometimes used my intelligence as a shield, Howard wielded his like a sword, brandishing doozies like 'When I was doing field research in Mauritius . . . ' As he talked, I couldn't help but smile—when I was a girl, I used to tell my friend Jennifer that I had an eccentric millionaire uncle who travelled the world 'collecting specimens,' who would one day come back and take me on his expeditions. Howard was eccentric millionaire scientist uncle out of central casting, except perhaps a little more effete than I'd have imagined as a girl; a little more wine decanter than pith helmet.

At some point, I succumbed to the gravitational pull of the bookshelves and let myself wander over, as Howard followed. Besides dozens of novels, the shelves were lined with thick art books, from the Renaissance and Flemish masters, to books on Dadaism, the Bauhaus, and numerous individual architects and artists—Corbusier, Zaha Hadid, Eva Hesse, Joseph Beuys, Rachel Whiteread. Howard pulled out a monograph on Albrecht Dürer, and as he slowly leafed through the pages, we spoke about Dürer's woodcut of the rhinoceros he had made without ever having seen one. In their quiet way, these books communicated to me that Howard was my kind of person. Someone who wanted to feel part of the conversation; the immortal conversation of words and images that began with the first humans, and would continue long past our deaths, perhaps even past our extinction as a species, carved on the sides of cliffs, and beamed through outer space. As a girl growing up, eating baloney sandwiches for dinner while my mother worked the night shift, a desire to enter that great, thunderous conversation was a desire to liberate myself from the silence of poverty. The silence of a one-bedroom apartment without books. The silence that comes, not from any lack of intellect, but from the lack of time and means to nourish it.

After a few moments, Howard's much younger partner, Jo, walked over to us. Jo felt as calm and deliberate as calligraphy. She was a yoga instructor who spoke without a single unnecessary or unconsidered word. As I rambled about switching to decaf, and arguing with the phone company that morning, she listened as if excavating layers of meaning in my words that I wasn't even aware of, nodding and hmm-ing like a therapist. For some reason I didn't find this annoying, perhaps because it seemed to come so naturally to her, and I actually began to find the effect strangely calming. I later watched her interacting with others in the room and wondered what it must feel like to move through the world with such an effortless grace, like a swimmer in a calm, cool lake.

By contrast, when I sat down on the couch, I got locked into conversation with Leslie, a woman in her mid-forties wearing an expensive-looking cashmere sweater who broke into frequent little insecure laughs. Everything about Leslie seemed sharp—her features, her voice, her anxiety. She was fiercely intelligent and uncertain, like so many women our age. Probably a college-era eating disorder. Definitely on LinkedIn. She talked to me about her cocker spaniel Toby, who had spent the morning puking his guts up all over her carpet. All I was really dying to ask her about was the hum, but she didn't let me get a word in. The vibe I got from Leslie was that she was successful and unhappy. I could picture looking over in slow traffic on the highway and seeing her talking away on Bluetooth in the regulated micro-climate of her SUV.

Though I'm sure she was powerful, professionally, financially, I immediately felt a certain empathy towards her; even a kind of protectiveness.

When Leslie got up to use the washroom, I noticed a man sitting by himself on one of the kitchen chairs by the coffee table, so I went over and sat down beside him, a handsome but taciturn former soldier named Damian. For reasons he didn't elaborate on, he had been off on disability for the last few years; long enough for him to grow a truly regrettable goatee and ponytail. It was a testament to his natural good looks that these self-sabotaging features didn't override the rest. He reminded me of a roadie, wrapping up mic cables after a Kid Rock concert. I was fielding some pretty strong toxic masculinity vibes from him, but I tried to be generous; I was sure Damian had been through a lot and seen more than his share of horrors. I asked him a few questions about the hum— when he'd begun hearing it, what it sounded like to him—but he seemed embarrassed and evasive, like I was asking him about some dark fetish. Eventually I abandoned the effort, and he seemed all the more relieved for it.

Beside us, on one of the armchairs, sat Nora Delgado; a heavy-set, soft-spoken woman in her mid-forties with deep acne scars. She was the mother of Kyle's friend Julian, and I suppose the reason why Kyle and I had ended up in that living room. I leaned over and introduced myself, and we exchanged a few polite words. I didn't mention that I used to teach her son. And I certainly didn't mention that though this was our first time meeting, it wasn't the first time that I had thought about her. Julian once wrote a short story for my class, about a Guatemalan woman who crossed the Mexican American border with her infant son, and began life as an undocumented migrant, living out of a motel in Texas. The woman worked at the motel as a cleaner, in exchange for accommodation, and had to fend off the sexual advances of the motel owner. When I asked Julian about the story, he denied it was auto-biographical. And yet, there was something about the mother in the story that felt so specific and vivid, I couldn't help but feel she contained some residue of truth. Either way, I gave him full marks, despite the story being about half of the requested word count.

Standing next to us was a young woman with an easy smile named Seema, who, I overheard, was a medical resident at the General. She had a cherubic face, a boyish haircut, a neck tattoo, and a gold nose stud. I admired the casual transgression of her style, in a suburb where black skinny jeans stood out. As she spoke, Seema hid her hands inside the sleeves of her roomy flannel shirt, and sometimes tucked her mouth behind her shirt collar while listening; not in a shy way, but like a cat playing with an empty bag, full of excess, restless energy. She was the youngest in the room, after Kyle, and the two of them had naturally drifted into conversation with one another. They seemed to be comparing notes on the hum, sharing timelines and theories. I wanted to join them, but I got the sense that Kyle needed some space.

He was wearing a baggy black t-shirt with a picture of Heath Ledger's Joker on it. His conversation with Seema had allowed him to avoid making any eye contact with me, right up until Howard convened the meeting and suggested we all take a seat, and even then, Kyle barely managed a glance in my direction. It seemed like an eternity since we had last spoken, and I had felt the absence like a physical ache. I wondered what lie he had told Brenda before leaving home that morning; or if she had even noticed. He looked worn down. But then, we all did. There was a palpable sense of exhaustion in the room. We were a circle of broken spirits, animated with the faint hope that perhaps, at last, we were on the brink of some shared catharsis.

Howard essentially began the meeting by saying, Look, I know you have all been struggling with this noise, and it's confusing, but

I know exactly what it is, and you have nothing to worry about. And frankly, though that seemed like a bit of a ludicrous thing to say, it was exactly what I wanted to hear right then and there in his mahogany voice. The easy confidence with which he made that overarching claim made it almost seem plausible. He then began guiding us through a kind of thought experiment.

How many times do you think lightning strikes the Earth in a given day? he asked smiling, obviously enjoying presiding over this small captive audience. Anyone?

Damian shrugged and broke the silence by guessing twenty-three.

I think it's higher than that, Seema said.

What would you say then? Howard asked her.

A few thousand maybe. Say five thousand?

Five thousand, okay. Anyone else?

Leslie said she thought five thousand sounded about right. Howard asked Kyle what he wagered.

Five thousand five hundred, Kyle replied, which made the group laugh.

What is this, *The Price Is Right*, Seema joked. Five thousand five hundred and one!

Howard waited a moment for any last-minute guesses, and then said—So it's actually eight million times a day, which elicited more laughter. Which works out to about a hundred times a second, he continued.

Twenty-three, Damian repeated to himself, chuckling.

I was like *twenty-three*, Seema said, I've seen twenty-three bolts in the same storm.

So that's about three billion times a year, Howard continued, and so as you can imagine—He suddenly looked up and stopped. Oh, hello.

Everyone turned to see an elderly couple standing in the entryway to the front hall. With no sound of knocking or the doorbell, it was as if they'd been conjured from thin air.

Please, come in, Jo said, waving them into the room.

Sorry we're late, the man replied, stepping forward. He wore a baby-blue dress shirt and seemed athletic for his age, like he might be a member of a tennis club.

Howard rose from the couch to shake the couple's hands. No, no trouble at all, he said.

The door was unlocked, the woman said with a coy smile, burrowing her neck into her shoulders.

We got a bit turned around, her husband added.

He keyed 'Sierra' into the GPS and I said I think it's Sequoia, but—She raised and dropped her arms, laughing, but clearly not yet over the irritation. Jo reassured them that it was easy to get turned around in this area.

We were just talking about lightning, Howard said.

Lightning, okay, the woman said, as Jo took the couple's matching fleece jackets from them. Lightning in what way?

I take it you're Dr. Bard, the man said, before Howard could answer his wife's question.

Yes, but please—call me Howard.

The man introduced himself as Tom, and then introduced his wife, Emily. Hello, she said, with a little wave to everyone. Her glossy manicure suggested migrant labour, but her haircut suggested a Republican voting record. She leaned in towards Howard, and motioned to Jo in the entryway—And sorry, can you remind me your daughter's name?

Jo's not my daughter.

Oh, pardon me, Emily replied, stricken.

Please, Howard said, gesturing to the empty chairs.

Leslie rose to greet Tom and Emily. I'm Leslie, she said, shaking their hands. Tom cocked his head slightly and said she looked familiar. I'm a real estate agent, she replied, with a stretched smile.

Ah. I've seen your lawn signs.

Yup, she said, with a little trilling laugh. I get that a lot.

Jo returned from the front hall as the rest of us introduced our-selves, in turn, to Emily and Tom. To make myself useful, I poured out a few glasses of water from the pitcher on the coffee table and began handing them to anyone who looked like they wanted one. I poured some water into Kyle's empty glass of ice, and he thanked me without meeting my eyes.

We also have coffee or tea if you'd like, Jo offered.

No, water's just fine thanks, Emily replied as she took her seat.

I wouldn't mind a coffee, if you're offering, Tom said. Just black. Jo nodded and headed for the kitchen.

Oh don't make her, Emily muttered, you just had one.

Please, that doesn't count. Tom looked at the rest of us, and, leaning in as if confiding, said Emily kept a French press filled with coffee on the counter for days, and then just heated up cupfuls in the microwave.

It's very practical, she said with an open face.

It's savage.

Tom and Emily obviously enjoyed performing the hapless cou-ple. I've always wondered about couples who argued and teased each other in front of others. It almost struck me as a perverted form of affection. Mostly, I found it embarrassing.

So. Three billion lightning strikes, Leslie said, slapping her thigh.

I liked Leslie. Where would the world be without A-type women slapping their thighs, keeping things on track?

Howard ran his index finger along his brow. Yes, so I was just saying—three billion lightning strikes a year, all over the world. A hundred every single second. That builds up a huge electromagnetic charge in the atmosphere. And this atmospheric charge resonates. And by resonates, I mean that it creates an actual sound wave. A very, very, very low hum at a frequency of 7.83 hertz.

You're saying lightning is causing the atmosphere to hum? Seema asked.

Essentially, yes.

She lifted her feet off the ground, to sit cross-legged on the couch. And this is, like, accepted science? she asked.

Howard laughed. Yes, absolutely.

Well you never know. There's a lot of bullshit out there.

Okay, I liked Seema too.

It's called the Schumann Resonance, Howard said. We've known about it since the early fifties.

And it's just, like, humming all the time, or—?

Exactly, so—Howard extended his arm towards Seema to apologize for cutting her off—you have these constant global electromagnetic resonances generated by lightning strikes in the cavity between the Earth's surface and the ionosphere. Have you ever blown across the mouth of a bottle? he asked, addressing the question to Seema.

Uh, yup.

So just as the space inside a bottle has a specific resonant frequency, which you can hear when you blow across it, lightning, in the Earth's case, is like the breath over the bottle. And the Earth's resonant frequency is 7.83 hertz.

Tom raised his hand—I'm sorry, I know I came late to the conversation, but what the heck are we talking about here? Are you suggesting this is the sound we're hearing?

Well I suppose that's the controversial bit.

Tom frowned. Uh-huh.

Anything much below twenty hertz usually just drops off for humans, Howard said. I glanced at Kyle, but he didn't turn my way. Below that range, we mostly just feel sound waves as a kind of physical pressure, Howard continued. Some mammals like whales can hear as low as seven hertz, but for humans to hear 7.83 hertz is—

Impossible, Tom said.

Most would say so, yes, Howard said, but there are some folks, myself included, who suggest it's not. Just—exceedingly rare.

So hold on. Tom reached out into the middle of the circle like he was stopping traffic. This, this thing—and I'm sorry if I missed this—but is this something you read about in an article?

I was the dean of Virginia Tech's Department of Geosciences for eighteen years, Howard said. I've published many articles about this.

This resonance?

Yes.

Oh wow, Emily murmured.

Howard's a famous scientist, Leslie said, without irony.

Howard chuckled. Well I wouldn't go that far but I—

Are there famous scientists? Tom asked. I don't think I could name you one.

Emily rolled her eyes. Of course you could.

Don't think so.

Stephen Hawking, she offered.

Yeah, but he doesn't count, he's dead. Obviously, I can name famous dead scientists.

Jo returned with Tom's coffee on a little saucer—Ah, thank you, thank you.

Elon Musk, Damian said.

Tom snorted. Hardly.

I should mention that Jo was actually a former grad student of mine, Howard said, smiling at her.

Jo closed her eyes, a moment longer than a blink, as she wiped a strand of hair from her face. Yes, well, she said, I eventually realized academia wasn't going to nourish my soul.

Looking around the room, there was something I found a bit creepy about sitting in a circle with other strangers. It reminded me of the Quakers, or an AA meeting. My discomfort was probably rooted in a disdain for religion and self-help and group therapy, which I knew was rooted in my own arrogance. And maybe in my fear of being vulnerable. That's just how I was raised. I inherently mistrusted people seeking to be healed or helped or enlightened. Or maybe I just have a natural aversion to groups. To group dynamics, group think, group activities. I've always been wary of shared, collective experience. That said, there was something about Howard's erudition and professorial charisma that somehow put me at ease.

I tried once more to catch Kyle's eye. I wondered what he was making of all of this. I was conscious of him being a child in a room of adults. Not that he came across that way, though; he held himself with a subdued and mature confidence. I was sure that he would have some very funny insights about this group. I smiled, thinking of the impressions he might make of Damian, or Leslie. Tom and Emily were definitely a bit OK boomer. Personally, I felt myself sort of drowning in the conversation. It was the first time in days that I'd been surrounded by so many people; so many voices.

As if picking up on this, Howard brought his hands together and said, Listen, I hope you all don't mind me just jumping into this. I know it can be a lot to absorb at first. I just figured this is what we all came here to talk about.

Your theory, Seema said, bluntly.

I'm sorry?

If I were you, Howard, I wouldn't presume to know what we came here to talk about. With all due respect, you've been dominating the conversation since we arrived, and I barely know anyone in this room or their experience of this hum, which we've all been desperate to talk to someone about. So while I appreciate your thoughts, I would also like to hear from some of the others.

Howard looked chastened. No that's, that's fair enough, he said.

To be honest—Tom waded in—I don't buy that this is some natural phenomenon.

Damian mumbled his assent.

This is something new in our neighbourhood, Tom continued, and I'm here to discuss strategies for tracking it down and dealing with it.

I'm in the same boat, Seema began, but—

So why don't we focus on that?

—but I'd like to understand what people's experiences of this thing are first. She gestured to Emily. Like I have no idea who you are, Seema said, or if what you're hearing is even what I'm hearing. Or how long you've been hearing it.

Emily's posture straightened. Well, she said, Tom and I are here because I saw the ad in the library. We were just going out of our minds with this noise for a good two months by then.

It's been two months for me too, Seema said.

Damian and Leslie both nodded. Same, said Nora.

We weren't sleeping, Tom added. Were having horrible headaches.

The noise was so bad, Emily continued, I'd have to turn up the TV to drown it out. We started keeping the TV on twenty-four hours a day. So I can't tell you my relief when I saw that ad, I just . . . Emily trailed off and Tom placed a hand on her knee.

Sorry, but what—what ad are you talking about? I asked. Damian unfolded a piece of paper from his pocket and handed it to me.

Oh I wish you hadn't ripped it down, Howard said, with a frustrated laugh.

As I looked at the poster, clearly designed and printed out on a home computer, Jo explained how she and Howard had put up a few notices in public spaces around the area.

Just to see who might be out there and interested in talking, she said.

Along the top of the page, in red sans-serif letters, was the question: *Can you hear The Hum?* Seeing the words capitalized like that suddenly made it A Real Thing which existed in the world. Below this question was a description of the sound, its side effects, and an email address.

Seema had seen the poster in the organic grocer's beside the mall. Damian had seen it at the community centre. It struck me as curious that neither Kyle nor I had come across one; nor Paul or Ashley for that matter. Though frankly the poster was so plain and innocuous I could have stared right at it on a lamppost and not even noticed.

I'm not sure what I was expecting, Howard said, clearing his throat. This is quite a high turnout, really.

You should've posted it online, Damian said.

Well we wanted to start small, Jo said. To find a group of neighbours who we could really talk to about this.

Damian admitted that he posted about it on Reddit. Jo looked taken aback—What?

To help spread the word, he said.

I'd really prefer if you didn't, to be honest, Howard said, clearly uneasy.

This is not just our neighbourhood, Damian replied, leaning forward. What about the rest of the world? This hum is affecting everyone, and only some of us are waking up to it.

Right, well—

Only some of us are tuned in.

—we can't exactly start with the whole world, can we? Howard said. It's a big house but even I don't have that kind of room.

Any more people would have made it difficult to have a proper conversation, Leslie said. And I get the sense that's what we all need right now, she added, looking at Seema. Am I right?

I need to talk, Nora said quietly, and everyone turned. The bangles on her wrists clinked as she folded her arms over her generous bust. Her thick black eyeliner made her already penetrating eyes seem enormous. I need to be listened to. Nobody is listening to me. My friends, my family, no one.

There was something plaintive yet forceful in her voice. To hear another grown woman give words to my desperation sent a chill through me.

Me neither, I said. I mean this—I held up the folded-up poster—I-I-I think I need to show this to my husband.

Nora said hers would be furious if he knew she was here.

Jo looked perturbed—Really?

Oh yes, Nora said, gravely.

Mine too, Leslie said.

My girlfriend keeps telling me it's in my head, Seema said.

I said that sounded familiar, and Jo asked us why our partners made us feel like this. Leslie suggested that they were scared for us. I said I thought they felt threatened. It suddenly seemed so clear to me that, of course, those who loved us felt threatened by the fact that they couldn't help us. They couldn't accept that there was no room for them in this mystery.

My husband thinks I need medical help, Leslie said. Not a 'stitch and bitch,' in his words.

A what? Nora asked.

Like, a knitting circle.

That sounds rather dismissive, Seema said. And gendered.

Leslie said her husband put his fist through the wall the other night, out of frustration.

Oh my god, Seema said, horrified.

Leslie insisted that he was not a violent person. Seema raised her eyebrows. Like he would never hurt me, I know that, Leslie said. It was very atypical of him.

Everyone's been acting different, Damian said. It affects everyone.

Jo gave Leslie a purposeful look and said, You tell us, though, if he does that again, okay? Leslie moved her mouth about her face and nodded.

Yeah that's not cool, Seema said, rolling up the sleeves on her flannel shirt like she was about to punch the guy out.

Emily looked at Tom and put her hand on his. I guess we're lucky that we've had each other, she said. But of course our kids think we're, you know—She twirled her finger around her temple, and chuckled.

Oh come on, Tom replied.

They do, they're very concerned.

Sure, but that's different than thinking we're going senile or something.

I didn't say senile.

Well.

Theytheytheythey've been treating us differently.

Because something *is* different.

They think we've lost our marbles.

No they don't.

Yes they do, they think we're sick.

I don't want to—Tom waved away the conversation as if it were a fly, and the circle went quiet. I suddenly saw a lifetime of Emily being waved away like that, and I felt sorry for her. She seemed unfazed by it. If Paul had done that to me, I would have grabbed his hand and slammed it on the coffee table.

As the ten of us sat there I became aware of the fact that The Hum—for it was now capitalized in my consciousness—was the loudest thing in the room. I felt this realization slowly occur to the others. Here we all were, sitting in what anyone else would perceive as total silence, tormented by a noise that only we could hear. I found this somehow disturbing and comforting at the same time.

I can barely work because of it, Leslie said, eventually. I'm so exhausted and frayed, my nerves are—totally frayed. I'll be showing clients around a property and I can't concentrate on what they're saying. They'll be asking me questions about central air or the backyard and it's like I can't hear them. One time I just broke down in tears right in front of this young couple. They had no idea what to do, poor things.

She started to laugh. I can laugh about it now, but—She shook her head, with a rueful smile. Well anyway, eventually I went to a psychiatrist.

I did too, Seema said.

Really? Nora replied, frowning.

Leslie nodded. Oh yeah.

I've never thought I was crazy, Nora said.

You're lucky.

Anything that's a bit different or inconvenient we just pathologize it, don't we? Jo said, looking at Leslie.

Leslie nodded and looked down at her lap. She took a deep, quaking breath. I've been made to feel so—punished, she said, her voice snapping like a twig. I've been so punished for this. It was like no one could help me. My doctors made me feel crazy. They prescribed me all of this medication, because I was getting depressed. Even, if you can believe it, they made me start taking antipsychotics.

Jo leaned forward—What?

They thought I was delusional.

That's unconscionable.

I've been completely gaslighted, Leslie said. I would wake up in the morning and look in the mirror and think—you're crazy. That's what I was conditioned to think. And that medication, let me tell you, it really does a number on you. On your mind, on your body. It's only been a month and I've gained like fifteen pounds. And I'm angry, she said, eyes widening, tearing up. Mostly I'm just really, really angry.

Jo reached out to place her hand on Leslie's knee, and in that moment I felt something inside me unlock. To hear a story so close to my own, told back to me like that. I suddenly saw Leslie's courage. The courage of her getting up in the morning, getting dressed, leaving the house, facing others, sharing her most vulnerable self with a room of strangers. And then, before I could really think, I was speaking. The words just tumbled out of my mouth.

I lost my job because of it, I said.

Jo turned to me, stunned. What?

The others murmured their shock.

I'm so sorry Claire, Howard said.

My life is—I raised my arms and dropped them into my lap. I made to laugh but something inside me gave way, collapsed, and a sob heaved from me instead, like a mudslide. Jo took hold of my hand and knelt down beside me as I cried. I was completely mortified. Me, crying in front of a room of strangers. When was the last time I had cried? I honestly couldn't remember. Ashley would have grabbed me by the shoulders and told me to pull myself together, woman. And yet, at the same time, I remember thinking—God this feels good. It felt so damn good to release like that. To have a space held for me. To let myself be soft—soft? Was that the right word? Vulnerable, yielding, porous, exposed, open. Either way, it felt beyond my control. Jo's eyes stared up into mine, but I could barely see her through my tears.

Kyle's a student of mine, I said. I suddenly felt the need to tell them the truth. I needed to make them understand, make someone understand, even if they were strangers, in fact all the better for it. *Was* a student of mine, I clarified. I cleared my throat. I saw Kyle shifting uncomfortably in his chair. I could feel his surprise and anxiety radiating from across the room. I told the circle about the meetings after class, the drives, Ashley's intervention, the showdown.

So they fired me, I said, my voice rasping. I cleared my throat and wiped my hand over my eyes. Well, suspended me pending further review, I continued. Which means I'll be terminated officially next month after a hearing. I have no idea what to do. My husband won't talk to me about it anymore. My colleagues have basically completely cut me off. I'm like a-a-a leper.

Jo squeezed my hand. I smiled down at her kind face and thanked her. I then looked up at the others, at the care and concern on their faces, and felt a little burst of gratitude for each of them, and for the space they'd made for me to be heard without judgement. The last face I settled on was Kyle's, and he looked ashen. I wanted to reach out and hold his hand. I wanted to apologize and reassure him at the same time. Instead, I turned back to the others and said if they knew I was here with Kyle now, they would probably call the police.

Tom mumbled something that I missed. I looked over and saw that his body language was very closed off.

But what are our options, I continued, posing the question in his direction. Who do we have to talk to? I know I shouldn't be saying this, I mean you're basically strangers, but I just—

You can trust us, Jo said, giving my hand a final squeeze before returning to her chair. I nodded, and I told her that I knew that. And I did. For some reason, I already did trust them.

I can't believe they fired you for this, Howard said.

Seema said even if I lost the hearing, I should sue for wrongful dismissal. I told her that I couldn't even imagine having the energy or wherewithal to do that at the moment.

I'm honestly just trying to get up out of bed every morning, I said. I still feel shell-shocked. But I'm not going to let them intimidate me into pretending that I'm not experiencing this. And neither is Kyle, and that's why we're here.

That's right, Leslie said, nodding, as the others echoed agreement.

I can't tell you how good it feels to be able to tell you all this, I continued, bolstered. When it all started, I was completely—

I'm sorry, Tom cut in. I don't mean to be insensitive, but can I suggest we focus our energies on actually figuring out the source of this hum and addressing it?

My face flushed hot. I felt like a child, scolded. Leslie glared at Tom. That is what we're doing, she said.

No, that's not what we're doing, he replied.

Tom, people have felt isolated, Jo said, trying to defuse the tension.

I know, but I don't think it's productive for us to sit here licking our wounds—

Emily placed her hand on his knee. No one is licking their wounds, dear.

—or letting this become some kind of-of wallowing.

I felt a volcanic rage building in me and tried to find somewhere to look that wasn't Tom's face. Wallowing. The word made me think of a sow in shit, roiling in the mud. I was not wallowing, I was not a dog licking her wounds. Even in that moment I knew Tom was speaking of a uniquely feminine grief and suffering when using those animal metaphors.

I think it's important people feel free to talk in a safe space, Jo replied.

A lot of us have been struggling, Seema said.

Tom raised his hands—I have been too!

So then—

Do not silence me, I erupted at Tom, shaking. I hadn't meant to get so loud.

I'm not.

Yes. You are.

I'm just saying we need to focus on productive outcomes.

Oh, I'm sorry for being so unproductive, I said.

Jo suggested that we were all trying to get a handle on this and that we needed to be patient.

And Tom, people around this circle are saying that they need to be listened to and heard, she said.

I wouldn't mind a bit of that myself, he replied. What I don't need is an emotional support group, to which I just shook my head, astounded. Jo told him that this was not what this was.

Maybe some of us do, Seema said, which frankly wasn't useful because that's not what this was and that's not what I needed, and I resented the implication that I did.

And what about those of us who want to talk about solutions? Tom asked.

We will get there, Seema said.

Well maybe, I began, those people can have a little bit of compassion for the rest of us who need to build ourselves back up first because we have been made to feel like shit and abandoned by our friends and family, okay?

Silence fell over the circle. Tom looked down at the floor. I couldn't bear to be dismissed by another man in a dress shirt, I literally couldn't bear it a second longer.

Okay, Howard said. Obviously we all have our different agendas and reasons for being here.

I don't have an agenda, Tom said, slow and pointed.

And we will do our best to be respectful of that, Howard continued. To listen to one another while, yes Tom, at the same time—

Don't, don't say my name like that, Howard. It's not just about listening to each other and working together. We need to reach out to our city councillor about this, and we need to start applying pressure on them to investigate what the hell this thing is.

There will be time for that, Seema said, with mounting frustration.

The time is now, Tom replied. I don't want to live with this any longer than I have to. I've lived with it long enough already.

I think it's very natural, Howard said, when we're upset and confused to want to blame someone, the government or some corporation, when in actual fact it is something much larger and more complex.

Do you know how I know your theory is bullshit, Howard, no offence? Tom asked. Howard extended his hands, giving Tom the floor. I had a conference in Phoenix last week. I got in a plane, I flew, I landed—Tom said, illustrating this trip with his hands in miniature—and I didn't hear The Hum. I walked around Phoenix for three days, and never heard it once. So do you know what that tells me? That tells me there is a localized source. Something in this city, or even in this neighbourhood that is new, and that we—

The Hum has been reported around the world, Howard interrupted, and if you didn't hear it in Phoenix maybe that's because the traffic was louder. Or maybe you just didn't want to hear it. But it was there. And it's in Japan and Paris and Sydney, I can assure you.

Go online, Damian said to Tom. Look at some message boards. It's not just in our area.

Tom sat forward in his chair, until he was perched on the edge. I've been living in this neighbourhood for almost twenty years, he said, when most of this was just dirt and foundations, and I can tell you something has changed, and it's affecting, *adversely* affecting our ability to live and enjoy our lives, and I am not just going to sit here and let someone tell me that it's because of lightning. There's been lightning my entire life, Howard. This is new. And, *and*—he continued, fending off Howard's interjection—the longer we delay, the more precedent they have to suggest it's not a pressing crisis. I think our first step should be to try to find as many other people as possible who are suffering from this.

Seema sat forward on the couch to mirror Tom's stance, and said, Can I point out that Claire just told you that you silenced her, and yet you have continued to dominate the conversation? We have heard what you have to say.

Frankly, I don't think you have.

Tom, please, Emily said, closing her eyes.

I'm encouraging both of you, Seema said, glancing at Howard, to be mindful of who is taking up space in this room.

And who is being listened to, Nora added, widening her already wide eyes.

The presence of the two women of colour in the room suddenly felt super-charged.

Tom turned to me, and apologized, about as sincerely as I reckoned he could manage. I nodded, accepting it, though feeling desperate to disgorge the anger that had gathered in me. I gave an Oscar-worthy exhale, which helped a little.

Claire, Jo said, it goes without saying that we're here for you. And we will be one hundred percent discreet.

Several of the others nodded, and I thanked them.

I think we should all agree now, Jo continued, that nothing that is said in this room is to be repeated to anyone else outside of this room.

Well how is that actually practical? Tom asked, massaging the bridge of his nose. If we're going to discuss strategies for tracking down and dealing with this hum we're going to have to interact with the outside world, he said. Jo made to respond, but Tom turned to me and said, I'm not talking about your personal dilemma, but I don't think an information blackout policy is the right—

I think there can be some nuance, Jo interrupted.

Well that's not what you just said.

Nothing personal, no personal details should be shared, she clarified. That has to be a baseline.

But there again, what exactly does that mean? he asked. Medical details? The impact on our lives? Those things are going to be important to share with the city if we're going to get them to investigate, or the companies who might be responsible for this.

Seema admitted that she had to agree with Tom on this one.

I think it's common sense, Leslie said, what is and what is not permissible to be shared.

Is it? Tom asked.

Seema shook her head. Yeah, I don't—

In my experience there is no such thing as common sense, Howard said.

And sorry, Tom said, turning back to me. But if you are not allowed to be seeing this—he suddenly turned to Kyle—sorry I forgot your name.

Kyle.

—Kyle out of school, then there are legal implications to us tacitly condoning it.

My stomach double knotted. There is nothing illegal about either of us being here, I said.

Tom pointed at me. You just said yourself that if your—

Are you not comfortable with it, Tom? Jo asked.

I don't know.

Well what are you saying? she pressed.

I don't know the dynamic. I don't know any of the details.

Howard suggested that maybe we should move on.

I suppose no, I don't, I don't feel comfortable, Tom said, crossing his arms. If you've been let go from your job and told not to associate with this student any further, and we are sitting here with the two of you, that feels wrong to me, no?

All we had is each other to talk to, Kyle snapped. Do you get that? And now we have you guys. Don't push us away.

Kyle's eyes were bright and fixed on Tom. He seemed transformed, no longer a child in a room of adults to be protected, but a man squaring off against another man, and for a moment I had the impression that Kyle was actually being protective of me.

Does anyone else have a problem with it? Jo asked, trying to keep control of the room. I turned to Nora and asked her not to tell Julian about Kyle and me being there.

I'm sorry but I don't lie to my son, she replied, stoically. I never have.

I'm not asking you to lie. I'm just asking for your discretion.

Please, Kyle said. It could cause a lot of problems for us.

Tom huffed—Like what, are we talking criminal charges here?

Who's Julian? Seema asked.

Mrs. Delgado, I'm begging you, Kyle said. Nora looked pained with indecision.

If this is going to work, we need to support each other, Jo said.

Okay, Nora replied, with reluctance. Okay.

Seema pointed to Nora, Kyle, and me—So you three know each other already?

I play ball with Julian, Kyle clarified. I talked with him about The Hum once, and he told me about his mother, he said, nodding to Nora.

And I work for Howard, Nora said, which surprised a few people, including me.

She's transcribing years' worth of old audio recordings from my research, Howard said, looking over at her with a somewhat apologetic smile. It's hundreds of hours.

I've started hearing his voice in my sleep now, Nora said wearily, to which we laughed.

So wait, all of you—? Seema turned to Leslie—And you already knew Howard and Jo?

Jo's my yoga teacher, Leslie confirmed.

Huh. Seema nodded, furrowing her brow as she traced the lines of connection in her mind.

Jo said she taught clients out of her home studio, in the basement; usually in one-to-one sessions, tailored for each client's specific needs and capacities. She was also trained in body and energy work. She said she tried to offer clients holistic, multi-pronged approaches to their physical, mental, and spiritual well-being.

I've been doing yoga for a couple of years, Emily said. It helps my arthritis.

Or causes it, Tom added, chuckling. If you're making yourself into a human pretzel.

Leslie told Emily that she should really consider doing sessions with Jo. She's amazing, so patient, really lets me go at my own pace.

Maybe I should. Emily looked at Jo. Are you expensive?

Yes, replied Leslie, which got a few laughs. But the core strength is worth it. You should show them your peacock, she said to Jo.

Jo laughed, and waved Leslie off—Not right now.

Tom leaned in—Her what?

Why not? Seema asked.

Yes! Leslie cajoled. The rest of the circle joined in, encouraging Jo, and telling her how much they wanted to see 'her peacock,' which I gathered was a yoga pose.

Are you serious? Jo asked.

It's incredibly impressive, Howard said.

C'mon! Leslie pushed.

Jo raised her arms in surrender. She cleared the water pitcher and glasses off the coffee table, placed both of her palms down in the middle, and proceeded to balance the rest of her body in a perfect plank. The group cheered and laughed. It was a truly impressive sight, though I was a little worried about the coffee table flipping or giving way. It must have been well-built. I don't think mine would have held up quite so well. The thought of me planking on my own coffee table caused me to snort a laugh, which I turned into a cheer, as I clapped encouragingly for Jo. She was really holding the pose.

Incredible, Emily said, shaking her head.

Wouldn't want to mess with her, right? Leslie said.

Jo then evolved the pose into an even more precarious and impressive hold, bringing both of her legs forward and out beyond her, such that her bum was now resting on the backs of her arms. This really sent the group into spasms of delight. People were whooping and clapping, even Tom. Half of the circle was standing. Damian sat back in his chair, hands in his pockets, but smiling. Jo then dismounted from the table and did a little bow. The whole episode was a glorious and slightly surreal release of tension. I can't quite explain how, but it felt like we were collectively forgiving Tom for his antagonism earlier, and his eager laugh seemed to suggest he picked up on this. I then wondered for a moment whether Jo, while seeming reluctant to do so, had actually somehow engineered the moment with exactly that emotional reset in mind. The more I thought about it, the more it seemed likely that she was operating on an intuitive plane beyond any I could aspire to.

Leslie slid her arm over Jo's shoulder—When the time comes for you to have babies, you're just going to bang, bang, bang, she said, pumping her fist low down.

Oh god, Jo blanched, still laughing.

That's what destroyed my abs, Leslie continued. My Caesarean.

Jo patted Leslie's abs—Well we're getting there.

She then sat back down in her chair, and those of us standing returned to our chairs too.

Les and I were meditating in a session a couple of weeks ago, Jo said, and I could tell she was struggling. She couldn't focus. I remember your body was just—vibrating, with anxiety. I asked you about it, and it came out that you could hear The Hum too.

Then I-I just started crying, Leslie said. You must have thought, who is this crazy woman? I was so relieved.

And then a couple of days later we learned that Nora could hear it too, Jo said.

Everyone looked at Nora, who nodded slowly, and fiddled with the small gold crucifix at the end of her necklace.

At first I thought it was because I was listening to so much of the recordings, she said. I thought it was like a—like hearing damage.

That's so weird—Seema said, narrowing her eyes and shaking her head—that all three of you, like, I mean it's almost like a virus catching or something.

That's when we figured, okay we need to hold a meeting, Howard said. We realized there were obviously others around, nearby.

There's probably loads more, Seema said.

Damian nodded—Hundreds. Maybe thousands.

Probably a lot of people just suffering on their own, Jo said.

But why now? I asked. Why here?

Howard leaned forward, his elbows on his knees, and his hands clasped together. From my experience, he said, there seem to be certain places in the world where, for whatever reason, small clusters of people can suddenly hear the Resonance more strongly.

Tom resumed massaging the bridge of his nose, and Seema rolled her head back, both of them evidently irritated at Howard rehashing his theory.

Over the years you just hear about these people, Howard continued, ignoring their restlessness. A couple dozen in Sausalito. A bunch of folks, all from the same neighbourhood in Windsor,

Canada. And in some cases there's an obvious, you know, source
that's eventually discovered like a nearby factory or—

Exactly—Tom said, gesturing towards Howard—that's why
we—

But, Howard ploughed on, holding his hand out, there are tons
of these cases around the world where people complain, authorities investigate, and there's absolutely no explanation. And that's
because they're not thinking about the bigger picture. They're
focusing on wind turbines and factories. They have no conception
of geophysics.

But why do you think we can feel it more strongly here? I asked.
And all of a sudden?

Howard talked persuasively, with calm assuredness, but I just
didn't understand why now, why us?

Well it's not exactly all of a sudden, he said.

Because two months ago they opened the new highway extension, Tom said, with a little flourish of his hands as if he had just
performed a magic trick. Emily clicked her tongue in admonish-
ment, but Seema laughed, and pointed at Tom.

Okay, I'll give you that, Seema said.

Am I right? Tom asked.

Seema nodded—There's no question it's the highway.

Thank you.

Nora looked confused—The highway?

They opened the new extension in the spring and there's been
a low roar ever since, Emily explained. Just half a mile from here.
No sound barricades or anything.

And I reckon it's been driving coyotes into the neighbourhood
too, have you noticed? Tom asked. Way more walking around the
roads these days.

C'mon, there's been more coyotes for years, Leslie said. Ever since
they started building all those new subdivisions out by Solar Valley.

Well there's been even more recently, trust me, Tom replied. Even our dog is suffering. Two months ago he started acting up. Eventually we had to put him on Prozac. Kyle chuckled, and Tom's face hardened—Why is that funny?

It's actually very bad, Emily said. Kyle covered his mouth and coughed, as if to suggest that was what he'd been doing all along.

It's not funny, Tom said.

He's always been a bit of a highly strung dog, but recently it's become too much, Emily said. And he's probably been picking up on our stress too.

What I'm saying is, as much as I appreciate your, you know, your theory, Howard—Tom said, rolling his hand in the air—I think it's time for us all to get real here.

Is science not real enough for you, Tom? Jo asked, a subtle new edge in her voice.

Lightning humming in the atmosphere? No, it's not real enough for me and I'll tell you why.

This is an objective, verifiable natural phenomenon, Jo said.

Yeah but a highway's also pretty objective and verifiable, Seema countered.

If this was a natural phenomenon, we would have all heard it ages before now, Tom said, and Seema gestured towards him in agreement. It would be something widely reported, he added.

I've heard The Hum my entire adult life, Howard said. And it is, actually, widely reported.

The group sort of did a collective double take at this. These statements felt like flares lobbed into the room.

Sorry, you've heard it all your life? Seema asked, incredulous.

Since I was a grad student.

Then it's not the same thing, Tom said, shaking his head. You have some kinda condition.

So you've had to deal with this for thirty-odd years? I asked.

For me it's not something to 'deal' with, Howard replied. It's a gift.

This also sent a small shockwave through the circle.

Gift, Nora said.

I feel privileged to hear it, he said.

Tom rolled his eyes—Oh give me strength.

Howard explained that, of course, he didn't realize what it was at first. He had just begun his grad studies on atmospheric noise and was in his bed one night when he began to hear The Hum.

Not that I made the connection, he said. I went to the doctors and they told me I had tinnitus but I didn't buy it. The symptoms didn't match. But eventually I figured it out, I realized, My god I can actually hear the Resonance. I'm sure it was there all along, very faint in the background, but now I was finally noticing it, and once I noticed it I couldn't un-notice it. I told my colleagues and they thought I was crazy. They thought I was just falling too deep into the research and losing my head. But I never stopped hearing it. And I've spent my entire career researching it. My wife, my kids, they never heard it. And then I met Jo who—

You're saying you've heard it for years, Tom interrupted, when all the rest of us have suddenly begun hearing it two months ago.

Tom, would you like me to tell you about how variations in global temperature or water vapour in the upper troposphere affect how and where the Resonance is heard? I've spent three decades studying the Resonance and you won't let me speak for three god-damn minutes about it without interrupting me.

It's a basic question of logic, Howard.

I know you're both very keen to get started on that letter to our city councillor, so don't let me hold you back, Howard said, gesturing to Tom and Seema. But I can tell you this is a lot more complex and, frankly, sublime than a highway extension.

Kyle suddenly cleared his throat, and we all turned to look at him. For what it's worth, Claire and I also think it's something in the area, he said, looking over at me. Don't we?

Um, well . . . I replied, faltering. That was our first impulse.

That's still my impulse, Kyle said, holding my gaze.

I nodded, as if to suggest that it was still mine too, but I turned to Howard and told him that I was also very interested in what he'd been saying.

We've actually spent a lot of time looking for it, Kyle added.

But we haven't had much luck, have we? I said.

It's a work-in-progress.

I told the group about the various sites we had visited, about the measurements we had taken, and then, removing it from my purse, I showed them the map we'd been making, charting the coordinates of each possible sound source, in the hope that some trend or hot spot might emerge. Everyone seemed amazed. Tom even clapped, in an awkward, lone echo of our collective fun moments earlier.

Now this is what I'm talking about, he exclaimed. This is what we need the city to be doing with a proper team. No offence, Tom said, gesturing to me, but a proper, systematic survey of the area.

And what has your survey turned up? Howard asked me.

Well, we uh—haven't found a match.

Yet, Kyle added.

It's really impressive, Seema said. She asked to see it, and I passed her the map.

Nothing's been low enough, I said. Everything is fifty, sixty, seventy hertz. Nothing sounds like our hum.

Tom asked Seema to see the map, but she said that she wasn't finished with it yet, so he rose and perched on the armrest beside her.

The thing I agree with, with what you're saying, Kyle said— turning to Howard—is that whatever this is, is like, super low.

Like, barely something this thing—he held up his phone—can pick up.

That's why the city should be doing this properly, Tom said, looking up from the map. He asked us if we had measured the sound coming from the highway.

Kyle looked at me and then back to Tom. No, we, uh we didn't think of it, he said.

Tom pointed at the map—That's why we need experts.

I thought you weren't interested in listening to experts, Jo replied, coolly. Howard gestured to her to drop it.

I really thought we would find it, I said. Some evenings it felt like we were so close. Like we might turn a corner and there it would be. I told the others that I kept imagining it might even be this very small thing I would find, like in the back of a neighbour's shed or something, that I could pick up and smash to pieces.

God, wouldn't that be nice, Leslie said. Nora nodded, seeming to savour the thought.

I wondered how they each pictured the source of the noise in their minds. Did they see it as an object? A place? I had spent nights lying in bed trying to imagine it. Sometimes it looked like a big subwoofer speaker in an abandoned warehouse. Other times, I pictured some forlorn bungalow on the edge of town, with all of the blinds drawn. And other times it was some kind of natural phenomenon. Like a large fissure in the earth. Or a mysterious cave in the desert.

When I find out who's responsible I want to hurt them, Damian said quietly. Howard asked him if he really meant that. Damian nodded—Yup.

You think there's someone responsible for The Hum? Howard asked.

Of course. Not one person, but a group.

And you want to hurt them?

Howard, I'm a military man. I find and remove the enemy, that's my training.

This is not your enemy.

It's just my nature.

Howard turned to me—And The Hum, you want to destroy it too? .

Isn't that why we're here? Seema asked.

Of course I do, I replied, meeting Howard's gaze. I didn't see how he could be asking me this, after everything that Leslie, and Emily, and I had said.

Why?

Because it's ruining my life.

Is it really, though?

Haven't you been listening?

Or is it the people, the way people are reacting to your hearing The Hum that's ruining your life? he asked.

No, trust me, it's The Hum and it's fucking up my life and I want to stop hearing it as soon as possible, I told him, punctuating the end of my sentence in the air, with my thumb and index finger together.

But you can't, that's the thing, Claire. Once you hear it, you can never stop hearing it.

I shook my head and told him I didn't accept that.

I'm afraid you're going to have to, he said.

Well I won't.

But you can learn to live with it. And not only live with it but come to see it as something that augments your life.

Augments! Seema scoffed.

I'm not trying to upset you, he said. I'm trying to give you the facts you need to help yourself.

I told him that it needed to stop.

Well . . . it won't.

It will, it has to.

Claire—

I need it to.

And how do headaches and nosebleeds augment my life exactly? Seema asked.

The Hum is incredibly powerful. And it can do extraordinary things, if you let it. But if you fight it, it will hurt you.

Right, Seema replied, obviously unconvinced. She shot me a look of vexed complicity.

You need to transform your relationship with it, Howard said.

What does that even mean? I asked.

Well that's what we're here to discover, he replied.

That's not why I'm here, Tom said.

Seema chuckled—Yeah, sorry, me neither.

Tom rose from his perch on the sofa beside Seema, and clapped his hands—Right, well, I think I should go. I'm obviously here under the wrong pretext.

Emily told him to sit down, and Lesley seemed to want him to stay too, for some reason, but he wasn't having it.

I sure the hell didn't come here to be lectured to, or sit in a circle trying to make ourselves feel better, Tom said. Or 'transform' my goddamn relationship with something.

Just sit down, Emily said, exasperated.

If he wants to go, just let him, Jo said, gesturing towards the front door.

Tom looked at Howard—I came here today to get to the bottom of this.

And that's exactly what we're trying to do, Howard replied. We're trying to access the truth of this.

And you've done nothing but assume you have it, Seema countered. You're not willing to entertain that this might be something else, and it feels like there's no space in this room for anyone—

We are, excuse me—Jo interjected—we are making space. That is exactly what we're doing.

No you're not, not a genuine space for discussion.

This is about you gathering a bunch of folks together and advancing your cause or whatever, Tom said. Well count me out.

I don't have a cause, Tom, Howard said, sounding suddenly exhausted.

You have a very specific framework that you're operating in, Seema replied, creating a little box with her hands in front of her.

You want to know why I'm here? Tom asked. He picked up the piece of paper and brandished it. This to me, he said, this to me, looks like a neighbourhood association meeting or something. Am I the only person who thinks so? Because that's what we actually need here.

Just go, Jo said.

Tom looked down at Emily—Come on.

No.

I'm not staying.

Well I am, she said, folding her hands in her lap.

Tom looked at her in disbelief—Why?

Because I want to. I feel invested.

Invested?

You're welcome to go, I'm not keeping you.

Invested in what?

In this conversation.

This fucking Resonance stuff? he asked, gesturing towards Howard.

Why are you being so aggressive? Emily asked.

Tom looked dumbfounded—I can't even believe you right now.

Just—she gestured towards the door. Tom turned to Seema, hoping to find an ally in her, but frustrated as she was, she had no intention of leaving. He then looked over at me, but I didn't meet his gaze. Howard's words had gotten under my skin, and I was far from finished with working them out. I also couldn't imagine leaving without Kyle. Tom scanned the circle one last time, giving us a little sardonic wave, and walked out of the house, closing the door behind him with a bang. Emily looked around the circle and apologized to everyone, in the quiet that followed.

No, I'm sorry, Howard said. Really.

For what? Leslie asked. You didn't do—

No, I came on too strong, he said. This is brand new for all of you, and I've had decades to process this. I got too excited and just jumped right in, I'm sorry. I think that kind of spooked Tom. It's just that I've been wanting to do this for so long, I can't even tell you. And there are such exciting breakthroughs and discoveries that lie ahead of us.

Just then, to everyone's surprise, Tom walked back through the front door, and into the living room. Emily sighed—Let me guess, you forgot your glasses.

Tom gestured towards the bay window—There's a man sitting in a white car in the driveway.

A look of confusion passed over Jo's face—What?

Who is he? Leslie asked Tom.

I have no idea, but he looks agitated.

My phone began to buzz, and my heart sank. Oh my god, I whispered. I got up and, as if in a kind of trance, I crossed the room to the window. Paul's car was parked in the driveway, and he was standing beside the open driver's-side door, with his phone to his ear. I tried to catch my breath. Jo asked me if it was my husband. I heard Tom mutter Christ. Jo appeared at the window beside me, and I told her that I didn't know what to do. She put her arm around my shoulders. I felt like I was going to collapse.

How does he know? Kyle asked, somewhere in the background.

I turned away from the window and Jo led me back towards the sofa, trying to calm me.

He's walking to the house, Seema said, looking out the window.

The phone was still buzzing in my hand. How was this happening? My mind raced back. Where did I slip up? Did I leave some kind of clue? My phone hadn't left my side in days. I told Ashley about the meeting ages ago, the night of Kyle's phone call, but how did she know the date, the address? Had I said those things aloud? I couldn't remember now. Jesus Christ. How could she have possibly remembered? We hadn't even spoken about it since that night. Was she just waiting to test me; to see if I would go? Did she even have a game today? I felt myself spinning out, and my knees gave way, and I was down on the sofa.

Do you want us to deal with him? Tom offered, crouching down beside me. Our eyes met, and I felt a moment of gratitude for him. I told him I didn't know what to do.

He's not coming in here, Jo said, as if casting a protective force field around the house.

Not if you don't want him to, Howard said, looking at me.

I'm—I began to say, but what was I? Scared? Humiliated? An idiot? The phone was still buzzing and buzzing, and I couldn't take it, so I answered the call. Paul? Are you—? But before I could get the words out, there was a pounding on the front door, followed by several rapid doorbell rings.

Everyone stay where you are, Howard ordered, now standing.

Is he going to try to hurt you? Leslie asked, wedging herself down beside me, and putting her hand on my thigh.

No, no, I told her, but that made me no less afraid of his anger and intensity. Paul was my gentle giant until he wasn't, until he was just a giant, shouting me down.

It's okay, love, Emily said, we're here for you.

Do you want me to answer it? Tom asked Howard, but Howard held up his hand, and shook his head. Howard steeled himself, walked over to the front door, and opened it. From where I sat, I could just glimpse his back in the doorway, at the far end of the hall.

Can I help you? Howard asked.

Yes, you can. Paul's voice came low and steady from the other side of the door, just beyond sight. My wife's inside and I need to speak with her.

And who are you, sorry?

Paul Devon, my wife's name is Claire. May I?

I watched as Howard blocked him from entering—No, you may not.

I'd like to see her please.

Well I'm afraid she's indisposed at the moment.

I glanced at Kyle, and he looked back at me from across the room with an almost unsettling calm. He didn't seem afraid or upset, just resigned, as if he had half expected this would happen. Had I as well? Maybe we had both known, deep down, that we would be caught, that it was inevitable, but we chose to come anyway. What other choice did we have?

I'm not leaving without my wife, I heard Paul say.

Yes, you are, Howard replied.

Excuse me?

I'm asking you politely to leave my—

And who the hell are you? Paul interrupted.

I'm the home owner.

What's your name, home owner? Howard didn't answer. I said what's—?

Dr. Howard Bard.

Are you keeping me from my wife?

Your wife doesn't want to see you.

Oh yeah? Is that your professional medical opinion?

I suggest you leave right now before I—

Before you what? Before *you what*? Get out of my fucking—

Paul threw his weight into Howard, causing Howard to stumble back, and for a split second I saw Paul coming through the doorway, but Howard grabbed hold of his arms and forced him back outside, which I have to say was extremely impressive given Paul's size. I could hear them scuffling on the front step, and I closed my eyes. I knew I could have put an end to all of it, but I felt completely overwhelmed. In the past I would have met Paul's fury with my own, but I was already spent. I felt totally frayed. Exhausted. I couldn't even muster the strength to be afraid, or angry. I heard Paul threatening—I'm going to sue you so fucking bad.

You go right ahead, and I'll—

Claire!? Paul called out, his voice breaking. I know you can hear me!

Go on, I told myself, get up, shout back, he's trying to haul you off like some mule on a rope. The others surrounded Kyle and me, and I felt moved by their protectiveness. They barely knew me. I could have been a maniac for all they knew. Surely only maniacs prompted scenes like this. I heard Howard threatening to call the police.

Is Kyle Francis in there? Paul asked Howard, out of breath.

Who?

Don't play stupid, you know who I'm talking about.

Then things fell quiet outside. What was going on? Had Paul stormed off? I was just about to stand up, when suddenly there was a loud *bang* on the bay window. Everyone startled and turned to see Paul with his palms against the glass, peering into the room.

I can see you, Paul shouted, his voice muffled, I can fucking see you!

Kyle jumped to his feet, yelling back—Come at me, you think I'm afraid of you old man?

Howard suddenly appeared in the window and grabbed Paul's shoulder, but Paul swung him around and slammed him up against the glass. Emily clasped her mouth, and Nora murmured a prayer in Spanish. Paul then disappeared from view and, anticipating his next move, Tom dashed to the front door to shut it—but he was too late, Paul burst into the house, through the front hall, and into the living room, everyone recoiling and gasping, and jumping to their feet. Paul's brow was split, and bleeding. Kyle, for the first time, looked genuinely afraid and, instinctively, I stepped in front of him, sheltering him with my body.

Let's go, Paul said to me, panting.

No.

Jo told him to get out of her house.

Claire—Paul began.

Don't, I said, with the force of a punch. Howard re-entered, limping slightly. It seemed he had maybe rolled his ankle. Jo ran over to tend to him.

It's okay, everyone, I announced. He's going now.

Is he? Paul said, taking a step towards me.

Yes.

If I walk out that door, and you're not with me, that's it, he said.

That's it? What did he mean, that was it? I was taken aback but was ready to call his bluff. I threw my arms up and shook my head.

So that's it? You're choosing this over me? he asked, gesturing around as if at a fetid swamp.

Are you making me?

Me? You have made all of this.

You're forcing me to make that decision.

Make it.

I could feel the heat of Kyle's body behind me, like a frightened rabbit that, through some strange conspiracy of fate, had fallen to me to look after.

Yes, I said.

Yes what?

I swallowed—I'm choosing this.

Paul gestured to Howard—This piece of shit?

Just go.

Paul glanced once more around the room, at each and every person there, as if committing their faces to memory. He then turned and looked at me as if he couldn't quite work out who I was. As if I was some sort of changeling. I'm right here, Paul. I'm standing right in front of you. But he couldn't see me. I saw his confusion. His lack of recognition. And I watched as he considered the entirety of our love, weighed it in the balance, and decided to go. I watched as he turned, and walked out, and I listened as the door closed behind him, not even a slam, but a quiet click of resignation. I listened to the scuff and clack of his shoes on the front walk, for that's how quiet the room was. I listened to him open and close his car door, start the engine, pull out of the driveway, and disappear down the street.

9

PAUL DIDN'T MOVE OUT RIGHT AWAY. THE THREE OF US lived as strangers in the same house for another four excruciating months. I lost the hearing with the school board. I kept going to the meetings on Sequoia Crescent. They became all I had. They were the only times I had any actual conversations, as Paul and Ashley had all but shut me out, I suppose as a kind of punishment, or maybe as a way of protecting themselves. Looking back, I realize our dynamic had become a Catch-22—they wouldn't talk to me as long as I kept going to the meetings, but I had no one if I didn't go to the meetings, no contact, no affection, no communication. Paul and I had tried never to go to bed angry with one another in all of our years of marriage, and so for us to now be living in a perpetual war zone of passive aggression felt like uncharted territory. We communicated through empty milk cartons left on the countertop, or by the intensity with which a drawer

was shut. Even the sound of Paul urinating in the bathroom down
the hall could feel like a rebuke aimed at me.

Initially I went to the meetings once a week, on Monday evenings, and then twice a week, on Mondays and Thursdays, and
then eventually we began meeting on Saturday afternoons as well.
The meetings grew into a potluck scenario where we would each
bring a dish, which gave me a reason to cook as Paul and Ashley
had started fending for themselves at dinner. People put a lot of
effort into their contributions. Nora pulled off some serious sorcery
with her *chiles rellenos*, which were basically peppers stuffed with
meat, vegetables, and spices, and then fried in egg batter. She also
made this dessert called *rellenitos*, a kind of Guatemalan doughnut
which consisted of cooked plantains with refried beans, sugar, and
cinnamon. It was so delicious I literally swore under my breath the
first time I bit into one. I have to say, to look at him I might have
assumed Damian would have been a bag of chips and salsa kind of
man, but he brought trays of glazed ribs and barbecued chicken.
Leslie and Jo held down the vegan camp with eggplant lasagne
and lentil chili. Emily wasn't a cook, but she bought nice pies and
banana loaves, and I tended to bring salads and side dishes, which
weren't flashy, but there were never any leftovers.

Paul exiled me back to The Gym. I was still managing only
about three hours of sleep a night and was probably becoming
increasingly erratic, though at the time I felt I was slowly getting
stronger and clearer in my thinking. I stopped seeing Dr. Gompf
and refused any other kind of medical or psychiatric intervention,
mostly at the urging of Howard and the group, who helped me
see that my medicalization was for the benefit of those around
me, to help contain and mute me, rather than my own. They
helped me see that dulling or numbing my perceptive capacity
was a kind of violence; a self-inflicted wound. Rather, I started to
ask—how could I transform my relationship to my own sensitivity

of perception? How could I transform my relationship with the sounds I was hearing? To The Hum? If this was a natural phenomenon, how could I learn to live with nature, as opposed to in opposition to it?

It's important for me to assert my agency in all of this. I was not brainwashed. I was not coerced. Of course, the more that I insist that I was not brainwashed, the more it is used as evidence against me now that I was. But I do not see myself as a victim or a dupe, and I never once felt like one at the time. I chose to engage and believe and participate in these meetings and the conversations that occurred therein. There was a genuine climate of care, compassion, and intellectual inquiry at work in Howard and Jo's home. I felt trusted and heard. I think all of that has been lost in the reporting of the events that followed. This, in no way, is meant to dismiss the serious allegations that have since emerged about Howard, and which are before the courts at the time of my writing this. But speaking from my lived experience alone, the house on Sequoia Crescent felt like a refuge for a group of well-meaning, hard-working, and exhausted people who were just doing their best to get to the bottom of their own suffering.

Quite apart from the sense of community, one of the key things the meetings gave me was a pride of purpose. They restored an element of dignity to my life. I was done with being fucked up. I was done with being wrong. I was done with being a patient. I actually started keeping a journal during this period, which I will spare you the details of—it's all rather solipsistic and quotidian— but what I was struck by, when re-reading it for the purposes of this book, was how lucid my writing was at the time. It was not the chaotic rambling I expected it to be. It was methodical, considered, and measured. I didn't hurl myself into the embrace of the group in some unthinking, unguarded way; I retained all my usual

cynicism and skepticism, and really wrestled with how vulnerable
to make myself, how much to expose, how much to let in. It was
incremental. Contrary to how Paul may have seen or thought of
me I was, recognizably, myself through it all. As I read the diary, I
took comfort in that.

Then one evening I came home, and Paul was gone. His Ford
Escape wasn't in the driveway. Ashley was staying over at her
friend Julie's again. It took me a good two hours to realize Paul
had moved out. It wasn't until I opened our closet that I realized
something was amiss. I then wandered into the ensuite and noticed
his toothbrush, razor, and shaving cream were gone. He had taken
just the bare essentials. A single carload. He texted me later that
night to say he would be staying with his friend Nathan for a few
nights while we figured out what would happen next. I liked that
'we' in his text message, as if it was going to be some kind of conversation or negotiation between us.

Apparently, he and Ashley had already discussed all of it, which
frankly just felt cruel, but I suppose from Paul's perspective I was
acting unilaterally without consultation, so he felt at liberty to do
the same. He later told me that he hadn't wanted to have some
big showdown with me and felt that this was the gentlest way for
everyone. Ashley had refused to move out; she liked her room, and
there was too much on her plate with school and soccer to contem-
plate uprooting. A part of me couldn't help but wonder whether
Paul actually asked her to stay, to keep an eye on me. In the end,
Paul lived with Nathan's family for two weeks before finding a
small studio apartment by the Home Depot, in a generic new-build
with views of parking lot all around. I told myself it was a temporary solution. After nearly two decades of marriage, you don't
throw in the towel after a few bad months, or even a bad year. That
wasn't Paul's nature. But then what did I know about nature? Was
anything I had been doing in my nature?

Nature in Revolt. Those were the words on the news chyron one night, regarding the historically high temperatures that spring, and how it was affecting mating seasons, and migrations, and aquifer levels, and forest fires. Perhaps my nature was in revolt. Or perhaps my nature had always been revolt.

I couldn't help but feel, around this time, that the news chyron spoke of a larger disquiet that was settling over the neighbourhood; a sense of unrest that made itself known in small and innocuous ways. Shopping carts tipped over in empty parking lots. A burned-out couch just off the bike path. Foxes copulating in driveways. As I jogged past neighbours' homes in the early morning, and glimpsed them in their bedrooms getting dressed, or in their kitchens eating breakfast, it occurred to me that The Hum was working on people's minds and bodies whether they realized it or not. It was affecting their moods, their digestion, their sex life, the way they felt about their husbands and wives and kids. One night, from my bedroom window, I watched our backyard neighbour swimming laps back and forth underneath his pool cover. He must have been at it for an hour. I kept wondering—what happens if he got caught under there? Who would save him? It would take me at least five minutes to run downstairs, pull on some shoes, and dash around the block to his front door, and then who would open the door for me, I wasn't even sure anyone else was home. People probably had no idea why they were doing half of what they did.

I never looked for omens or placed much stock in coincidences. But there was something about my thinking around that time that made me begin seeing them everywhere. Perhaps the meetings were honing my perceptivity, or conditioning my brain not to disregard the sights and sounds that felt incongruous. When these moments appeared, I did not discount them as I once had, but tried to make space for them to reveal to me whatever it was they held. For instance, on my jog one morning, just as the mist was burning off, a coyote darted out into the middle of the road. I stopped, and I stared at him and I realized, to my delight, that he was the same coyote I saw the night I first noticed The Hum. The same white tips on his ears, the same white triangle patch on his neck. He was much larger now, almost an adult. His coat was shiny and thick. His large, bat-like ears stood upright, flicking back and forth, perceiving sounds I could only imagine. I stood there admiring him, and he looked back at me, letting me admire him. And I talked to him. Look at you, I said. You're the most perfect thing in the universe.

I took a cautious step towards him. I didn't know whether I should look him in the eyes or not. I didn't want him to think I was menacing him, so I fixed my gaze somewhere just below his, like Kyle had done to me when I entered Howard and Jo's living room for the first time. I crouched down and slowly stretched out my hand. It was trembling. What was it to touch something so wild? Had I ever touched a truly wild animal before? No, I didn't think I had, which struck me as remarkable, in four decades. Maybe once, when I held an injured sparrow as it died, after smacking into our patio door. But an injured wildness, a compromised wildness, didn't count. I looked up and met the coyote's eyes again. Only four or five metres separated us. He held my gaze, unblinking. He lowered and extended his head ever so slightly towards me, as if bowing, flattening his ears as he did. Did this signal a greeting, or a pending attack? With knees bent, I made to take another step forward, but he startled and darted off into a nearby yard. I stayed crouched in the street, heart beating, until a car beeped its horn behind me.

The other wildness I attempted to reach out and touch during that time was Ashley. I gradually got closer, day by day. A text message returned here. A thirty-second conversation in the kitchen there. I started calling her Boo Radley, for her spectral presence in the house, or sometimes the more hip-hop-inflected My Boo, or even Boo-urns, a reference from *The Simpsons* that cracked a smile on her face. There was still a strict moratorium on my attending her games, not that I could bear being seen by former colleagues and students and their parents anyway. The unspoken reason why I would never again be invited was that she blamed me for her fall from grace. She had been one of the strongest on her team at the start of the season, but by May her coach more or less had her benched.

A strange thing happened during this time, and the best way I can describe it is that I think my body began to mourn the absence of Ashley in my life, even though we were still living together. It mourned the loss of our emotional intimacy, and it did so physically. I would be going about my day and suddenly feel the sticky warmth of her nine-year-old hand in mine. Or while looking in the bathroom mirror, my arms, my chest, would suddenly remember the total surrender of her weight as I picked up her five-year-old body. One night, when she was staying over at Julie's house, I'm not sure what possessed me but I walked into her bedroom and sat down on the edge of her bed. I suddenly felt her hair in my hands, when it was long, and she was twelve and in bed with the flu, when even her hair felt hot to the touch. I ran my fingers slowly through it, which seemed to be the only thing that gave her any comfort. It was our way of talking, when we had exhausted all of our words.

Then, on an evening in May, Ashley found out that she hadn't gotten into her top two schools for soccer. I was having a bath when she walked in without knocking, sat down on the edge of the tub. She pulled off her socks, and stuck her feet in the water, and I held her calf and her thigh as she cried.

I should drop a radio in there, she eventually muttered. She tried to turn her grin into a frown, but it became a tiny laugh instead.

We then talked for the better part of an hour, our first real
conversation in months, as the soap suds dissolved and the water
grew tepid, and it was in that chilled and guilt-ridden state that I
agreed to the absolutely insane proposal of hosting the prom after-
party at the house, on the condition that I would stay over at a
friend's house that night. There was a plunging sensation in my
stomach the moment the words came out of my mouth, though
how could I have said no? I knew that conversation was as much
an olive branch from Ashley as the party would have to be from
me. I also knew Ashley had probably suffered some loss of social
capital at the school which this would go a ways to rectifying, and
I think somewhere in the back of my mind it felt triumphant in its
sheer unlikeliness that I, of all people, should be the parent to host
the prom after-party, and that maybe it would signal to Paul, and
my former students and colleagues, and anyone else who cared to
notice, that I was in a different and much better headspace than
they had ever imagined.

So that is how I found myself, three weeks later, standing on a
chair, taping up blue and gold streamers in the dining room. Ashley was blowing up balloons in her bra and underwear, with her
face and hair fully done to the nines. I could count on one hand
the number of times I had seen her in makeup before. The dining
table was laden with plastic-wrapped veggie and cheese trays, bags
of chips, two-litre bottles of soft drinks, paper plates, plastic cut-
lery, stacks of napkins, and a wide array of wine and liquor. Old
Town Road blasted through the Bluetooth speaker.

Oh I have to show you my banner, Ashley shouted at me.

What?

I made a banner to hang on the wall.

I can't—Hey Google turn down by five.

The music quietened, as Ashley picked up a paper banner and
handed me one end.

I wanna tape it over the door.

She climbed onto another chair, and we taped it to the wall. Once unfurled, the banner read It's All Downhill From Here. I told her that Congratulations would've taken fewer letters.

She shrugged—Yeah, well I'm a realist.

Speaking of which, I put two condoms in your purse.

She shot me a look—Mom.

I asked her if Liam was coming.

Do you think I care?

I laughed.

What?

You're such a terrible liar.

I honestly don't, I don't care.

Okay, I said, my eyebrows disappearing behind my hairline.

The next track on her playlist began and she ordered Google to turn it up by eight, and we danced as we continued decorating. When Ashley was little, I used to draw the blinds, and play eighties club hits on full volume until we were sweaty and exhausted, and collapsed on the floor in a giggling heap. I used to love how into it she would get; the look of deep concentration on her face, her little arms pumping, her hips jutting back and forth.

I checked my phone, and then shouted to her that it was a quarter to six. She left the living room and returned holding her metallic rose-gold prom dress.

I hate it, she said, without affect. It looks like an iPhone.

I began helping her into the dress and reminded her that she had picked it out.

I know, I hated them all.

I told you, you should have gone with the tux.

Just then, the doorbell rang. Shit, shit, she said.

It's fine.

It's not fine, I'm not ready!

I helped her into the dress, one leg at a time, and zipped up the back, before she dashed to the door to answer it—to find Tom and Seema standing there.

Hi, Tom said, holding a large reusable grocery bag. Sorry to bother you, but is your—

Mom! Ashley called.

I walked to the front door and greeted Tom and Seema, with a little laugh of surprise and confusion. I hadn't seen either of them since the first meeting, nearly four months earlier. Neither of them had come to the second one. I had taken Seema's number, though, and we'd been messaging on and off since.

Come in, I said. Hey Google, turn off.

The music stopped and, in the ensuing quiet, The Hum retook its place as the dominant noise in my awareness. Seema told Ashley she looked gorgeous. Ashley gave her a polite smile, and I explained that it was prom night.

Oh god, of course. We can come back later, Seema offered, but I waved away the suggestion.

No, no it's fine, her friends are coming by to pick her up any minute. We're hosting the after-party.

Without saying a word, Ashley turned, and bolted up to her bedroom, stumbling on her dress halfway up the stairs. She had no idea who these visitors were, but she must have assumed they were two Hummers, as she called us. Ashley had never met another Hummer before, and I wondered if Seema's nose piercing and tattoos and other signifiers of countercultural alignment, even her age and ethnicity, were making Ashley re-evaluate who a Hummer might be.

Seema apologized for dropping by unannounced, no doubt sensing the tension their arrival had caused.

I'm not sure if you saw my last message, she asked, walking past me into the dining room, and taking in the decorations.

Yes I did, I said. I'm sorry, I kept meaning to reply.

There's been a subsequent development, Tom said.

Oh okay. Well here—I pulled out chairs for them at the table and motioned to the mounds of junk food and liquor laid out. If anything strikes your fancy—

I wouldn't mind a Johnnie Walker, Tom replied. If you're offering.

I cracked the bottle, and poured him a shot into a plastic cup, before deciding to pour myself one as well.

Are these kids of age? he asked.

Well. You know how it is.

Seema asked if I was worried about them trashing the place, and I laughed. I'm serious! she said.

No, I know! All the valuables have been locked away.

God, I'd be so anal, she said, shaking her head and looking around.

Tom took a sip of whisky—I guess you'll be around to keep an eye on things.

Oh no, I'm out of here. They don't want Mom hanging around.

Seema was amazed. You're a saint, she said.

I told her I was seventeen once too; I got it.

And where will you go? she asked.

I'm staying with Leslie, actually, I said. From the group, I clarified, in case they had forgotten.

Oh, that's nice, Seema replied, somewhat muted.

Tom looked into his drink and seemed to stew on something for a moment. I wanted to say—I'm very sorry about you and Paul separating. Emily told me.

I nodded and thanked him.

This has taken an incredible toll on all of us, he said.

I glanced over at the cardboard boxes still stacked in the hallway beside the door to the garage.

You see those boxes over there, down the hall? Those are all his, I said.

When Paul first left, it sometimes felt like he was just away on a business trip, and then I would see those boxes and it would become real again. He had planned to swing by a couple of weeks earlier to grab them, but something came up. Then he was supposed to come by the day before the party, but he never showed. I texted him three, maybe four times, to remind him. I was sure, then, that he was just doing it to annoy me. But they were his things, not mine, that were going to be sitting out in the hallway when forty teenagers descended on the place. If I had felt magnanimous I would have carried the boxes into the garage for safekeeping, but I didn't.

Tom cleared his throat, and I turned back to look at him. Well, we uh—we don't want to take up too much of your time, he said.

No, especially not on a night like this, Seema said.

Then, without another word, Tom pulled out a charred hunk of metal from his reusable shopping bag and clunked it down on the dining table.

What on earth is that? I asked.

This, Claire, is my mailbox. Someone set it on fire last night.

What?

They're trying to intimidate us, Seema said.

Tom leaned back in his chair. We've been lobbying the city, the governor, our congressman, he said. And nothing. The city didn't even write us back. So we went to the media with it.

I know, I said, I watched you on TV.

He gestured to the mailbox emphatically, as if to suggest his television appearance precipitated the vandalism.

Just because of one little interview? I asked.

And the articles in the papers, Seema said.

But who would've done it?

Tom started counting off on his fingers—Someone from Grenadier, someone from the city, angry neighbours who think I'm wrecking their property value—

Neighbours?

Oh yeah. I've had some nasty arguments.

Seema said there were hundreds of people who had a vested stake in The Hum not being investigated. They know how much it could cost them, she said. So they're trying to shut us up.

I asked her how they would even know where Tom lived, and she shrugged—Anyone can find out where anyone lives.

You got to be careful, I said.

She shook her head. No, we've got to go bigger, she said. That's how we stay safe.

Unless they really go after you.

Tom rapped the tabletop with his finger—If those fuckers think they can scare us, they picked the wrong fight.

We've got to keep this in the public eye, Seema said. Which is why we need you. We need critical mass. We need as many others as possible to speak to the media to back us up.

But—

We've been canvassing the whole neighbourhood looking for others, Tom said, handing me a flyer.

The flyer was a lot more slick and detailed than the notices Howard and Jo stuck up. Seema said that they had been much more methodical in their outreach as well, knocking on doors house by house, street by street. I asked if they had found others.

Tom nodded—Oh yeah.

A handful, Seema clarified.

It's a slower response than we would've liked but—

We expect some people to sit with it for a few days and call us, Seema said, as I read through the flyer, which looked like a pamphlet you would find in a doctor's office for depression or menopause.

Maybe them just knowing about The Hum will make them think, wait a second, I do hear something, Seema said.

Most people will sign a petition but aren't willing to talk about their experience, Tom said. And what we need are testimonials. Your experience, the way you articulated it at Howard's? That's the kind of story we need to get the severity of this across. And listen, I know you and I didn't hit it off right away, and I'm sorry about that—

Yeah well neither did we, Seema said, glancing at him.

But you seem like a very reasonable, sensible woman, and we need someone like you on our side, he said to me.

They looked at me, expectant. They had obviously poured days and weeks of work into this, and I admired their drive, but our paths had diverged. They were on a completely different journey with this than I was. They were still stuck in the mindset of that first meeting, seeking to form some kind of neighbourhood association, and determined to find a physical source. My thinking, the thinking of the rest of the group who had continued to convene at Howard and Jo's week after week, had evolved and deepened in ways Seema and Tom couldn't even begin to grasp.

I'm sorry, I said, handing their flyer back to them. But I can't.

Seema motioned to the charred mailbox—Don't let this scare you, Claire. There's strength in numbers.

I took a moment to choose my words carefully. I'm learning to find peace with The Hum, I said.

She frowned—But you don't have to put up with it.

But I'm not 'putting up with it,' I said. I've chosen to welcome it into my life.

Tom muttered Christ, and looked down at the floor.

Seema's face hardened—So Howard's got you then?

He has not got me, I said, I have an independent mind, thank you. I just don't buy anymore that it's some blast furnace or highway. I mean listen.

I paused and the three of us sat there, surrounded by balloons and half-hung streamers, listening. It's atmospheric, I said. It's completely encompassing.

Tom sighed and swilled what was left of the whisky in his cup— Claire, Howard's theory is complete nonsense. It's—

It's like the science equivalent of fake news, Seema said.

I told them that I thought it was very easy to be cynical, and a lot more difficult to open yourself up to the possibility of discovery.

Pretty much all scientific theories are discredited at first, I said. String theory, dark matter. The Earth revolving around the Sun wasn't too popular at first either, if you recall.

Seema extended her hand towards me, over the tabletop. I'm a medical resident, she said. I'm used to a lot of pseudoscience and alternative cures.

I suggested to her that she should read about it and inform herself, and that it was all online if she cared to look.

Oh, Tom said, raising his arms, it's online, it must be true.

There are many reputable sites—

This wavelength that Howard is talking about, Seema cut in. There is absolutely no way the human anatomy can hear it. It's not physically possible.

I suppose that's the nature of discovery, isn't it? I replied. What once seemed impossible is re-evaluated and reconsidered.

You really believe him, she asked. She posed this more like an accusation than a question.

Well I'm not surprised you don't, I said. The two of you never even gave him a chance. You came in with your minds made up, and when something else presented itself, you were out of there. You barely got any explanation whatsoever, and then you never came back. You have no idea the full scope of—of revelation around this.

That was, perhaps, an indelicate word choice.

Revelation, Tom scoffed. Please. Enlighten us.

You don't actually want to know.

No, I do, he said.

Only to mock it.

Well I sincerely do, I want to know, Seema said. And I absolutely won't mock it.

I met her eyes—As a doctor you might actually appreciate this. We've been learning about brain waves.

Okay.

I'm sorry—brain waves? Tom said. Is that a thing?

Seema sighed—Of course it is, Tom; have you never heard of a brain scan before?

Well I don't know.

Well maybe stop talking then.

They're the fluctuations of the electric current in the brain, I explained. And scans show that the brain lights up when brain waves hit 7.83 hertz.

The Schumann Resonance, Seema said. I nodded, impressed that she remembered from the first meeting.

Right. Exactly. And at that specific frequency, whole areas of our brain that we never normally use suddenly burst into action. We only otherwise use about ten percent of our brain at any given time.

That's—that's a popular myth, she said.

Studies support it.

I'd like to see those studies.

And if that's the resonant frequency of the Earth's atmosphere, I continued, then we've spent millions of years on the planet evolving under its influence. Every cell, every living thing. So naturally our brains want to synch with it. And all kinds of living things do. Whales, birds, bees—they all use the Schumann Resonance to navigate. And for our health and well-being we need to learn to tune ourselves to it.

Tom chuckled—Tune ourselves?

Yes.

And how does one do that, exactly?

Well that's the question, isn't it? I explained to them that people have been trying for millennia. The chants of Buddhists. The Hindu Om. The drone of church organs. Didgeridoos.

All kinds of faiths, maybe every faith, has been trying to do just that; trying to achieve transcendence by tapping into the Resonance, I said, hearing myself trying and failing to articulate the full splendour and complexity of the discussion at Howard's.

Tom downed the last of his whisky—I'm not religious, so—

Neither am I, I said.

—so I haven't felt that impulse to uh *tune* myself with anything, he said, before turning to Seema. Have you?

Well—

With a hum?

No, but—

Just forget religion for a second, I said. Have you never had a moment where you just felt perfectly in rhythm with the universe? Where you're thinking perfectly clearly and everything seems to make sense?

Maybe after a good cup of coffee, he said, reaching for the Johnnie Walker and uncorking it.

I have, Seema said.

Have you? he asked, with bemusement.

There's a kind of euphoria to it, isn't there? I continued. Well just imagine if you could feel like that all the time. And 7.83 hertz is the frequency of our brain waves during meditation and dreaming. It's like a gateway to deeper states of consciousness and creativity.

Seema exhaled. Claire, the thing is—

And none of it strikes you as bullshit, Tom cut in, pouring himself a fresh shot.

No, it doesn't. And I'd appreciate if you didn't infer—

From upstairs in her bedroom, Ashley's voice suddenly thundered—It's bullshit! It's bullshit it's bullshit it's bullshiiiiiit.

Tom raised his eyebrows and stifled a laugh. I closed my eyes. Please just go, I wanted to tell them. Five minutes ago I was helping my daughter into her prom dress, I'd been busting my ass for days to make this a special night for her, and this was the last goddamn thing I needed.

Listen, I said, eyes still closed, I can only speak to my experience.

And have you experienced this transcendence? Seema asked, with compassion. I opened my eyes and looked at her.

Not yet fully, no.

Do you believe you will?

I don't know, I said. I hope so.

She said she sensed a skeptic in me.

Well that's my nature. I question.

And have you questioned this?

Of course I have; I resent your implication.

I'm not implying anything, I'm just—

I'm not a gullible person, Seema.

I never said you were.

And I can tell you that things have begun to make a lot more sense to me.

Since Howard?

Since—since having this information to draw on, I said. The air does feel like it's vibrating. The humming is louder at night. And it seems to be coming from everywhere, and yet nowhere.

And so then you start trawling the Internet for blogs, Tom said, with cool detachment, that parrot this theory back to you until you're in this little echo chamber of people who don't know a damn thing about science because we're barely taught the basics in school by nutjobs like you.

Seema told him to stop. He took a sip of whisky. I noticed movement out of the corner of my eye, looked over, and realized Ashley was now sitting halfway up the staircase, watching. Good, I thought, I wanted her to hear what I was about to say. I turned back to Tom.

Tom, the Earth is making us aware of itself in the most extraordinary way. And you can choose to listen or can choose not to. But I am listening. Because I have been given the gift of being able to. And so have you.

I looked at Seema. And so have you, I said. So why say no? Why not commune with the Earth on a more sensitive and fundamental level than most people could ever imagine?

Tom looked down at his mailbox, and then back up at me— With all due respect I think you're a lunatic.

I nodded—Lunatic. Madwoman. Witch. Yeah. I know the story, Tom. Those who see differently—

Oh yeah, you're a martyr, he said, rising from his seat. A real Joan of Arc.

He picked up his mailbox and made for the door.

And what about Emily? I asked.

What about her?

She believes it too.

We don't talk about it.

Well let me tell you, she believes.

Tom flashed me a pained smile—I know.

He glanced at Seema, and then up at Ashley on the staircase. He saluted her, and then walked out through the front door into the gathering dusk.

I don't know how you stand him, I said to Seema, as the door shut.

She shrugged—He's the only person willing to help me figure out what this actually is.

I downed the last of my whisky like a movie mobster and dropped my cup into Tom's empty one. I know you think I'm a lunatic too, I said.

She smiled and shook her head. I told her I was sorry that I couldn't help her, and she said she was too.

So you really don't think the Resonance exists, I said.

Claire. I know that's maybe the more exciting or poetic explanation, but honestly? Our hum? It's just some industrial white noise. And I'm going to find it and I'm going to deal with it. On top of all the other shit I have to do in my life.

She made a little doleful laugh to herself.

Like I'm—I'm pulling eighteen-hour shifts at the General, she continued. Tom's retired, so he can, you know—I can't spend all my free time on this. But I just know if I don't, it's not going to happen. Like can you imagine Tom doing this on his own? He'd get into an argument while handing out flyers and punch someone in the face. You laugh but he almost did.

I wished her luck. She rose, thanked me, and wished me the same. She then told me to be careful. Thanks, I replied, but I think you're the one who has to be careful.

She considered this for a moment, and made to say something, but smiled instead. She turned, wished Ashley a happy prom, and walked out the door.

I looked over at Ashley on the staircase, slumped in her dress.

Let me fix your hair, I said. She ignored me, picking some lint off the carpeted step. C'mon. I motioned to her to come down and join me in the dining room, but she didn't move. I walked over to the staircase, climbed halfway up, and sat down beside her.

I'm completely alone, she mumbled.

I'm right here.

No, you're not. You've been taken from me. This thing has taken you and now it's taken Dad, and everything is fucked forever.

And you can't see it because you're inside of it, and so are they, with their stupid petition and flyers. It's like a mass delusion, she said, swirling her hand in the air.

Just because you can't hear it, doesn't—

I can't because it's not there. You're all caught in this—this hysteria and you don't even—

Hey Miss Feminist—

I know, I know but it is, Mom, it just fucking is. Like that medieval dancing plague or something.

Howard has spent his career devoted to this.

So? Mom, a priest spends his entire career devoted to God, that doesn't mean I have to give a shit about what he has to say about it.

But this is something that exists, okay, this is science.

To Howard Bard it exists, Mom, not to the rest of the world.

He's an internationally respected academic.

Oh please.

He has more degrees than a thermometer!

Yeah so did, like, Robert Mugabe.

I started to laugh, and Ashley smiled, in spite of herself—It's true. I wrote an essay on him.

Howard's not a tinpot dictator.

No he's just a—tinfoil-hat dictator.

He was dean of geosciences at Virginia Tech for eighteen years.

Yeah, before he was fired, she said, widening her eyes.

I told her the administration was completely threatened by him.

Do you know how hard it is for an old white man to be kicked out of a tenured teaching job? she asked. He was dean for Christ sake, he'd practically have to murder someone to lose his job.

He was a renegade who totally revolutionized the department.

She buried her face in her hands for a moment, and then looked up at me—You're not on stable ground, Mom, and honestly? It's scary. Because people, when you're in this state, they'll take advantage of you.

No one's taking advantage of me.

You are not yourself, and you're not in a strong place.

Yes I am and don't—You think I'm a weak person? A weak person, Ash, would have just ignored it and wished all of this away. A weak person would be still at school teaching and coming home, and just, just carrying on like everything was hunky dory.

I pointed to my chest—I am battling. I am going to battle every single hour of the day.

I'm not saying you're a weak person, I'm saying you're—

And I can't do this alone, okay? I need you on my side. You can't let your dad turn you against me.

Whoa whoa, she said, holding up her hands, as if I just drew a gun.

I know he's trying to.

Don't start—

He's telling you I'm bipolar, isn't he?

She looked away, down the staircase—Who else is he going to talk to?

Has he been telling you that?

Our conversations are private.

He shouldn't be off-loading that on you, I said, shaking my head.

Who else has he got?

I need you with me on this.

On what? she asked, turning back to me, indignant. On Howard? On The Hum? No, I'm sorry. I love you, but I'm fucking scared for you.

Scared of what?

Of the complete disintegration of your life!

I couldn't bear to look her in the eyes, so I stared down at my feet on the stair. I touched the tip of my big toe, poking through the small hole it had worn in my left sock.

I wish you could just be happy for me, I said. I have found a community of people who care for me and love me.

They do not fucking love you, Mom. I'm your daughter, I love you. Dad loves you. These people barely know you.

They know me better—Ash, they know things about me that even your dad doesn't.

That's fucked up.

No, it's not. Because they treat those parts of me, and my life, and my story with a care and a, and a compassion that even he could never muster.

That's just bullshit, she muttered.

Well it's not, and I wish you'd stop dismissing me, it hurts.

You think this hurts you?

I tried to explain how I had found a space where I could be truly free and uninhibited for the first time in my life. A space where I felt truly safe.

Do you know how rare and precious to me that is? I asked. I don't understand what you are so afraid of.

That Howard's a fucking psychopath, she replied.

Her phone buzzed, and she pulled it out of her bra to check it— They're outside.

Without looking at me, she got up and descended the stairs.

Ash, wait.

I hurried down after her, and put my hand on her shoulder— Have fun tonight, okay?

She mustered a faint smile—Just promise me you'll be gone when we get back.

I told her that I would. And don't leave your drink unattended, I called as she walked out the door. I watched as she hurried down the front walk, waving to her friends Sophie and Jess, who whooped and cheered while leaning out the windows of a white Escalade. If they saw me in the doorway, they pretended not to. I closed the door, turned back to the half-decorated dining room, and felt the wind escape from me like a punctured tire. The room was a mess. There was still so much that needed doing. I crossed to the table, sat down, and poured myself another whisky, before glancing up at Ashley's homemade banner.

10

UNTIL THAT EVENING AND MY CONVERSATION WITH ASHLEY on the staircase, I don't think I fully grasped the extent to which hysteria was a psychic wound that we as women still bore; a wound inflicted from centuries of our symptoms, our instincts about our own bodies, our pleasures and afflictions, always being the first to be discounted and discredited, even by other women. Even by our own daughters, as the case may be. It was a wound that we still carried, because we could, at any moment, have an entire history called upon to silence us in a word, in an instant. And in the eyes of my family, of those who loved me most, I was now the hysterical subject.

I was the woman in Ancient Greece with a womb wandering through my guts like a feral dog for having sexual desire, or anxiety, or depression, or whatever other feeling was inconvenient for my husband. I was the melancholy woman prone to demonic possession and witchcraft. I was the woman sent to the Alpine sanatorium, when my husband no longer wanted to deal with me complaining about his mistresses. Too much sex. Not enough sex. Too much female seed becomes venomous if not released through regular climax, don't you know. Too much menstrual blood. Not enough menstrual blood. If I was living a hundred years ago, less even, I think it's entirely possible I would have been subjected to electroshock therapy for hearing The Hum, and maybe a hysterectomy fifty years before that. And I have the feeling that Paul would have very lovingly and supportively allowed it.

I was the one who first told Ashley the story of the dancing plague. The plague started with a woman, naturally, named Frau Troffea, who on a clear summer morning in Strasbourg in 1518 began dancing in the street. Neighbours gathered to laugh and clap and cheer her on. But it soon became clear that something was wrong. Frau Troffea danced and danced for six days without stop. Her husband and children brought her water, and shoved pieces of bread and cheese into her mouth to keep her alive, for she wouldn't even stop to eat; and as discreetly as possible, they did their best to clean her whenever she soiled herself. By the end of the first week, more than thirty others had joined Frau Troffea, and by the end of the first month, there were four hundred dancers, most of them women. Some of the dancers dropped dead in the street, sweaty and red-faced, from exhaustion and strokes and heart attacks. At the height of the mania, around fifteen people were dying each day. The doctors of Strasbourg ruled out astrological or supernatural causes, and instead attributed the dancing to 'hot blood.' Some prescribed bleeding, but others suggested the only cure was for the afflicted to dance day and night until they had danced out their mania. So the city gave over two guildhalls and the grain market to the dancers, and when these spaces filled up, the city hired a band of musicians and built a giant outdoor stage. But, perhaps unsurprisingly, this only encouraged more people to join in. Soon, people from all across the land were pouring into Strasbourg to dance to their deaths. It is still not known why the mania began, or how it ended.

While writing this book, the obvious question that struck me was—Whatever happened to Frau Troffea? I could find no mention of her fate in any article, despite nearly every single one identifying her as the first dancer. A few details also differed from my memory of the story. Like for instance, there's not a single mention of her husband and children bringing her food or cleaning up her shit as she danced. I suppose that was my own hopeful invention. I did, however, find an image of an engraving by Hendrik Hondius from 1624 called *Dancing Mania on a Pilgrimage to the Church at Sint-Jans-Molenbeek*. Hondius based his engraving on a drawing made nearly eighty years earlier by Pieter Bruegel the Elder, who had been a witness to the events.

In the foreground of the engraving are six figures. Two middle-aged women are held by men on either side. The men have their arms hooked through the women's arms, and grip the women's hands, but it isn't initially clear if the men are dancing with the women, or restraining them. In the distance, two men appear to be carrying a woman away over a low bridge, while nearby, another woman sits in a stupor by a creek. The more I looked at this image, the more I realized that the women were the only ones being portrayed as wild. Raving crones to be wrestled by their concerned menfolk. The women are not rendered sympathetically; they're homely and heftier than the men who attempt to subdue them. In other words, they're comic subjects, meant to be mocked and scorned. It feels like a knowing elbow nudge, from Bruegel to Hondius, one man to another, about the inherent and eternal madness of women. Madness as our nature. We only need the slightest provocation to break free from our homes, from our domesticity, and flee into the wilds, for our menfolk to come chasing after us, and carry us back to civilization, back to our senses.

When I found this image, my eyes lingered over the figure of the woman on the left-hand side of the group. Her gaze is angled towards the sky, and her brow is furrowed with intensity, as if trying to challenge God. She is gazing beyond the moment, beyond herself, and the strictures of her body, and the social order that attempts to restrain her. She is gazing upward to the heavens, to the birds that circle above, to a divine mystery that she alone seems attendant to in that chaotic moment. In her look I do not see madness.

I see resolve.

11

KYLE WAS NOT INVITED TO THE PARTY. ASHLEY AND I HAD
been extremely clear about this fact. So it was with considerable
surprise that I pulled into the driveway the next morning to find
Kyle walking out the front door. And not only was he walking out
the front door, but he was accompanied by Paul. And not only was
he accompanied by Paul, but he was helping carry one of Paul's
cardboard boxes down the front walk and load it into the trunk
of Paul's car.

What the actual fuck is going on right now? I murmured to
myself.

After loading the box into the trunk, Paul and Kyle both looked
over at me sitting in my car, and gave me polite nods as if this
wasn't the most surreal scene any of us had been privy to, as if
my former student who precipitated the implosion of my marriage
wasn't helping my husband move out of my party-ravaged house.
They then turned and disappeared back up the front walk. I sat

there for a stunned moment, before climbing out of the car, and hurrying after them into the house.

Stepping through the front door, I noticed where there once was hardwood floor, there was now a carpet of deflated balloons, crumpled streamers, discarded corsages, and plastic cups. A framed Georgia O'Keeffe print formerly hanging near the staircase was missing, replaced by smears of god-knows-what on the walls. And the glass front of the ornamental clock in the front hall was smashed.

Morning, Ashley said from the staircase. She was wearing her PJ Harvey t-shirt and plaid boxers and was watching, with serene disinterest, as Kyle and Paul negotiated which box to lift next from the pile in the hallway. Paul turned and gave a furtive little wave, and said he had texted Ashley last night to let her know he was coming over.

But my phone died, she said, as if that were all the explanation needed.

I looked at her with what I hope she read as bewildered rage, and then back down the hall at Kyle, who flashed me an apologetic smile. His shirt was stained all down the front with what looked like cola.

What are you doing here? I asked him.

I know, I'm sorry, I—

When I saw him last night I threw my drink at him, Ashley said, sounding vaguely proud.

And then dragged me upstairs—

Well we weren't going to have it out in front of everyone, so yeah I took him into your bedroom because—

What?

—because there were people in mine, and—

You went into my bedroom?

Our bedroom, Paul corrected.

So we could have somewhere to talk—

We agreed—

I know, I'm sorry, but we had a talk, she said, turning to Kyle. About everything that's been happening, your little group, these meetings—

The meetings? I asked, feeling like I was scrambling up a sand pile. What, what did you say?

Nothing.

I wanted to know if he really believed, Ashley said. All this shit about the Resonance, did he really, did you really believe it? she said, looking at him.

I can literally hear it, Kyle replied. That's like asking me if I believe in gravity.

And then I asked him what Howard wants.

Wants, I said. In what way?

Like what's his agenda, Ashley said.

I put my overnight bag down, and steadied myself against the wall.

He's a scientist, Kyle replied. He's interested in the truth.

He's your leader, Paul said, looking at me.

He's not our leader, I replied, exasperated. We're all equal, we all lead, we all contribute.

Right, Paul said, nodding, dismissive.

Well it all sounds majorly fucked up, Ashley said.

Why, because you don't understand it? Kyle asked, in a measured tone. Do you think you understand the whole world? You don't think there's room for things no one can explain? Is there nothing left to discover?

Ashley turned to me, and said, matter-of-factly—Kyle's here because his mom kicked him out of the house yesterday, and he had nowhere else to go, and I felt sorry for him.

What? I looked at Kyle. Your mom—?

Kicked me out. Yeah.

Kyle—

She found out about the meetings. You can't hide shit from my mom, she's like the CIA.

I told him he could crash here for the night, Ashley said. I figured you'd probably prefer that than letting him wander the streets.

Well of course.

And then I came home to find him on the couch, Paul said. And we had a pretty damn heated exchange, let's say. Well I was heated.

Just hearing this was giving me stomach cramps.

But we had a talk, didn't we, Paul said, looking at Kyle.

Kyle nodded.

What kind of talk? I asked weakly.

That's between us men, Paul replied.

He actually said 'us men,' I kid you not, like he'd just given his son the sex talk, and I would have laughed if I hadn't felt so close to stress-vomiting. In retrospect, Paul must have been unbelievably stressed as well, to have said something so dumb; he was never very good at performing calm when he wasn't. Either way, I found his answer both disquieting and irritating.

And then, Paul continued, at the end of it, Kyle very kindly offered to help me with these boxes.

I see, I managed to breathe out.

You're not thinking of letting him stay here, are you? Paul asked me.

Paul, I have no idea, I've just walked through the door. I haven't even had a cup of coffee yet.

Because I don't feel comfortable with him staying here.

Well it's not your decision.

I still own half of this house.

Oh right. So what half are you taking with you?

You're just going to let him sleep on the couch? Claire Devon's House of Strays?

It was just a night, Ashley said, flinging her hands up.

Claire, do you get how this would look? After everything?

I turned to Kyle and asked him if he had somewhere else to stay. He puffed up his cheeks as he thought, then exhaled—I'm sure I can figure it out.

But do you? I pressed.

I don't know.

What about Luke or Mohammed?

You're joking.

Or Jay?

His family doesn't have the room.

Are we seriously having this conversation? Paul asked.

It's not our responsibility, Ashley said to me.

Of course it is.

Paul flushed with indignation—How?

Because I'm a human being.

Really, it's fine, Kyle said. It's not your—

There must be someone, Ashley said.

I've asked Rory for a night but I haven't heard back.

What about like an uncle or aunt? Paul asked. Grandparents?

It's just me and my mom.

Well you're not staying here. I'm sorry.

Yes he damn well is if he has nowhere to go, I said. I do, actually, have some responsibility.

What's your mother's phone number? Paul asked Kyle.

I held my finger up at Paul—Do not, *no*—

I'm calling and resolving this right now.

You're going to make this a thousand times worse.

Worse than him moving into your house?

His mom should know, Ashley said.

Paul leaned in towards me—He is her goddamn problem, not ours.

And then, whether to curry Paul's favour, or because he felt he had no other choice, Kyle recited his mother's home phone number. Paul grabbed his own phone out of his pocket, and had Kyle repeat the last four digits as he dialed. Paul held the phone up to his ear, and we waited, breathless, for the call to go through.

Is this her real number? Paul asked Kyle after several rings.

Yes, of course.

She's not answering.

It's nine in the morning on a Sunday, Ashley said. She's probably still sleeping.

She'll be at church, Kyle said.

Church? Paul looked surprised. Right. Didn't even occur to me.

The call went to voicemail and Paul began leaving a message— Hello, Mrs. Francis, this is Paul Devon speaking, Claire Devon's husband. I'm sorry to be calling you so early on a Sunday—He wandered off into the kitchen while recording the message, stepping over balloons and piles of paper plates.

Kyle looked at Ashley, and then at me—Well I'll see you later, he said, turning and walking out of the living room, towards the front door.

I followed him to the door, and tried to stop him—Kyle, wait.

But he charged outside and down the front path without turning around, as I felt white-hot anger flare up in me. I turned around to find Ashley right behind me.

You're such a little shit, I said quietly.

Excuse me?

You knew your dad was coming this morning, and you invited Kyle to stay over knowing this would happen.

Are you insane?

Did you want to embarrass me? I asked. Punish me?

You've fucking lost it, woman.

Make him think I can't possibly be left on my own?

I was trying to do the right thing!

I stared at her, shaking my head. I knew in my gut that she had seen Paul's text the previous night. Just as she had seen Brenda's text, and never warned me. She knew Paul would be there that morning, knew I would come home to this ambush. I had never spoken to Ashley like that before. I didn't recognize myself. And in that moment I didn't recognize her either.

Your phone is dead, I said, mocking.

It is.

Show me.

No.

Show me your phone.

I'm not a child.

No, you're a liar.

She set her jaw, just as Paul returned from the kitchen holding the espresso machine with both arms—I'm going to need someone to help me unload the boxes on the other end.

I'm coming with you, Ashley said. Lemme just grab my bag.

She bounded up the stairs towards her room.

Ashley, come on, I called up after her. Your father has no second bed, no bedding, no kitchen supplies.

I looked at the espresso machine in his arms—Well, no useful kitchen supplies.

I can host her for a few days, Paul said. Maybe she just needs some space.

Well a studio apartment doesn't have much of it.

I don't think it's healthy for her to be here right now, with you like this, and with him hanging around.

With me like what? What am I like?

In a cult! Ashley shouted down from upstairs.

I felt like she had just slapped me across the face. A cult. Before
I could reply, Paul said—Let's call a spade a spade, Claire.

I'm sorry, what?

You believe in a totally illogical delusion.

Paul, you believe in talking snakes and the parting of the Red
Sea and a God who somehow has a son who he sent down to Earth
to be born to a virgin woman—

Okay, okay—

No really, how many people have to believe for it to stop being a
delusion? If I'm in a cult, you're in a far bigger and more fucked-up
one than I am.

You've completely—he made a spinning gesture with his hand
to signify that I had unravelled, I suppose, that I was spinning out
of control—I mean look at you, look at this place.

She just threw a fucking party, I said.

With underage drinking and adults nowhere to be seen.

As we argued, I thought, Was this really what Paul and Ashley
had been thinking all along? That I was in a cult? I found this
completely astonishing. For them to say this was to suggest there
had been some disjuncture in the continuity of my being. I was
not, in their eyes, fundamentally the same person they once knew.
I couldn't be. Not if they truly believed their accusation.

Ashley bounded down the stairs with a duffle bag slung over
her shoulder, and tossed her phone to me, which I barely managed
to catch.

It's dead, she said.

I handed it back to her without looking at it. What did it even
matter? I felt like bursting into tears, or perhaps flames, like a car
slammed at high velocity. She grabbed the last box from the front
hallway, and walked out with Paul, who closed the door behind
them with a look I had never seen him give me before. I held the

look in my mind for several seconds after he had closed the door, parsing it out, until I realized—it was pity. Paul, my cornflake-faced giant from Amarillo, had every possible emotion at the disposal of a heterosexual man, and he chose pity. He might as well have chucked an egg at my face before closing the door. One parting addition to the mess of my house, my life.

12

THE GROUP HAD CONTINUED TO CHANGE SHAPE OVER THE
winter, and into spring. At one point we had three new members,
but then Pierce—the bald architect who came to one session, and
said next to nothing—never came back. The other two newcom-
ers stayed. The first was Shawn—a witty, loud, and effete man in
his early thirties, with something of an equine face: big nose, big
eyes, big teeth. The second was Mia, also in her early thirties—
a self-described 'antifa' who worked with autistic teenagers and
spent winters living and working at an 'eco farm and wellness
retreat' in Oaxaca, Mexico. She had been arrested the year prior
for blocking the construction of a new natural gas pipeline. I can't
recall how either of them found out about the group. It's possible
it was through Damian's post on Reddit. Either way, both of them
had heard The Hum for months, and suffered in isolation. Like
most of us, they were initially reticent to adopt Howard's theories

wholesale, but gradually became some of the most active partici-
pants in our exchanges.

Shawn, in particular, was wickedly funny and really livened
up our sessions, which, if you ask me, risked getting a little self-
serious at times. He was an incredible baker, and had actually
won a reality television show for amateur cooks a couple of years
earlier. I never watched it, but Leslie did, and was evidently a bit
starstruck. He was constantly bringing in homemade confections
like gluten-free carrot cake with cinnamon cream cheese icing, and
vegan white chocolate fudge brownies. His true gift, though, was
the exacting comic dissection of everyone and everything. Nothing eluded his notice. He would pick up on people's little habits
and foibles and tease them about it, though always in a way that
made them laugh hardest of all, and always in a way that somehow
highlighted his own shortcomings and neuroses. I also noticed that
he had the ability to seem incredibly forthcoming, and yet somehow he never ended up revealing that much about himself. I never
worked out, for instance, if he had a partner. I was never even particularly clear what he did for a living, other than 'work in retail.'
And yet I always knew, in hilarious and intricate detail, the story
of his last, ill-fated haircut, or visit to the dentist.

Mia, on the other hand, had a millennial righteousness that I
found both admirable and intimidating. At her first meeting, she
introduced herself and her gender pronouns—My name is Mia.
I go by she, her, her. Emily and Nora had no idea what she was
talking about, so she explained. And then everyone else, I suppose
feeling a bit put on the spot, went around and introduced themselves the same way—Howard. He, him, his, and so on. Everyone
except Damian. And to be honest, I was a little indignant at first
too. I thought: take a look at this group, is this really necessary?
But then I caught myself and thought—is this what it is to grow
old? To become defensive and resentful when confronted by my

own assumptions and biases? By new modes, new sensitivities? I couldn't help but wonder what Ashley would make of this exercise. She and Mia would probably get on very well. Either way, Mia's presence engendered a new self-consciousness around language and conduct within the group; which, for men as prone to micro-aggressions as Damian and Howard, was probably no bad thing. That's not to say she stilted our dynamic, though. She made it more thoughtful and humane.

Damian continued to say very little during meetings. Sometimes his silence felt like a black hole sucking energy and light out of the room. But he was never disengaged. His eyes would flit from face to face, as if sizing up everyone's comments against his own internal value system. He also did this thing where, while keeping his mouth closed, he seemed to clean his teeth with his tongue. I couldn't tell if it was some kind of macho affect, like a cowboy with a toothpick, or a nervous tick, but either way I had to avoid looking at him while he did it. That said, he was always very gentlemanly, he would make a specific point of saying hello and goodbye to me, and nodding when he agreed with something I said. I could tell on some level he respected me. And I have to say, a part of me was slowly warming to him.

We had a covenant of privacy within the group, in which deeply personal details could be shared with the full knowledge that nothing would leave the room. Trust and honest communication were essential. While Howard and Jo led our meetings, we agreed to make decisions by consensus, and tried to share speaking time as much as possible. We knew we were stronger together than any of us would have been individually in seeking the truth about The Hum, and that our success would hinge on our ability to stick together and overcome our differences. And so we each pledged to do so.

By June of that year, we were meeting five times a week. On nights we weren't, I would miss the others so much I would spend most of the night messaging them on our group chat. I couldn't bear rambling around the house alone. Some nights Ashley would reply to my WhatsApp messages, but mostly all I could hope for were the two blue ticks indicating she'd read them. Kyle and I used to message most often, sometimes twenty or thirty times a night, mostly processing things that had come up in the meetings, or sending each other dumb memes—but that all stopped abruptly after the prom after-party. The only messages Paul sent me were angry missives about my living off our joint savings, but what choice did I have? I was still fighting the teachers' union about severance pay, and considering my options for an unlawful dismissal case, all the while carrying the bills for the house.

I found myself calling Jo a lot, when I was lonely. I never used to be a phone person. But I found I began to rely on her guidance and insights—about Ashley and Paul, about feeling like a pariah among my friends and colleagues, about feeling adrift without purpose, about my fears around future employment, and what I was supposed to do with the rest of my life. She sometimes just led me through breathing exercises. Kyle once joked that she had become my spiritual guru. He said that to irritate me, as he knew my aversion to anything New Agey.

He then told me that I had something of a secular Western arrogance about me. That I was too closed off to the possibility of wonder. He kept sending me Simone Weil quotes about making space inside myself for the divine to enter. *Grace fills empty spaces, but it can only enter where there is a void to receive it, and it is grace itself which makes this void.* I told him that I found Weil's mystic Christian koans slightly insufferable. I preferred my voids empty, thank you; I didn't need God cramming himself in there. I was a dyed-in-the-wool atheist, a pragmatist, and I took pride in that. I felt it was actually an important position to defend in an age when reason, logic, and facts felt so assailed and devalued. That said, when Jo led us through guided meditations, and said that we were approaching

a great mystery, I could tangibly feel this, even if I might not have
fully understood it. It did feel as if we were collectively scaling a
mountain towards something. Perhaps a shared catharsis, or some
greater understanding of The Hum and its potential.

Because Jo seemed to rise with such grace above the daily
drudgeries and degradations of life, she could sometimes feel a little remote, particularly when presiding over our meetings. As if
she had ascended to a higher plane, just out of reach. But in those
phone calls, she made herself completely open and available to me.
We spoke very candidly about my situation with Kyle. Her early
relationship with Howard was also a fraught educator-student scenario, though of course quite different than ours. It meant a lot to
me that we were able to open up to one another about it, and sort
of fascinating that we were coming at it from opposite sides of the
dynamic. Jo said she had been dazzled by Howard when she first
met him. He commanded a great deal of respect at the university
at the time, and in their field.

He looked a lot younger back then too, she said to me one night
over the phone, with an apologetic laugh. I pictured her sitting
somewhere secluded in their house, perhaps upstairs in their bedroom, or maybe in her studio, perhaps wrapped in that turquoise
Mexican blanket she sometimes draped over herself during meetings. She confided in me that Howard had had a bit of a reputation
for sleeping with students.

Not necessarily his own, she clarified, but just . . . other students
at the university.

I heard her take a sip of tea, from her favourite fired-clay mug.
She said she was always aware of the power imbalance between
them, and that bothered her. She also began to feel alienated and
judged by the other graduate students.

Eventually it became a really oppressive working environment,
really toxic, she said. And then Howard started getting all this flak

from the school for his research. All kinds of people were trying to tear him down. And he just said you know what, I don't need this, and he quit. And I sort of felt like I had to quit with him. We'd become a unit. The thought of staying there and completing my studies without him felt, just, impossible.

For some reason her voice, isolated on the phone, reminded me of that surrealist Méret Oppenheim sculpture of the teacup, saucer, and spoon wrapped in fur. A hard thing wrapped in unlikely softness. I couldn't remember what the piece was called, but I made a note to find the image and send it to her. I was sure she'd get a kick out of my mental association. She always seemed interested in how the mind worked and drew connections, in slips of the tongue, and what our dreams revealed about us. I suppose rather like the surrealists, she was invested in the world of the subconscious. How, in an instant, the mundane could become extraordinary.

I heard her take another sip of tea and hold it in her mouth for a moment before swallowing. She admitted to struggling, for years, with living under Howard's shadow. For years, their friends would be his colleagues, or doctoral students from other countries making pilgrimages to their home to meet with him.

I began to feel like his personal assistant, she said. Sorting out his calendar, booking his travel, even answering his emails sometimes. It really got to me.

Her voice was quiet on the other end of the line. She then said that for years she felt she was just a kind of appendage. I asked her if she regretted how things had unfolded, and she said no, she was much happier and fulfilled doing what she did now. She said she was not a fatalist, but believed, with regard to her career, that things had taken the course they did for a reason.

If you look at it one way, she said, what we're exploring now with the group sort of combines both of my worlds. The scientific and the spiritual. Not that you want to call it that, I know.

As a group, we mostly avoided speaking about spiritual matters, as it was clear we were all coming at things with very different frames of reference. One afternoon, a week after the prom party, Nora mentioned how she felt God was communicating with her through The Hum.

I don't mean like I'm Teresa of Ávila or anything, she said, with a self-conscious laugh.

Saint Nora! Shawn proclaimed.

I mean in the way He communicates with us all the time, she continued. Through sunlight, through the wind, through the smile of a stranger. I really do feel this.

Damian nodded, and said he felt the same way. I know this is something holy, he said, surveying the group as if challenging us to suggest otherwise. Howard said he thought it was important that we treat The Hum as a phenomenon to be explored, and not to try to fit it into our own preexisting belief systems.

But of course we're going to try to, Nora countered. That's like when some Christians tell me not to fit evolution into my belief system. Well I'm sorry, you don't get to choose what you put in, and what you don't.

Howard pointed out that this was, in fact, the exact opposite scenario. It's not religion saying disregard science, he said, it's saying let's not turn this science, or whatever it is, into religion.

Well as someone with faith, everything is God's doing, Nora said.

Usually I stayed quiet whenever the conversation veered in that direction. My feeling was: let people make of this what they will, as long as they don't begin to circumscribe my ability to do the same. So it's science for some, and divine for others. And industrial white noise for yet others. Whatever it was, it still kept me up at night. My migraines persisted, as did the nosebleeds, though much less frequently. That hadn't deterred me, though, from welcoming the mystery of The Hum into my life. I had chosen to be the one in control of this new condition, this new awareness, and I wanted to understand it fully. Because if I was not in possession of it, then it was in possession of me.

I would say that I was about eighty-five percent certain that what we were doing on Sequoia Crescent didn't constitute a cult. It didn't have a dogma. No one was seeking to extract money from me, or force me to pledge myself to anything or anyone. There was no hierarchy, no talk of the end times, no mythology or holy book. But Ashley's and Paul's words lodged like splinters that I couldn't quite pull out. In my dark hours, I sometimes wondered if what we were engaged in was more akin to a conspiracy theory. A theory that a group of us had bought into in isolation, and could no longer see the forest for the trees. Science seemed to be on our side, but maybe I was only paying attention to the articles that were. I was having profound encounters with The Hum, sensations that I knew beyond any doubt were real, but what if I was self-inducing them, or they were the result of some other phenomenon?

I began reflecting on this during a conversation one meeting, led primarily by Damian, Leslie, and Mia, about government surveillance and the Deep State. Damian had gradually become more and more fixated on the idea that the Deep State—which, when pressed, he loosely defined as the military, the government, and Wall Street—had been aware of the Resonance for some time and had intentionally kept it secret. During this conversation, which the others entertained for far longer than I expected, there were some very strongly held sentiments about the NSA and metadata and Facebook, but it didn't seem like there was an awful lot of nuance or detail. It felt more like a kind of collective purging of anxiety. Their sources always seemed vague—something read on a blog, or in a tweet, or mentioned by a friend. I found Damian and Mia, in particular, connecting dots where there weren't any necessarily to connect, and drawing conclusions which required more than a few leaps of logic. The few times I pointed this out, I was accused of thinking 'what they want' me to think—though whoever 'they' were was never quite defined. So eventually I just submitted myself to the chaotic flow of conversation, like a kayaker plunging through cataracts without a paddle.

What I found most amusing, though, was that it gradually emerged that Damian and the women were approaching their paranoias from completely opposite ends of the political spectrum. For instance, Mia and Leslie both loathed Trump, whereas Damian refused to outright dismiss the QAnon conspiracy. I had heard about this QAnon stuff in the news but had only the vaguest understanding of what it was all about. As Damian explained it, the conspiracy (not that he called it that) alleged that numerous liberal Hollywood actors and high-ranking Democrats had been running an international child sex trafficking ring, and that Trump feigned collusion with the Russians in order to enlist special counsel Robert Mueller in an effort to expose the ring and thus prevent a coup led by Hillary Clinton, Barack Obama, and liberal philanthropist George Soros. That's the essence of it at least, as far as I understood it. I could barely keep a straight face as Damian explained all of the shadowy saga's numerous subplots, twists, and pseudonymous online players. He suggested that parts of it had 'maybe been blown out of proportion' but seemed to otherwise believe it was true.

There were a few other points of conspiratorial divergence amongst the three of them. Leslie, for instance, believed the measles vaccine led to autism, whereas Mia said the anti-vaxxer movement 'melted her face off,' especially given her line of work. All three of them, however, agreed that September 11 was an inside job, as did Nora. Damian arrived at this belief only after his two tours in Iraq. Perhaps unsurprisingly, given their backgrounds in science, Howard and Jo both seemed wholly unconvinced by these alt-narratives. Shawn, being Jewish, also had no time for conspiracy theories, as he found most of them anti-Semitic at their root, in some form or another. He had a gorgeous way of sort of staccato hissing with laughter to himself, not quite loud enough to interrupt, but just enough to register his complete disdain for what was being theorized. Emily, meanwhile, remained mostly silent; though I couldn't tell whether out of polite opposition, because she was being gradually persuaded, or because, frankly, she just couldn't follow the conversation.

When, in my adult life, in my own free time, of my own free will, had I sat in a room talking with someone like Damian or Emily? When had any of us, for that matter, spent time making friends on the other side of the ideological chasm of our country in the last four years? Though it shouldn't have come as any surprise, I was nevertheless struck, when looking at Emily, with her immaculate white-blond bob, and collared blouse under her country club cardigan, and her talk of garden parties and canasta clubs, that she and Damian—who seemed to me to be the personification of a comments-thread troll, with tinted aviators, tinted pickup-truck windows, a sum total of ten minutes a week spent on personal hygiene—shared an identical vision of who should be leading our country.

The old me would have cut anti-vaxxers and truthers out of my life like Kevin Spacey was cut from that Ridley Scott movie. I think it says a lot about the patience and compassion I was cultivating through the sessions that I could still feel a kinship with people with whom I so fundamentally disagreed. Howard and Jo had created a space where that was possible; where radically divergent ideas could be shared without anyone feeling assailed or invalid. That said, despite the tangents, Howard invariably steered the conversation back towards the sensible and productive, which was critical. I would never have stuck with the meetings otherwise.

I would bet that you could have assembled, at random, ten Americans in 2019, and found the same level of conspiratorial thinking as existed in our discussions on Sequoia Crescent. I sincerely believe that it wasn't anything unique to this particular group of individuals. It was simply the new register society was operating in. I told Kyle one night, after the meeting where the QAnon stuff first came up, that I remembered a time when conspiracy theories were niche and a little shameful, like kinky porn, not public camps of identification like religions or political parties, to respectfully 'agree to disagree' with. As we walked to my car, I said that it felt like the result of a society losing trust in itself and its institutions. Kyle didn't seem nearly as unsettled by it as I was. He pointed out that there *were* insidious cabals and secret societies of elite, privileged men in this country that exerted untold influence over government and global finance.

I don't blame the Damians of this world for feeling like they're being conned, he once said. Why should someone like him trust the government or Wall Street or Silicon Valley?

I had to admit that I couldn't disagree. Kyle said a part of him actually admired anti–status quo thinking.

Yeah, but there's no truth anymore, I said. Just opinions.

He pointed out that it had ever been thus. Even the idea of objective truth, as proved by science or law, was a recent invention.

All we've known for millennia has been hunches and impulses and opinion, he said. Who's to say that isn't our true nature?

I should make clear that this kind of conspiratorial thinking only ever reared its head a few times in our many meetings, and I'm probably letting future events colour my recollection of things by spending so much time writing about it here. I was deeply invested in the group, and had a genuine affection for each and

every member, even if there were elements that occasionally unsettled me. Sometimes, the elements that unsettled me unlocked the
most profound revelations. The most obvious example of this was
the first time that all of us tuned.

We were sitting in a circle in the middle of Howard and Jo's living room. Our eyes were closed. The older among us were sitting
on decorative cushions from the couches. The furniture had been
pushed back against the walls, and the coffee table had been moved
into another room to give us space. The ten of us sat quietly, but
not in silence, for there was no such thing as silence, as I had come
to learn. We were listening to the infinitely complex aural tapestry
unfolding around us, and we were giving ourselves over to it. As
we became aware of a sound we named it so as to isolate it, exam-
ine it, and incorporate it into our being.

The neighbours' wind chime, I said.

I could hear its soft, random tinkling through the bay window.
It reminded me of clinking glasses being carried by a waiter. My
grandmother's garden, filled with tiger lilies. The hot summer wind.

After a long moment, Leslie murmured—Wind through the
trees in the backyard.

And yes, I could hear it too. Its hushing, like the waves on a
beach.

There was another long pause, in which the air was thick with
concentration.

There's a bird, Mia said.

Two birds, I think, Nora said, a few seconds later.

A dog began to bark in a distant backyard, and Emily and
Kyle both noted it at the same time. After another minute or so,
Damian remarked on the car that could be heard driving slowly
past us, down the crescent.

It's braking at the stop sign now, he said. And it's turning—

Which direction? Jo asked.

Left, towards Sanderson.

We continued this for the better part of an hour, listening with exhausting intensity, until Jo said—And now I'm going to ask everyone to slowly bring their awareness inside the room. Paying attention only to the sounds they hear within these four walls.

I could feel a shift in our collective consciousness, as we began to tune ourselves to the intimate sounds immediately around us. It was as if someone was turning the manual zoom on the camera lenses of the room, and we were being pulled deeper into it.

The air conditioning, Leslie said, after some time.

Emily mentioned the clock, ticking on the mantel.

My breath, I said, and Nora echoed it back—My breath.

The cracking of my ribs, Leslie said.

We fell quiet again for a while, until Howard said—There's a . . . faint whistle in my nose, when I breathe in.

My socks on the carpet, Emily said.

Shawn remarked that he could hear Kyle rubbing his hands on his pants.

I can hear that too, Kyle said, prompting some laughter from the group. They're sweaty.

My heart, Mia said, after a moment.

Yes, Emily replied.

My heartbeat, several others murmured.

The crack of my back, Jo said.

The sound of my swallowing, I said. My saliva. My teeth in my head . . . clacking together when I close my mouth.

Emily's stomach, gurgling, Damian said.

Emily laughed—I was going to say!

Several more sounds were identified, but gradually we fell quiet. Once it seemed we had exhausted the possibilities of the room, Jo guided us to listen deeper.

Go further. Can you hear your blood? Circulating inside of
you? She paused. What about your nervous system? Can you hear
the high-pitched whine of your own nervous system?

I tried to listen for it. I felt the others in the circle doing the same.

What else? Jo asked. Listen deeper. The Hum is there. Louder
than ever. Inside the deepest part of you. I want you to focus the
entirety of your awareness on it.

I was straining with every fibre of my being.

Frame out every other sound until only The Hum exists, she
continued. Let it grow louder. Let it fill your body. Let it fill every
space between your cells. Between the molecules and the atoms
that make up your cells. Between the infinite, vibrating space
between the electrons and protons. This is the only sound. The
original sound. The sound that predates life on Earth. The sound
that made us. The sound that will unmake us and remake us
an infinite number of times. As The Hum fills all of the empty
space inside you, you become more Hum than human. You become
nothing but sound. Vibrating as one frequency, across the entire surface of the Earth. Infinite, expansive, resonant. Until any trace of
you is obliterated and you become boundless, until there is no dis-
tinction between our bodies. Release yourself into this boundless-
ness. Release yourself. Release yourself from the confines of your
bodies and let the sound erase you, erase you, erase you, erase you,
release you, release you—

Jo incanted like this for some time, and I began to hear people
breathing deeply around me. After a while, I could hear my own
breath deepening. A feeling began to overtake me that I can best
describe as a kind of ecstatic wholeness. It seemed to emerge from
somewhere deep within my pelvis and expanded infinitely outward
into a glowing warmth.

Oh my god, Leslie gasped.

What? Emily asked.

Oh god.

I can feel it, Mia said.

Damian said he could too. Jo encouraged us to keep focused.

Holy shit, Kyle muttered.

It's happening, Mia said.

Yes, I said.

Welcome it in, Jo said.

We're tuning.

I don't feel it, Emily said.

Me neither, said Nora.

Once again, Jo instructed us to focus.

And then—my god—I felt it intensify even further, that ecstatic warm expansion.

It's surging, Howard said.

Oh momma, Shawn groaned.

Yes, Damian said.

The power of all of us here combined is extraordinary, Howard said.

The Hum was getting louder but not just growing in volume but growing in every possible manner. It seemed to be penetrating every part of the room, my body, filling every available space, between every molecule, every atom. And just when it seemed to have saturated everything, it intensified further, and the space between spaces, between bodies, seemed to collapse.

Ugh my god.

The heat.

Yes.

Oh wow.

Holy shit—I can feel it now.

Good.

I think me too.

Do you feel it?

Yes.

Expanding inside you?

Yes, I think so.

I'm getting hot.

Uh-huh.

Me too.

Yeah.

Like a lot.

Ughhhhhhh, someone moaned.

Yes.

Like—

—burning, like—

Ugggghhhhhhhhhh my god.

Let it fill your stomachs now. Let it fill your lungs. Let it fill your throats and out through your mouths ahhhhhhhhhhhhhh—

And then a low, guttural hum emerged from within us, from within the circle. I wasn't even conscious of producing the sound, but it produced itself from within me, moved through me, and through various registers, shifting like a murmuration of starlings, like resplendent light, who knew the body—bodies together— could make such a sound. Sounds erupted from us, unleashed and orgasmic sounds, unrecognizable and inhuman sounds until I was moving, we were moving, standing now, moving through space, space moving through us, thrashing our bodies, swaying in ecstatic transport, The Hum expanding infinitely within us until it was a scorching white heat—until there was a *smash*, and we were ripped from our deep-state back into the room. Everyone fell silent and blinked open. Looking around, I realized that Leslie had knocked a lamp over. It lay in several pieces on the floor.

I am . . . so . . . sorry, she said, not quite fully returned.

Howard waved it away—It's fine.

Everyone collapsed back into chairs, and onto the floor, exhausted, collecting themselves. I felt momentarily gripped by the most intense embarrassment. I couldn't look anyone in the eye.

Okay, everyone, Jo said, let's just take a deep breath.

Large exhales from around the room. I glanced over and Leslie seemed to be hyperventilating. Emily put her arm on her shoulder—Les?

Jo came over and sat down beside them—Deep breaths, love, deep breaths.

Leslie nodded. Gradually, she began to calm.

Wow, Mia said, as if not yet fully emerged from a dream. Her face had a sheen of sweat, and there were strands of hair in her mouth, which she gently pulled away.

That was—Shawn looked for the word.

Insane, Kyle said, in wonder.

It wasn't insane, it was beautiful, Emily said.

I know, that's what I mean.

It's not insane.

Felt absolutely amazing, Leslie said, still catching her breath.

Mia motioned over her stomach—That heat.

It got super intense, Kyle said. I thought my chest was going to explode.

I felt like I was going to orgasm, Leslie said, deadpan. The group burst into laughter. I'm serious, she insisted.

No, honestly, Shawn said. For real.

Me too, Damian said, laughing. It was the first time I had seen Damian laugh. It made him look softer and younger.

Well I sure must have been doing something wrong, Nora said, crestfallen. Jo asked her what she felt and Nora shrugged.

Did you feel anything?

I wish. From the sounds of it.

But you heard The Hum?

Yes of course, I hear it always.

Did you feel it expand inside of you? Jo asked. Nora shook her head. Did it get louder?

A little, maybe. Maybe I focused on it more clearly.

It got so loud for me I almost couldn't take it, Mia said.

Howard gave Nora a sympathetic smile—Give it time. There's no rush.

Leslie gestured to the mess on the floor—I really am sorry about the lamp.

Honestly, don't worry, Jo said, it was a gift from his old boss.

I still feel like I'm burning up, Kyle said. Like—here. He reached over, took my hand, and placed it on his forehead. His skin was hot to the touch.

I'm still hot too, Mia said, and Damian said he was as well.

I'm hot . . . and I'm wet, Leslie said, matter-of-factly, prompting more laughter.

Good god, Emily said, looking playfully mortified.

Just saying!

Amen, Shawn replied, with solemnity.

Was that the tuning? I asked, looking to Jo, and then to Howard.

It was, just for a moment, he replied.

But what exactly happened?

You just felt it.

I told him I didn't know what I felt.

How did you do that? Mia asked Jo.

I didn't do a thing. That was all The Hum. You just opened yourself up to it. It can give you migraines and nosebleeds or it can, well—

Make you cum, Shawn said.

Yes.

Kyle looked both bemused and slightly repulsed—Seriously?

If you let it.

Have you? he asked Jo.

I shot him a look.

I have, actually, she replied, nonchalant. Shawn burst into a braying laugh.

Just from the sound? Emily asked, astounded.

It's more than sound, Howard said.

Shawn was absolutely delighting in all of this—You've honestly had an orgasm, just from The Hum? And you're only telling us this now?

Despite all the levity, Jo remained stony-faced. To be honest, Howard and I really struggled with whether to share this—deeper aspect of The Hum with you at all.

It's very powerful, Howard said. And very easily misunderstood.

Right, well don't hold back on us, Shawn replied, splaying his hands. We can take it.

Well that's our hope, Jo said, still not conceding to the general giddiness of the room. Hopefully we've established enough trust.

Everyone quietly exchanged glances. The group appeared a great deal more certain and enthusiastic about what had just happened than I felt, even Nora and Emily and the ever-serious Damian, which surprised me, being the more conservative three among us.

I hope I don't freak you out when I say this, Jo began, but a few times, not often, but a few times when I've been able to tune, and stay in tune . . . I've had a ten-minute orgasm.

Shawn's jaw dropped. Get the fuck out.

Hands-free.

Leslie seemed to almost choke on a laugh.

Emily shook her head in awe like a daytime talk-show audience member. I found myself wondering when Emily, buttoned-up and pushing seventy, might have last experienced an orgasm of any sort. I got the feeling there wasn't much happening in that department

between her and Tom anymore, and somehow, I struggled to picture her working magic with a suction dildo in the shower.

There was one afternoon I came eight times, Jo said. And I
honestly could've kept going too.

You must've gotten nothing else done, Mia said, with a mixture
of knowing and reverence.

It was a Saturday.

Clear the calendar! Shawn was laughing, full teeth and gums.

I think when you figure out how to have eight hands-free
orgasms you just make the time, Mia said, sliding back in her armchair and putting her leg up over the side.

And how about you, Leslie asked Howard. Have you been able to?

I have, yes.

Hands-free?

Howard nodded, as if being asked if he flossed.

I knew we had been working towards this for some time now,
towards this 'ecstatic interconnectedness' that Howard and Jo had
been referring to, but somehow this aspect of pleasure, of tantric-
like transcendence unsettled me, or at least took me by surprise. I
asked them how any of this was even possible.

The Hum makes it possible, Howard replied. It suffuses everything. And it can affect us on a fundamental level.

Yes, but I just don't understand how—

Stop trying to understand, he said, moving his hand slowly
through the air as if wiping a fogged mirror. It's about experiencing. Did you feel it or not?

Yes. Very much.

So just let yourself feel it.

For me it almost got too intense, Damian said.

Mia nodded—Same.

Damian said he didn't think he could keep going—The sound
kept expanding, I thought my rib cage was going to burst.

Goodness, Emily said.

Or my skull.

It almost hurt, Mia said, but it was also, I mean—

Incredibly pleasurable, Kyle said.

There was something about Kyle experiencing 'incredible pleasure' in my company that, frankly, freaked me out. Perhaps because
it risked rupturing some threshold between us. The threshold that
still maintained the acceptability of our continued association.

It's very strange but I could taste iron in my mouth, Shawn said.

Nora looked confused—Iron?

Yes. At one point I thought I'd maybe bit my tongue and was
bleeding but I wasn't.

It affects everybody differently, Howard said. It's working on a
cellular level. For me, near the end, I had the feeling of being on
the verge of something. And I don't mean an orgasm or anything,
but on the verge of—of manifesting something.

I think I know what you mean, Mia said, and I noticed both
Kyle and Damian nodding.

It's hard to explain, Howard continued. But all of us together—
I felt myself pushed closer towards this . . . thing . . . whatever it
is . . . that will come. And I don't mean—

Everyone laughed, except me. It has nothing to do with that,
Howard added, with a smile.

Jo turned to me, and frowned—Claire, what's wrong, love?

Everyone looked in my direction. I opened my mouth and
closed it again, trying to find the words. I just feel a little . . . shook,
I finally said.

That is totally understandable, she replied, which caused something in me to seize.

No, it's not, I don't understand, and Howard telling me not to
overthink it doesn't help me, that just frustrates me more. I digest
things through logic, okay? I'm a logical person. I believe in science.

But this is science, Jo said.

It's also more than science, Howard said.

I held up my hands—I'm not interested in more.

Because more scares you, he said.

Because I don't need more.

But what if it's there anyway? Whether you need it or not?

He paused and studied my face—Science is the frame, Claire, it's not the whole picture and it's because of that attitude, because of the worshipping of science to the exclusion of every other kind of human experience, that nobody else knows about what we've just experienced. There's a reason this isn't global news, and it's because I don't have a job or a platform or any credibility anymore, and that's because I didn't play by the rules of science. But if you must know right now, in this exact second, instead of just letting us process this with our bodies, the science, the all-important science behind this has to do with the caudate nucleus in our brain stems, okay, which controls various states of arousal. At 7.83 hertz frequency the caudate nucleus becomes hyper-stimulated. In brain scans, it just *boom*, ignites like a fireball.

It's the most incredible thing to watch, actually, Jo said.

Most of us can only hit this frequency for a few moments during the peak of orgasm, Howard continued, without breaking eye contact with me. But what if we could train our brains to operate at this frequency every moment of the day?

Leslie said that sounded absolutely exhausting.

Oh no, quite the opposite, he replied.

Cumming twenty-four seven? I'd be wrung out. To which Shawn let out a single, percussive laugh.

Jo smiled, patiently—You won't be cumming. You'll be on another plateau of consciousness. A consciousness that continually activates the ninety percent of your brain that's usually dormant.

It would still be stimulation overload, though, wouldn't it? Leslie asked.

You think that but only because you're used to sleepwalking, Howard said. We spend our lives mostly brain-dead when we could be awake.

Wouldn't you prefer to be awake? Jo asked.

Of course, Leslie said, but ...

But what?

It's intimidating.

Shawn nodded—Terrifying.

Doesn't that sound liberating? Jo asked. To be alive like that?

But to have something re-pattern the way you think, I don't know, Shawn said. It just feels very major.

What about talking for the first time? Jo asked. Or walking, or swimming, or riding a bike. Or sex. But thank god you pushed yourself to do them.

I can't swim actually, Shawn said, but yes, I take your point.

Have you reached this state? Leslie asked Jo. This—other plateau?

Maybe for a few moments, Jo replied, looking at Howard. But we've never been able to sustain it for very long.

But is it all in the brain? I asked. I mean my body . . . I felt the heat and pressure and the sound.

Howard gestured to me—You see?

What is that?

Science can't explain it.

But I felt it.

So is it real?

Yes of course it is.

Because science would tell you it isn't. Science has no explanation for any of The Hum's physical manifestations. The heat, the pressure, the tingling, the pleasure, the pain, the nosebleeds, the headaches. But you have felt it.

Yes.

Did you? he asked Kyle. Kyle nodded. He asked the rest of the circle, and they all replied yes. Except Nora. She was poured into her chair, looking disconsolate.

I want to, she said.

You will, Jo said, placing her hand on Nora's thigh.

I really do.

Just give it time.

It's nuts the whole world doesn't know about this, Damian said, sitting forward on his chair.

In time, hopefully they will, Howard replied.

It's because it's been kept from us, Howard. There's no way this is the first time anyone's ever felt this. This is a phenomenon of the Earth, right? Others must have felt this at some point.

Howard made to answer but Damian continued—Like how come everyone isn't doing this all the fucking time?

No one has shown them, Mia said, pulling out her scrunchie and raking her hair with her fingers.

It doesn't make sense unless it's been kept from us. Systematically.

Damian, around the time I met Howard, I was really struggling, Jo said, using her calming voice on him. A whole number of reasons. Anxiety. Depression. I was on this regime of meditation and trance as a way of centring myself. And then when Howard became my supervisor, and the work we began doing with the Resonance, it all kind of clicked into place. Discovering we could tune to it—

It changed everything, Howard said, looking at everyone except Jo.

But then a researcher tells the university we're running a sex lab and that Howard's using mind control on them and the whole thing gets shut down.

Emily looked horrified—What?

It terrified people. If there are two things that terrify WASPy bourgeois academics it's sex and spirituality, Jo said.

So they just turfed you out? Shawn asked.

Howard sighed. It was clearly still painful for him to talk about.

We found ourselves outcasts, he said. And anytime we did try to talk to someone about it we were shunned. People had all these wild stories about us.

Oh god, Leslie said, and on campuses these things take on a life of their own, right?

Jo nodded—Which is why Howard and I have been so trigger-shy to go to that place with you all. We're both still scarred from what happened at Virginia Tech.

It just became our own little private revelation, Howard said. But of course you want to share a revelation, right? The more people know and can access it, the more its beauty and power is magnified. I'm not saying we're Copernicus here or anything, but can you imagine if he discovered the Earth revolved around the Sun and then couldn't tell anyone about it? It would be absolutely maddening. We've been sitting on this thing that we know can change people's lives.

Nora, what's wrong? Emily asked. I turned to see that Nora had teared up. In fact she seemed to be rocking herself ever so slightly in her chair.

Nothing, it's fine.

Come here, Jo said, extending her arms.

I'm just so frustrated with myself. I don't know what's wrong with me.

Nothing is wrong with you.

I want to feel it so much.

And then Nora broke down, her face contorting—I'm a good person. I work hard. I deserve to feel it.

I know, Jo said, stroking Nora's hair.

I hear it so strongly.

I know.

What am I doing wrong?

It will come in time, Howard said.

The way Howard said those words made me think of my father teaching me how to ride a bike when I was five, and then my teaching Ashley to do the same. The iridescent tassels on her handlebars. Her pink training wheels.

When? Nora asked Howard.

When your body is ready.

Is it because I'm stupid or something?

No, of course not, Jo said, soothingly.

Then what?

Here. Jo stood up and moved to the centre of the room. I want you to kneel in the middle of the floor, right here. She knelt down on the floor to demonstrate.

Kneel?

Yes, right there.

Nora stood and joined Jo down on the floor, with some audible bone cracks as she knelt. And now, Jo continued, I want everyone to kneel around Nora.

One by one we got to our knees and formed a circle around Nora.

Full circle, that's it, Jo said, like a kindergarten teacher, before finding her own place within it. We're going to tune ourselves, once again, to the Resonance and we're going to channel its full intensity at Nora.

Oh wow, Nora murmured.

And how exactly are we going to do that? Shawn asked.

Trust me, you'll know, Jo replied. Just allow it to work through you. And love—she leaned in towards Nora—you will feel it this time, I can assure you. I can't promise you something earth-shattering—

Eight orgasms?

No.

I'll settle for six, she joked. We laughed encouragingly, as a little smile danced across her face.

But you will feel something, Jo reassured. I want you to focus your full intensity on the sound of The Hum. I want you to feel it swell inside you and, as it does, I want you to picture the sound like a warm glow filling your body with light, okay?

Nora nodded.

Don't be nervous, Jo said. There's nothing to be nervous about.

Okay.

We're all here supporting and lifting you.

Thank you.

Okay. I want everyone to find their breath.

I watched as everyone closed their eyes. I wasn't sure if I was ready to do it again, and so soon. I had barely reckoned with what had happened the first time. But I closed my eyes, and tried to slow my heartbeat. After a long moment, I could hear Damian to my left and Mia to my right beginning to breathe deeply. One by one, I heard others do so as well, even Nora, though it was hard to distinguish one breath from another. We gradually forged a single breath. Breaths turned to gasps, which turned to groans, which gradually transformed into a kind of aural emission, a sustained, almost ritualistic humming, unconscious and libidinal, which grew in intensity, grew in heat, grew ever more expansive until we were swaying, frenzied, until my body was not my body, my breath, my voice, until nothing belonged to me, and I was just a portal of sound, until everything came undone, ruptured, and culminated in a thunderous climax, channelled through the vessel of Nora's convulsing body.

13

LATER THAT NIGHT, AFTER OUR FIRST TUNING, CARS CHIRPED, and headlights flashed as we all dispersed from Howard and Jo's. I glanced around for Kyle and noticed him walking off by himself down the street. I called his name and he stopped. I jogged over to him and asked if he was okay. He shrugged and took out his vape.

You left pretty suddenly, I said.

He took a puff, turned his head, and blew vanilla-scented smoke away from me—It's just a lot to process.

We stood there, in the middle of the street, watching the others find their way to their cars. I asked him if he was still mad at me.

Why would I be mad at you?

I told him that it felt as if he had pulled away from me over the last few weeks. Sometimes we'd go a couple of days without messaging. I asked him if he was hurt that I hadn't done more to help after his mom kicked him out.

He shook his head. No, it's cool.

How has it been staying with Mark?

He shrugged.

Are you on the couch?

I don't really want to talk about it.

I nodded. Okay. And then, after a silence, I said—I'm sorry. I feel like I failed you.

He breathed a little laugh out through his nose and shook his head—You've risked everything for me.

I'm not sure it's made things any better for you.

Leslie's car began to approach us, and we walked to the curb to clear the street. She gave us a little wave as she passed. We watched her red tail lights recede into the dark.

I miss our talks, Kyle said.

Me too.

He turned to look at me. His hair was plastered to his forehead. We had worked up quite the sweat during the tuning.

What did you think about all of this? he asked, nodding towards the house.

The tuning?

All of this, everything.

It occurred to me that it had been a very long time since Kyle and I had had a moment to ourselves to speak candidly about the group.

I think it's pretty extraordinary, I said. Don't you?

He nodded. I told him that it had kind of rearranged my whole frame of reference.

Does that scare you? he asked.

A little.

It scares me too.

Why do you think that is?

He considered this, as we watched Damian drive past in his pickup.

I think it's scary to know how far we can be stretched. To feel pleasure like that. Because it means that maybe . . . the things that we thought contained us, don't actually contain us. And that means everything is chaos.

But isn't that also exciting?

He smiled, but left the question unanswered. Why does it scare you? he asked.

I feel um . . . I cocked my head to the side, searching for the words. Sort of . . . reshaped, by this. You know?

The whites of Kyle's eyes glistened in the darkness.

And I guess in that reshaping I worry that some part of myself will be lost, I said.

What do you have to lose? he asked, which made me laugh.

You mean that I haven't already?

You don't believe in God.

This isn't about God, I said.

Isn't it?

I shook my head. No.

It's certainly about something larger than ourselves.

Maybe.

Is that why you're holding back? he asked.

I'm not holding back, I said, a little defensive.

Yes you are. I watch you in there. There's a part of you that doesn't want to let go. Doesn't want to give in.

He balanced on one foot on the curb for a moment. I like that part of you, he said. But that's also your fear. You're afraid of what might happen if you give yourself over completely. But I know you want to.

He stepped down off the curb. And so do I, he said.

The street was empty now. The others must have driven away without us noticing. I told him, for the record, that losing one's disbelief in God was still losing something.

And are you? he asked.

No. I don't know.

I thought about it for a moment. I told him that it felt a bit like I had been living in this small room my whole life, and then Howard and Jo opened this door to another room, and we had taken just the smallest step into it. And the new room was dark and massive. I couldn't even see its walls. Maybe there were no walls; maybe it was boundless. But I knew that all I wanted was to be in that new room.

Kyle looked at me. I want to be in that room with you, he said.

He then took a step towards me, coming inches from my face. I could smell vanilla smoke on his breath. He closed his eyes, and leaned in—and I stepped back.

Sorry, he said, opening his eyes, suddenly self-conscious. I shouldn't have done that.

Why did you?

He looked over his shoulder, and then turned back, brow furrowed—Because um. Well. I love you, basically.

My mouth opened of its own accord, but I said nothing.

I-I don't mean that I'm *in love* with you, obviously, he said, suddenly an awkward teenager again. Or maybe not obviously, I don't know. But I love you. And not like a teacher, or a friend, or a mother, or anything romantic, it's not like any of that. But it's something sort of between all of those things. Something there isn't a name for. I don't even care if you love me back but I just needed to tell you—

I do, I said, without thinking; without ever having admitted it to myself before then. I loved this possibly gay seventeen-year-old former student of mine in the same unnameable way he had just described, which, by acknowledging, meant that I was so much further gone than even I had thought myself to be.

He made a little laugh of relief, and looked down. He kicked a stone into the darkness—So where does that leave us?

I don't know, I said.

Standing on this street, I guess.

I guess.

I don't want to go yet, he said. I know we can't just stand here but, um. I kind of just want to keep talking.

I nodded, because I wasn't ready to drive home to an empty house. He suggested going to the nearby park, and I told him that I didn't think it was appropriate for us to be hanging around a dark park together after midnight.

And when's the last time we've done what's appropriate? he asked.

I smiled but stood my ground.

What are you afraid of? You are filled with the sound of the fucking Earth, Claire, you can do anything, you can be and say and do whatever you want because you have felt it, you have touched it, and you know how good it can be.

He then told me that he wanted to tune with me.

We don't know how, I said.

Of course we do, we just did.

But not alone.

If we want to enough we will, we'll figure it out.

He looked at me and he could see that I did. I wanted to feel it with him again; that ecstatic connectedness.

Please, he urged. Who's going to stop us? Who will even know?

We're probably being watched in the street right now, I said. This conversation. The fact that I'm not already at my car driving away.

So we better make a decision.

I shook my head, and looked down. He asked me what I was thinking. I told him that I thought we were in a very vulnerable and unstable moment in our lives, and that I didn't want to regret this.

Step into the new room, Claire, he said, starting to walk off while holding my gaze. There are no walls anymore.

The park bordered the back fields of the high school. Besides a small playground, and some bike paths, large swaths of it remained wild, making it a favourite spot for dog walkers and birdwatchers. We walked through the darkness, with only our phones to light our way. The sky was empty that night; no moon, and no stars. Just temporary constellations appearing and disappearing around us in the blinking of fireflies. Just the smell of mud, and wet sage, the sound of cricket song, and our feet rustling through the under-brush, snapping twigs and branches. Kyle said he could traverse the park with his eyes closed, and I joked that we pretty much were. He seemed to be leading us somewhere in particular, and I let him take me. I suddenly felt utterly unburdened by obligation. I had nowhere to be but here. No family to return home to. No job to wake up early for in the morning. I could stay out all night in this park with Kyle, and no one would know, and no one would care.

We arrived at a thicket of bushes and he parted some branches to reveal a narrow path. He walked through first, and held the branches back so that they didn't smack me in the face.

Careful where you step, he said. The ground was uneven, and raised roots snagged my feet, causing me to trip towards him. I put my hand on his shoulder and kept it there, so I could focus on looking down at the ground. We walked for what felt like three or four minutes, deep into the overgrowth.

God, what is that incredible smell? I asked.

Juniper.

He broke off a twig and handed it to me. I brought it to my nose.

Smells like a clear blue sky, I said. Or the colour indigo.

Or gin.

Oh yes, of course. You know, I bet I'm thinking of the Bombay Sapphire bottle, I said, laughing.

We're almost there. He then asked me if I was okay, and I said sure, why? There's nothing to be nervous about, he said.

I'm not.

Your hand is trembling.

And then I realized that he was right. He offered to turn back, but I said no. A moment later, we arrived in a small clearing, in the middle of which sat an orange family-sized camping tent.

Voila, Kyle said, gesturing like a doorman welcoming me into the foyer of a grand hotel.

Aha.

One sec.

He dashed into the tent and turned on several portable lanterns until the tent was glowing, warm and luminous. I saw his silhouette moving about inside, like a shadow puppet. I crossed the clearing, and poked my head into the tent.

Oh my god, I murmured, astonished.

Inside, the tent was fully furnished—an air mattress, quilts and pillows, makeshift shelving made out of bricks and boards, stacks of books, two lamps complete with fabric shades, pots and pans, bowls and cups, a portable stove, a metal basin, plastic jugs of water, an old traveller's trunk, an amateurish painting of a horse in a gilded frame, and a tattered Persian carpet on the floor.

Cozy, isn't it, he said.

How did you do this? I asked, marvelling, stepping inside, hunched over.

Luke and me built it in grade eleven, he replied. We'd come and smoke during our spares. But I just kept adding to it.

Look at all these books, I said, marvelling at his collection. At the top of one stack was his weathered and beaten copy of *The Magic Mountain*.

Did you ever finish it? I asked, picking it up.

The essay?

No, I know you never finished the essay.

I did so, he said, indignant but smiling. I suppose it would've been nearly impossible for him to pass the class had he not. He and I had never talked about my replacement at school, or really anything to do with school. We had a sort of unspoken agreement to avoid the subject altogether. Perhaps I let myself imagine he had never finished the essay as it was just easier for me to believe that. The thought of another teacher reading it caused a kind of jealousy-limned sadness to come over me, which I knew was ridiculous. Perhaps sensing this, he told me that it wasn't very good.

I'm sure it was.

No it really wasn't, trust me. I just phoned it in.

I told him that I was still working my way through the book. He looked surprised, and said he didn't realize I was reading it.

Didn't I tell you? I sat down on the air mattress, my back already starting to ache from bending over. I've been listening to the audiobook, I said.

Really? he said, crouching down beside me.

Well. I've slowed down a bit lately.

I told him that I had listened up to the passage where Hans Castorp gets caught in the blizzard and slips into a kind of death-bound reverie. His disoriented visions grow progressively darker until they culminate in the ritualistic slaughter of a child by two ancient, cultic priestesses. That's where I stopped, I said.

Oh but that part's so good.

Yeah, well—there isn't always an overlap between good literature and what I wish to put into my head before bed.

Kyle said that sequence made him think about how nature is neither kind nor cruel, but simply a force which is. It sustains life and destroys it, and is beyond our capacity to comprehend or control. And yet we always try. Again and again.

I smiled at his philosophizing, and told him that maybe I should try listening to the book when I wasn't half asleep.

Speaking of listening—He walked over to the trunk and pulled out an old battery-powered CD player. He sat it on the makeshift shelf, put in a disc, and pressed play. A jazz song kicked off with a plucky piano and a punchy trumpet line.

Well you've really thought of everything, I said.

Just the essentials.

Who is this? I asked.

Charles Mingus. Do you know him? I told him yes, I did, my grandmother was a jazz fanatic. This is his album *East Coasting*, he said. From 1953.

Kyle extended his hand to me in an invitation to dance but I declined, with a laugh—there was no room!—so he did a dorky and endearing little jig. I caught glimpses of the old man and the young boy who both inhabited him. He appeared to know the track by heart, anticipating its ebbs and flows. I couldn't imagine he had ever dared show this side of himself to any of his friends; at least not the ones I knew. Though sometimes I wondered how many friends he really had, or good ones, at least. He seemed both well-liked and utterly aloof. Had anyone even been calling around, wondering where he was? Was anyone worried about him? He dropped down beside me on the mattress.

Please tell me you're not living here, I said.

He looked around, like a proud homeowner—I think it's rather nice.

This is not—My chest felt leaden. For how long?

It's been a while now.

I shook my head. It's not right. You can't—

What? What can't I do? he asked, with quiet defiance.

I was suddenly outside of myself, looking at us sitting in that tent, in the thicket behind the back field of the school where I was once a teacher, and he was once my student, back in a time when both of us had families, and I was suddenly struck by just how much The Hum had stripped from us.

I landed a summer job at the Best Buy, he said, flatly. I'm making money. I have what I need.

Yeah, except running water.

I can shower at the gym.

I told him that was madness, considering I lived in a practically empty four-bedroom house just six blocks away. He could have an entire bathroom to himself. He looked down and picked at a bit of fluff on one of the ratty wool blankets we were sitting on—I can't just move in with you.

I'm not asking you to.

So then what happens tomorrow night? And the night after that? You going to kick me out? he asked, and I shook my head. Exactly, so then I'll just be living with you.

Would that be so bad? I asked. He gave me a wary look. What?

It's not appropriate, he said, and I smiled to hear my own word echoed back to me.

And letting you sleep in a park, is that appropriate? I asked. He shrugged. It's also not safe, I said, and he laughed dismissively.

Wolves?

Drug deals, I said, for instance. He batted away the suggestion. Kyle, I'm worried about you.

Then go, he said, suddenly cross, and gesturing to the half-opened tent flap. I don't need you to be my fucking mother.

Okay.

You're going?

I won't be your fucking mother.

We sat there in strained silence, letting the piano and trumpets do the talking.

I like it here, he said, eventually. I actually prefer it. And listen.

He leaned over and turned off the music, and we sat there listening. The Hum penetrated the night. The air seemed to vibrate with it. It's strong out here, isn't it? he said.

I can almost feel it in the ground, I replied.

Though even more noticeable to me in that moment, more than The Hum or the crickets, was the sound of our breathing. Kyle glanced at me and then slowly stood up. Stooped over, his head pushed into the top of the tent. He kicked off his shoes, and then casually pulled his t-shirt over his head to take it off.

I'm still soaked from the tuning, he said. He rooted around the tent for something to change into. His chest was smooth and ivory white. I could see the indents of each of his ribs. I heard Ashley's words *scrawny stoner* in my head. His abs were clearly definable, but more from virtue of his sheer skinniness. With his back turned to me, he unbuttoned his jeans, pulled them down, and sort of awkwardly stomped out of them, until he was wearing just his baggy navy boxer shorts. I looked down and picked up the record sleeve to read.

My posture isn't very good, he said. I looked back up, as he pulled on a pair of grey sweatpants, still shirtless. He tried to straighten his back a little, pushing his head further up through the tent. I'm working on it, he said. I'm worried I have scoliosis.

I smiled and reassured him that I highly doubted it. He then lifted his left arm, sniffed, and apologized—One downside is the shower situation. It's hard to keep up my usual . . . freshness.

You're usually fresh? I asked, eyebrow cocked.

Wouldn't you say?

That's not the word that comes to mind.

He laughed. Oh yeah, what is?

Mmm . . . musky.

What, like a-a dusty old attic?

No, not musty. I chuckled. Musky.

Oh, I was going to say . . .

Like the smell of the earth.

Or maybe more like the air after thunder. Or a birch, peeled of its bark. A thing can only ever be described in relation to something else. One body described by another. He stood there in front of me shirtless, neither performative nor self-conscious, as if daring me to study him. I suddenly felt as if I was in a different Mann novel altogether, on a beach, considering a beguiling Polish youth. Without another word, Kyle knelt down on the carpet facing me. And I moved off the air mattress and down onto my knees on the blanketed ground, facing him. And without ever touching one another, we closed our eyes, and gradually relinquished ourselves to the frequency of the Earth; to the most intense and bracing pleasure I have ever known.

Afterwards, I lay awake trying to gather myself until morning light began to seep through the tent's translucent walls. Another night with barely any sleep. But I was not tired. I had never felt more awake. Strangely, I felt little guilt or approbation over what we had done. It was not sex. It was an intimacy unlike any I had experienced. To say sex and tuning were akin because they both invoked intimacy and pleasure was to say rain was akin to an ocean, or breath was akin to wind. Lying there now in my sports bra and pants, without shoes and without a shirt, basking in a night's worth of accumulated body heat—the scene had all of the trappings of violation, transgression, obscenity. And yet I felt none of those things. I lay there in a wholly different kind of afterglow, thinking about limits. The limits we imposed upon ourselves, and the limits nature imposed. What were the limits of nature? I was aware of Kyle's chest slowly rising and falling beside me. We were cocooned in separate, mouldering sleeping bags that smelt of bygone camping trips. Mine had some sand in it; probably from some childhood excursion to a canyon, or a beach.

Kyle took a deep breath and stirred; stretching as far as his sleeping bag would allow before opening his eyes. What time is it? he asked, with the groggy languor of a bear cub.

I checked my phone. Just after six, I said. I sat up and suddenly felt very light-headed. I rubbed my face, reached for one of the plastic jugs of lukewarm water, and took a sip. I looked down at Kyle; he was lying there, eyes half closed, on the verge of falling back asleep. He smiled up at me and I smiled back, and sank down into my sleeping bag. We lay there for a long while, watching the shadows of bugs fly over the tent. I could hear a bee buzzing and gently thwapping the sides of the tent with its bulbous body. Performing its sacred, life-sustaining duties. Using the Resonance for its intricate, internal navigation system. Kyle told me that you could cure hay fever by ingesting honey made by bees from the local pollen affecting you.

Really? That astounded me, and yet, the natural world was full of miracles. Miracles we once knew, and had forgotten or mislaid.

He then turned his head to look at me, across a mountain ridge of quilts and pillows—Last night was surreal.

It was, I replied. And very—

Intense.

Very.

He reached over and wiped sleep away from my eyes. He then asked if we had done something wrong. I considered how to give words to what I had spent the last few hours turning over in my head. I told him no. We didn't hurt anyone. We didn't break any law.

But tuning, without the others . . . are we keeping something from them?

As I lay there, considering his question, it struck me that the world was filled with an almost unbearably beautiful and limitless grace, and it was only we who were limited, in our capacity to perceive it. And just as no one possessed that grace, no one possessed our capacity to perceive it.

It's ours to do with what we want, I said. He nodded and seemed satisfied with this answer. I eventually rallied myself out of my sleeping bag. He sat propped up on his elbows, watching me pull my shirt and shoes back on. I tried to convince him to come back to my house for a shower, and a proper breakfast. He refused, as I knew he would. I took a step towards the tent flap and unzipped it. Well, I said, you know where to find me if you need me.

14

THE YOUNG POET DEPARTS ON A QUEST AND FINDS HIMSELF
in the Otherworld. There, he is seduced by a fairy, or a goddess,
and experiences the ecstatic transports of the enchanted realm.
Tannhäuser finds Venus in her mountain paradise. Oisín is
whisked off to Tír na nÓg by Niamh on her white horse. But
eventually the poet grows homesick, and longs to return to his
former life. When he does, he realizes that years have passed.
The world he once knew is unrecognizable. Hans Castorp finds
himself in the Otherworld of the mountain sanatorium, and like
sand through his fingers, seven years of his life slip away. When
he finally emerges from his reverie, Europe is on the brink of
catastrophe.

I've been thinking about how variations of this story exist
through history, through cultures, because the force it speaks
of must exist. A force in the wild that operates out of time, that
seeks to lure us, fevered, into a state beyond reason; beyond the

commitments that otherwise bind us to our lives and the people we love. What is this force, and why does it seek to enjoin our souls with itself? Is it just a blunt phenomenon like gravity, acting with no purpose or intent? One star devouring another in the vacuum of space? Or is this wildness somehow conscious? Seducing us to abandon as revenge, as corrective, for the order we have imposed upon it.

The question I have is—Does the poet always know when he has left the mortal world, and entered the enchanted realm? And what if he doesn't remember the way back?

In the afterglow of the tunings, a profound and untrammelled joy came over me. The house felt empty and cavernous without Ashley and yet somehow, after the tunings, I was no longer concerned with my solitude. I loved Ashley, more than anything on Earth, and I loved Paul, but I also loved my life, for the first time in ages. I felt wonder again at being in the world and in my body, and at the limitless pleasures that existed beyond it, in transcending my body and reaching into yet unknown folds of existence and sensation. I was still only managing a couple of hours of sleep a night, and the headaches persisted, but at least now I felt there was a greater purpose at hand. A greater mystery to which to commit myself.

After breakfast I drove to the supermarket, and it felt good to be seen, and good to see others. The thing I realized was—no one cared! No one cared about who I was or what I was doing. They were completely consumed by their own solipsism. I felt genuine wonder at the bounty of the Earth as I moved amongst the produce, lightly squeezing grapefruits to gauge their firmness, and taking a full minute to assess the optimal ripeness of a banana bunch.

Each and every piece of fruit, each and every piece of animal in the cellophane-wrapped Styrofoam trays of the refrigerated meat aisle, every single stalk of wheat, millet, and rye rendered into the

loafs stacked in their paper sleeves lived and died under the Resonance. While in line at the checkout, I smiled to see a grown man
in front of me pluck a small pink pack of Hubba Bubba Bubble
Tape from the rack of chocolate bars and candy on display beside
the magazines. And then I realized the man was Damian! I said
his name and he turned. It was almost surreal to see him outside of
Howard and Jo's living room, and judging from the surprised look
on his face, he felt the same. There was something electric about
the two of us standing there together in public, both of us possess-
ing the most extraordinary secret. We made some small talk and
then, anticipating my remark, he lifted the Hubba Bubba Bubble
Tape and said—This is for my son, by the way.

I lit up—I didn't know you had a son.

He's four.

Wow.

His name is Elijah.

He pulled out his phone and showed me some pictures of the
two of them together—on the couch, at a fairground, eating pan-
cakes. In one photo, a young woman in sportswear was holding
Elijah. Damian explained that she was his girlfriend, Crystal; not
Elijah's mother. I wondered for a moment why Damian had kept
this part of his life private, but I got the sense that the situation was
complicated, and I couldn't help but admire him for feeling protective of these two, and resisting the group's tendency to excavate the
deepest parts of our personal lives.

We're headed to the splash park today.

I smiled and thought that, for the first time since I had known
him, Damian looked genuinely happy. I told him as much, and he
brightened a little.

Thanks, he said. I feel good.

I told him that I did too, and I asked him if he thought it was
the tuning. He nodded as he began unloading the rest of his

cart—cans of tuna, cereal, jumbo bag of toilet paper, protein powder, chocolate milk mix—and then looked back at me to say, You know, I think it is.

I didn't tell him that I had tuned again with Kyle; that we had plunged deeper into the Resonance than maybe even Jo or Howard have ever dared go, and we saw how truly vast it could be.

I don't know quite how to describe it, he said after a moment, but it's like, since we tuned, I feel a little less . . . I feel a little bit more immaterial, or something.

It was probably a little unfair to Damian to say that I was astounded by this observation, but I was. In a word, he perfectly articulated the sensation. I felt somehow immaterial. As if, caught in a certain light, you could glimpse right through me. It was almost dizzying to feel untethered to the things that once bound me to my corporeality, my mortality; the things that had burdened and worn me down, and reminded me I was a limited, flesh-bound event on the planet. I felt somehow beyond myself, beyond time, beyond death; or at least those containers didn't seem to concern me the way they once had.

But it's dangerous, Damian said leaning towards me, voice lowered, suddenly serious. Because now we know. And you can be sure that they know that we know.

His words unsettled me as I unpacked my cart. He stood beside me waiting, as the cashier ran my items through. I couldn't quite seem to dismiss his concern as I might have in the past. What if there were people, or forces in the world, that would seek to limit my access to this pleasure; this unlimited way of being? And if there were, who were they, and how would they intervene? It did seem to be the nature of our system that limits were imposed. Limits must always be imposed. Because something unlimited risked dismantling everything else that hemmed us in.

Hi, Ms. Devon. I looked up and realized the cashier was a former student of mine, Rory. He was a close friend of Kyle's, or at
least he was when I was still at school. He had a ratty face and
demeanour, though he was probably a sweet enough kid out of
class. He gave me a polite, perfunctory smile.

Hi, Rory. How are you?

I'm good, yeah.

Did you enjoy yourself at prom?

Yeah, it was good. Sorry again about the clock. I don't know if
Ashley mentioned.

He was lucky he had found me in such a blithe mood. I asked
him if he had seen Kyle recently. He shook his head.

We're not really talking much at the moment.

He then swallowed and looked back at his till, as he swiped
through my Greek yogurt. Are you? he asked.

I pretended not to hear his question over the bleep of the scanner,
and he didn't ask it again. And I pretended not to know, or care,
that he had probably had a hundred conversations with his friends
about Kyle and me, and that he would pull out his phone to message them all the moment I walked away. I paid for my groceries
and wished him a good summer. The sliding doors whooshed open
as Damian and I stepped out of the aggressively air-conditioned
supermarket into what felt like a physical wall of heat.

We began walking through the parking lot, the smell of baking
asphalt and Damian's cologne somehow both nostalgic, when he
turned to me, and said—I know I sound paranoid to you. I can tell
by the way you look at me sometimes, that you think that.

No, I—I don't really think so, I lied, feeling caught out.

But I have been on the inside of it, okay, he said.

We slowed to a stop as a uniformed teenager pushed a giant
conga line of shopping carts past us into the outdoor dock.

I was a drone operator in Nevada for five years, he said, squinting against the sun. Sitting in a bunker under the sand. Hitting convoys of jeeps in Syria. Or some house in, you know, northwest Pakistan or wherever.

He glanced at me to gauge my reaction. Just taking people's lives because that was the intel, he said. I didn't know the first thing about who these guys were. Most of them probably just boys, running around on rooftops.

We began to walk again. You watch and watch and watch these guys, he continued. You see them talking with their wives. High-fiving their friends in the street. And then you . . . you know. He stuck his pinkie finger in his ear and swivelled around. You can see them hear it coming too, he said. Just a second before.

We slowed our pace to allow a black sedan to back out of its parking spot ahead of us.

After I had Elijah, I just couldn't anymore, he said. I'd be throwing up. And having these dreams. And so after that I started working in military intelligence, for a contractor. I know, you wouldn't think to look at me. He winked and tapped his temple— Me and intelligence.

No, c'mon, I said, forcing a laugh.

But seriously, if you knew the shit they could do, Claire, you wouldn't sleep at night. The shit they know about us, he said, shaking his head. And I just saw the tip of the iceberg.

We arrived at Damian's large white pickup. Through the windshield I noticed Crystal and Elijah both sitting in the cab, Crystal buried in her phone, and Elijah sucking on a long blue freezie. Damian dropped his grocery bags down on the ground and looked at me—You may not like him, but lemme tell you, I'm glad Trump's cleaning out the FBI and the CIA. Those are sick places.

Damian turned and called Crystal's name. She looked up, smiled, and gave me a little wave. He motioned for her to come out, and she climbed down out of the cab. Damian introduced me as a friend from his 'study group.'

So you do exist! she said with a laugh. He's been so secretive about it.

She said, ever since he started going to our meetings however, she had noticed 'a real turnaround in his attitude.' Talking to Crystal felt like twisting the cap off a bottle of pop, as all the bubbles rushed to the surface. She told me she worked part-time as a manicurist, but wasn't getting the hours she wanted, and then pointed out her salon in the cluster of stores on the far side of the parking lot. She looked up at Damian and scratched his goatee, as he scrunched up his face. The more the three of us chatted, the more it struck me that he hadn't told her about The Hum. I wondered what he had told her about our group. From the way they were both talking, it felt like he had represented it as some kind of Bible study. I suppose we all had to find a way to suture the realities of our old and new lives together, in whatever way we and our loved ones could handle. But it seemed strange for him to have kept The Hum secret, convinced, as he was, that thousands more people could hear it. But then it occurred to me, looking at Crystal, and Elijah in the cab with his blue-stained lips, that perhaps Damian had kept this from them for a reason. Like so much else in his life, no doubt. As miraculous as The Hum had revealed itself to be, I would have shielded Ashley and Paul from it too, had I somehow been able to. Perhaps they would still be in my life if I had. Not being able to hear The Hum, when your loved one does, must be a special kind of confusing agony. After a minute or so of pleasant chat we parted ways, but not before Crystal offered me a friends and family discount at Infinity Nails.

As I drove home, I felt the same effervescence from earlier, though Damian's words lingered with me. Coasting through the neighbourhood, it felt difficult to square the pristine yards, children's basketball nets, and family minivans with the threat of surveillance and infiltration. I reminded myself that beautiful things didn't always need to feel fleeting or endangered. I tried to refocus my energies towards savouring this strange post-tuning lightness of spirit. As I did, I found myself picturing an iridescent film of oil on the surface of a puddle. The puddle was black and bottomless, so perhaps it was a lake. A lake of pure sensation. And the oil slick—what was that? Was that me? My life? How did one merge with the lake, or was I only destined to contaminate it? I slipped so deep into this image that I nearly ran a stop sign. An elderly woman walking a terrier shot me a death stare. I held up my hand in apology, which she didn't acknowledge.

I spent the rest of the morning in the back garden, among the fuchsia coneflowers, yellow tickseed, and silver-green lamb's ears. I had been neglecting the garden terribly, and it was almost beyond redemption, but it felt grounding to put in the hours. I was hidden from view by the backyard's fences; only neighbours in their second-floor bedrooms could glimpse me, but I doubted any would be up there in the middle of the day. At one point I sank my hands into the hot earth. I closed my eyes, and I could have sworn I actually felt The Hum thrumming ever so subtly through the ground. I got lost in the sensation, and let time slowly slip past me. Worms roiled through my fingers as I sank deeper into the pulse. Bugs alighted on my neck, and scaled my arms. I let myself become their landscape. I pressed myself down into it. Merged with it. I began to feel loose, like my soul could slip right out from my skin, like a shirt sloughing off a wire hanger. But as the minutes passed, this looseness, this imma-terial feeling that felt so liberating earlier in the morning began to intensify, as The Hum seemed to grow louder, until, in a quiet panic, I wondered—Was it overtaking me? Was I disappearing into it?

I walked back into the house, unsteady, and washed my hands in the kitchen sink. I tried calling Kyle, but it went straight to voicemail, which meant he still hadn't charged his phone. Was he feeling the same sense of slippage, of disappearance? I told myself to snap out of it. I was fine. Maybe just a little overheated from the sun. I poured myself a glass of water. I gripped the kitchen counter. I found its sturdiness reassuring. I pressed my fingers against its cool surface and the sensation seemed to confirm that I was still there, corporeal, interacting as a single body within the physical world.

Once I had gathered myself, I considered walking down to the park to check in on Kyle. I even considered calling Child Services—but on behalf of a seventeen-year-old? No. That would only complicate things, and he would never forgive me for it. I debated calling Jo to ask for her guidance about Kyle's situation, but then she would have an obligation to tell the authorities. I'd also be betraying Kyle's confidence. If he needed me, he would be in touch. I felt hot rage when I thought of Brenda kicking him out—and after putting me through the goddamn ringer. She excoriated me for showing a bit of kindness and attention to her son, and then threw him out on the street.

As I finished my glass of water, I tried to remind myself again of the joy I had felt earlier in the morning, but I found it seeping from me. I found myself missing Ashley's mordant laugh. The sound of her moving about in her room upstairs. Her books left tented on tables around the house. I found myself missing the timbre of Paul's voice. His smell in the sheets. His little touches, on my shoulder, on my back, to let me know he was there behind me, as I was cooking, or brushing my teeth. I took out my phone and hovered my thumb over Ashley's number. I imagined her scrolling through her phone, as Paul put a frozen pizza into the microwave oven for them. Surely she couldn't bear to live with him in that studio apartment on a pull-out couch for the entire summer. Maybe she had already begun crashing with friends. *Focus.* I was having what

Jo called 'a wobble.' A moment of despair, of doubt, of missing my old life, but I couldn't go back. I needed to push forward. I needed to focus on the unfolding miracle of now.

I slipped my phone back into my pocket just as the doorbell rang. I glanced out the living room window and, to my shock, saw Cass's red Toyota Prius parked in the driveway. I was stunned for a moment. I couldn't possibly imagine what she was doing there, and why on earth she would show up like that unannounced. I rushed to the door, hesitated, and opened it. Cass was standing there wearing a characteristically bright and billowy yellow blouse with one of her signature chunky statement necklaces. She broke into a big, easy smile. I smiled back, out of reflex. It was dizzying to consider how much my life had changed since I had last seen her, backing out of my classroom with that strange look on her face. How much I had lost. How much I had gained.

Cass.

Hi, love, she said, extending her arms. I let her hug me, but I was caught completely off guard by her presence, after not so much as a text message in months. When she finally pulled away, I told her that I was slightly mortified at the thought of her setting foot in the house, which I hadn't much reason to keep clean anymore. She told me not to worry in the slightest, though I registered her subtle disapprobation as we walked through the door and into the kitchen. She told me it was just an impulse, her stopping by on her way home from church. I still had a bunch of groceries left on the counter from my morning shop, which I began to put away to clear space. As I did, we made small talk, mostly about her summer plans, and who won *Drag Race* in the end, and the endless back and forth with the school's administration about doing *Kinky Boots* in the fall. She asked about Ashley's graduation and the prom party, which I glossed over. She then asked me how Paul was doing, and I told her she would have to ask him herself.

We're not really talking at the moment. Not since Ashley moved out.

Cass looked shocked—What? Ashley's gone too?

Yup.

She's living with Paul? she asked, and I nodded.

Cass stood there watching me as I put the last of the vegetables into the crisper, and a couple of boxes of crackers into the cupboard. I've been really worried about you, she said.

Have you, I replied, chilly.

Yes. A lot.

I thanked her, and I told her that I could have used that worry a couple of months ago, but now it was misplaced. I'm in a good place now.

Are you really though?

I am, I say, packing the reusable shopping bags into their holder under the sink.

Love, I don't mean to be rude, but I don't think you are. I mean look around. Paul is gone. Ashley is gone. You've lost your job. Your friends—

My friends, what?

Well we're all extremely—

My friends love and support me, I interrupted. And I see them three or four times a week.

Cass nodded—I'm glad to hear it.

I found it difficult to gauge just how much she knew. I wouldn't be surprised if Paul had texted Aldo at some point, or one of the other book club husbands.

The truth is, Claire, I didn't feel comfortable reaching out while school was still in session. It felt wrong somehow. Like I would be betraying the school, or betraying Kyle. I felt like I was in a really tough position.

I wanted to laugh, and tell her she didn't know the first thing about how tough this had been. I was not sure why I should be surprised; it was just like Cass to make all of this about her and her feelings somehow. I was just about to ask her to leave when she touched my shoulder and told me that she wanted me to know that she was there for me. She tried to make meaningful eye contact, but I wasn't ready to accept it, so I looked up at the ceiling. She then apologized for not doing more before now.

To be honest I just didn't know what to do. I didn't know how I could be useful.

She said she knew that she had failed me, and it had been eating away at her. I looked down and met her gaze. I really am sorry, Claire.

We began to talk a little about The Hum, mostly in generalities as I didn't get the sense she was able or willing to handle specifics. As we spoke, I prepared some tea and pulled out some digestives from the back of the cupboard. I told her about my struggles with isolation and depression after being fired, and I could tell it pained her to hear it. With the comfort of old friendship, and years of knowing my kitchen, she set out the teacups and saucers, and prepared the milk and sugar without asking. Once the tea was ready, we relocated to the sofa in the living room. As I spoke, I felt Cass really listening, which was something of a rarity for her, the natural-born talker. But she was listening, and I began to relax and open up more, as we inched our way back to our former intimacy. She then related to me her own struggles with loneliness and despair when she was going through chemo. I don't think I had appreciated, at the time, the extent of her feelings of alienation from Aldo, and her friends, and our colleagues at school. I was just about to tell her about my new-found lightness when, like a hawk swooping down on its prey, she asked—Have you considered inviting God into your life?

I stiffened. I felt like I had been Trojan Horsed. Infiltrated by an agent of God under the guise of concerned friendship. I had an image of Christ, like a virus, entering through a mucous membrane and replicating through my bloodstream until my defences were overwhelmed and I was converted. I cleared my throat and told Cass that no, I had not considered this invitation. Never, in our eight years of friendship, had she ever asked me this question. I understood, in that moment, that some dynamic between us had forever shifted, forever broken, for her to be doing so now. And I realized that she must see me now as being in a place of weakness that she had never seen me in before.

I want to tell you that I lit a candle for you after the service this morning, she said with tenderness. I've been praying for you.

I looked down into my cup, and took a deep breath. Do you not see how your prayers and candles deny me agency over my own condition? I asked.

She said no, she didn't see that at all. She told me prayer was actually about reclaiming agency in our lives.

I looked back up at her. Say I was to tell you that I was happy now, I said. Truly happy. You would say that was God's doing, and once again a man would get all the credit for my hard work.

She laughed a little at this. I told her that I didn't see suffering as a test, or a punishment, or a destiny to be fulfilled. I told her that I had found an unparalleled sublimity in The Hum; a pure and rapturous transfer of energy between the Earth and myself, my body, which she might call God or grace or the divine, but which for me needed no label or language. A mystery that I was only just beginning to grasp.

She nodded but I could tell she was perturbed. As I looked at her sitting across from me on the sofa, it struck me that this would likely be our last conversation for a very long time. Perhaps ever. It also struck me that perhaps Cass and I had never been more aligned. I suddenly recognized myself in her faith and conviction. And this should have repelled me, would have once repelled me, but somehow it didn't in that moment. I saw the ecstatic chord that had been plucked in her, and that had compelled her to share the gift of divine revelation with those she cared about; compelled her to drive over to my house on a Sunday afternoon in her red Toyota Prius to salvage my soul. In that moment I could almost see it as a generosity of the heart. I wondered, as I looked at her, if I would ever feel that same conviction one day, to share The Hum with others. Was this embedded in the genetic code of revelation; that it must be shared, multiplied, disseminated?

I suddenly imagined a hundred, a thousand people tuning together. City parks filled with tuning circles. Conference rooms. School gymnasiums. Stadiums. The entire human race rediscovering the primordial frequency with which we had fallen out of synch; entwining ourselves again with the Earth at a time when it needed us the most, when our continued survival as a species depended on it.

We finished our tea with quiet briskness and I walked Cass out. As I opened the door, the sun felt as bright as a camera flash. The street was quiet; even the neighbourhood dogs were too hot to bark. After hugging me goodbye in the doorway, Cass pulled away and, with a grave look, asked—It's not really true, is it? What they've been saying?

What who's been saying? I asked, the words snagging in my throat.

Everyone. The other teachers, our friends.

She looked at me confused.

You don't know what they've been saying? she asked.

Who would tell me if not you?

She squinted against the sun, and brought her hand up above her eyebrows—They're saying you're a rapist, Claire.

I felt the blood drain from my limbs—What?

In the statutory sense.

Oh good, I said, bitterly. Just a statutory rapist.

Unusually for her, Cass seemed to be at a loss for words.

And now's where you tell me that you disabused them of that, I'm assuming, I said.

Well how could I know? she asked.

How could you know that I'm not a rapist? Is that what you're asking me?

I don't know what happened between you and Kyle.

Are you serious?

How would I?

I asked Cass to look me in the eyes and tell me, in her heart, whether she really thought I had had sexual intercourse with one of my students.

She shook her head—I don't know.

You don't know whether I'm a child sex offender?

She glanced around, as if worried neighbours might overhear, but frankly I couldn't give a damn. Claire, I need to tell you that I saw you and Kyle once, waiting at a traffic light in your car. About an hour or so after school. It was down by San Mateo Road. I had just dropped off a package at the UPS office there, when I recognized your car. And then I saw that Kyle was in there with you, and I thought . . . well, that's strange. And then I saw the way you two were laughing together. The way you were looking at him. And I thought . . . oh no. Oh no, there's something happening here.

I made to say something but Cass held up her hand to stop me.

And whatever did or did not happen between you and Kyle, I don't know, that is between you and God. But I will say this. In that moment, I knew. I thought—she's in love with him. I could see it in your face. And I know you, Claire. I know you better than almost anyone else.

Cass fiddled with her car keys for a moment, before looking back up with an afflicted expression. And I didn't say anything, she said. Because I was scared. Because . . . I'm a weak person, maybe.

I don't know. I regret it. I regret not confronting you about it. Or talking to Valeria about it. But that's mine to carry.

I had nothing to say in my defence. I didn't even feel particularly defensive. There was something strangely edifying in Cass's clear-eyed recognition of my state, before I had recognized it myself. And yet, how could I explain to Cass that it was a love that superseded want, or need, or sexual desire, or any of the drives I had previously known to animate love. It was a love that fell beyond. A union of souls. A spiritual kinship. Was rape the only force we could imagine occupying such a powerful space between a grown woman and a boy who wasn't her son?

Cass reached out, took hold of my hand, and gave it a little squeeze, as if saying goodbye to a dying patient. She told me to take care of myself. I nodded and watched her walk off down the curving stone walkway towards her car.

15

THERE WAS A MAN LURKING IN MY BACKYARD. I NEVER SAW him, but I knew he was out there, pacing back and forth, setting off the motion sensor lights. At first I told myself it was just a coyote, but the lights kept flashing. Once a coyote was startled it ran off and didn't come back. Something, someone, was pacing back and forth. I knew it was a man. Women didn't lurk in backyards. I suppose I did come close to lurking in the Campaneles' backyard once, but not like this. Not menacing and persistent. It was just after midnight and I was sitting on the couch. The blinds were drawn, and the lights were off, so he couldn't see in. I wanted to go to the window and peek out, but I was terrified he would see me. He would see that I was a woman alone. Maybe he already knew that. Maybe he had been casing the house for some time, watching my comings and goings. I had to press my eyelids with my index fingers to stop them from twitching.

I don't think anyone who isn't a woman living on her own can fully appreciate the amount of time we spend imagining and fearing this exact scenario. The number of times we feel a presence behind us as we turn off the lights. Or catch a glimpse of something out of the corner of our eye, and whip around to find an empty room. Or the hours we'll spend lying in bed, listening to steps on the staircase, or the electric garage door opening, or the doorbell ringing so clear in the night that it startles us awake. Though of course there's never anyone at the door. The garage is always closed. There's no one else in the house, on the staircase, or hiding in the next room.

But this was different. The lights were on in the yard. There was someone out there moving. Just then I saw a flicker of shadow on the curtain. *Stay quiet.* What did he want? Why didn't he just break in? I thought about grabbing a knife from the kitchen but no, I could easily be overpowered and have it used against me. It occurred to me that it might be Kyle, but why wouldn't he just ring the doorbell? For a second I wondered if it might be Paul trying to spy on me. No, that was crazy. I was holding my phone in my hand, but I didn't know who to call. I could call the police. But I couldn't just call the police because my motion sensor lights were flashing; surely I had to actually see someone, some credible threat.

I tried calling Kyle but it went straight to voicemail again. Then I called Jo. She picked up on the third ring.

Claire?

It sounded as if I had woken her up. I apologized for calling so late.

What's wrong, love? she asked.

I explained the situation, while trying to hide the panic in my voice. She told me that I needed to find a way to look out the window to assess the situation.

I can't. Not from the living room.

What about an upstairs bedroom?

What if he sees me?

Claire, he won't see you peeking from a second-floor window.

I told her that if I got up off the couch, he might notice my shadow moving behind the curtains. You said the lights are off, yes?

Yes.

Then there're no shadows. Just go upstairs. You can do this.

Just then, the backyard motion sensor lights turned off, and everything fell into darkness. I stood up and crossed the living room to the hallway, with Jo still pressed to my ear. I could hear her breathing. Just knowing that she was there, listening, helped. I whispered an apology to her again, and she told me not to be silly.

You always know I'm here. At any hour.

I was halfway down the hall to the staircase when, out the window behind me, the backyard lights flashed on again. I told Jo and she said to stay calm and keep going. I reached the staircase, and began ascending into the black of the second floor. Through muscle memory, I reached Ashley's bedroom and pushed open the door. At the far side of her room, the venetian blinds of the window were open, casting slanting bars of light across her bed. I crossed the room, and with my shoulder against the wall, I turned and peered down, out of the corner of the window, into the backyard. The backyard was lit starkly by the motion sensor lights above the patio door. I watched for five, ten seconds—and saw nothing. No movement. There was no one there.

Nothing at all? Jo asked.

Nothing.

And the lights are still on?

Yup.

Somehow, this unnerved me more. If I could see a body pacing, if I could see an animal, or a teenager, or a man with a gun, then at least I could have attributed my fear. There was nothing more unsettling than absence. Jo suggested that perhaps the lights had malfunctioned, but in my heart I knew that wasn't the case. I knew that there was something out there, and that the lights sensed something that I could not. Jo told me to keep looking, and I did, for another ten whole seconds, but then the lights flicked off. In the ensuing darkness, the membrane between outside and inside collapsed. Whatever was stalking my house could suddenly be anywhere, could be downstairs, could be in the closet of the bedroom. Jo told me to focus on my breath, but I couldn't get a hold of it.

Claire, do you want me to drive over?

No. I don't want to put you in danger.

She told me she was pulling on her shoes—We'll drive over there right now.

Please don't get off the phone, Jo.

Okay, I won't, love. I'm just going to have to put it down to pull on my shoes though, okay? And then I can plug you into the Bluetooth once we're in the car.

Okay. Just don't hang up.

I won't. I promise.

In that moment, I felt an almost overwhelming love for her. I wanted to tell her, but just then I heard her calling for Howard, and explaining the situation to him, and bless his soul, without even a question asked, I heard him getting ready to leave the house with her. And then Jo's voice came back on the line, gentle and measured, checking in to see how I was holding up, and to let me know that they were both on their way out the door, and should be arriving at my place within the next five minutes. I just slid down and sat on the ground in the dark of Ashley's bedroom, like a piece of wallpaper ripped from the wall, waiting for them to arrive.

Jo talked to me on the drive over, and as they walked up my front path, and rang my doorbell. I opened the door, I hugged them both as if they had just rescued me after two weeks in a flooded cave. They turned on the lights of the hallway, and the kitchen, and the living room, as we moved through the house together, waking it back up. Howard drew the curtains in the living room and we all looked out into the backyard. Howard moved towards the sliding patio door, opened it, and stepped out. Triggered by his presence, the motion sensor lights above the door flicked on.

Nothing, he said, looking around.

Jo and I stepped out of the patio door into the lucid night. The air smelled of the flowering creosote bushes along the back fence. Jo took a moment to search the yard for footprints, but the only ones she found were my own, around the flower beds, from earlier that morning.

I'm so sorry, I told them. To wake you up and make you come all the way over here. I feel completely ridiculous.

Don't, Jo said, squeezing my shoulder. You're under a lot of stress.

I told them I was still not sleeping properly.

Still? Howard asked, concerned. He said he hadn't realized. He said most nights The Hum lulled him to sleep, like white noise.

I wanted to confide in them about tuning with Kyle the night before; about how far we had managed to go, and about how exhilarating and terrifying it was; about the almost joyful disassociation that followed in the morning; the feeling of being permeated by the Resonance until what was left of me was no longer clear; about how this feeling intensified over the day until I felt like there was nothing left of me at all, and how panic set in, until I felt completely swallowed by it. But I was afraid they would be hurt. Or angry. Or not understand. Though maybe they did. Maybe they knew exactly the feeling I meant.

In the end, I said nothing. Howard stuffed his hands into his pockets. Jo wrapped her arm around me and pulled me into her. I felt a little bit like their daughter. Or their pet. A beloved burden. I stood with them in the yard, listening to the sound that had brought us into one another's lives. I then looked up at the sky spattered with stars, and thought of Kyle lying in his tent, six blocks away, nestled beside his reading lamp with a book resting on his chest. I thought of Ashley and Paul in their studio apartment overlooking the parking lot, probably getting ready for bed, if not already asleep. And I thought of my bed upstairs, its cold vastness, and the restless night that awaited.

16

DAMIAN SLAMMED HIS HANDGUN DOWN ON THE COFFEE table. Leslie gasped, and Shawn raised his hands—Whoa, okay.

Put it away, Howard said, standing up.

We're going to be targeted, Damian said.

Damian, Jo said, putting her hand on his arm. It was midday, the living room blinds were drawn, and everyone was on edge. Though I didn't realize it at the time, this was the water pulling out before the wave.

We are going to be targeted, Damian repeated, stepping away from Jo's touch, and we can either sit here and do nothing, or we can—

I'm not interested, Howard interrupted.

Well you should be. People have begun connecting the dots, Howard. On 4chan, on Reddit. There're others out there who can hear the Resonance and they are being tracked down and they are being eliminated.

Nora looked alarmed—Eliminated?

All kinds of people can hear it.

I know, Howard said.

Melbourne, Bristol, Munich, Calgary, all around the world.

Of course they can.

And you read these subreddits and every one of them—fired from their jobs, hounded by police, mysterious deaths—

Oh come on.

You don't know 'cause you're not paying attention. Damian was beginning to raise his voice.

Emily looked confused—But why, I don't—?

Because they don't want us to know.

Who's 'they'? Shawn asked. You mean the government?

What's 'Fortune'? Nora asked. Kyle leaned in and quietly clarified that 4chan was a messaging board website, which didn't seem to do much to clear up her confusion. Emily motioned to Nora that she didn't understand either.

It's way above the government, Damian continued, sitting back down on the edge of his chair. I'm talking about the small cabal of power brokers who run everything.

Oh god, Shawn moaned, this is some Protocols of Zion shit.

They've known about the Resonance for centuries, Damian continued, ignoring Shawn.

Damian, look at my nose, Shawn said, pointing.

And they've used its power to secure their place at the top of the pyramid.

Do you see my nose?

This is bigger than the government, or the military.

Don't go there, Shawn warned him.

Damian finally turned to Shawn—It's not just the Jews.

Oh not *just*, okay great.

Shawn's heckling would've normally cracked me up, but I felt too enervated to laugh.

And they're listening to us right now, Damian continued, they've been listening to us this whole time, and trust me, they are going to move in on us.

Move in, Emily said, indignant.

Because we know their secret. They've been hiding this shit from us for centuries, but we are on the verge of unlocking it.

Damian—Howard made to intercede, but Damian pointed at him.

And they got you fired, Howard, from Virginia Tech, don't think they didn't, Damian said, before trying to face me. You too, Claire.

With as much patience as I could muster, I replied that I somehow doubted F. G. Saunders Secondary was on the radar of the Stonemasons or whatever.

It's the Illuminati, Claire, Shawn joked. *Eyes Wide Shut.*

And now your house is being cased, Damian said to me.

I never should have brought it up. I had only done so to explain why I looked so wan and tired that morning. The others seemed startled to see me as I arrived. Mia said I looked haunted. I hadn't meant to set Damian off.

We don't know that, Jo said, holding up her hand to Damian.

And Mia's computer's been hacked.

What? Jo asked.

Howard turned to Mia—I didn't hear about that.

Mia nodded—I called Damian the other night because I know he used to do cyber-related stuff, and um—

Why, what happened? Howard pressed.

Well. The cursor, on my screen, began to move on its own.

That can happen, Howard said.

What do you mean that can happen? Damian retorted. That means someone's hacked into her desktop and is watching her.

Howard exhaled, exasperated—Or the thumb pad could just be broken.

But it's not, Damian fired back.

That's the thing, Mia said. It's brand new.

A cursor moving on its own—Howard began.

Howard, this was literally my field of expertise, Damian cut in. I went over to Mia's house, and I saw for myself. You don't believe me? Aaron Alexis. Aaron Alexis, civilian military contractor. September 16, 2013, he entered the Washington, D.C., Navy Yard—ring a bell?—killed twelve people before taking his own life. Does anyone remember this?

I . . . I do, yes, Emily said, nodding and frowning.

He posted on Facebook right before he did it, talking about how he'd been hearing The Hum for over a year, and that he was on the verge of uncovering its mystery, but They wouldn't let him be. He got pulled over for a busted tail light, thrown in prison 'cause it was his third strike, lost his job, his wife, no custody of the kids. Doctors telling him he's crazy. Putting him on all of this medication.

Okay, Howard said, holding up his hands to get Damian to stop.

All because he heard it. All because he was trying to unlock its secret. And this is one story of a thousand.

Mia leaned forward, hands out, as if trying to get a grasp on some intangible thing in front of her. So you're saying—

October 3, 2013—Damian continued, Miriam Carey, a young mother and dental hygienist. Reported hearing The Hum to local authorities and started getting hounded. Phones tapped. Strange calls. Cars parked outside her house. Eventually she snapped and drove all the way from her home in Connecticut to Washington, D.C., and tried to drive through a White House security checkpoint and she was chased by the Secret Service—you can watch this all on YouTube—chased by the Secret Service to damn near

Capitol Hill where they riddled her car with bullets, killing her. With her young daughter in the car.

Damian, you're just describing people with mental health problems, Jo said.

No, see, that's exactly, that's *precisely* what we've been told, he shouted back at her. He was getting worked up now. Jo shot me a sideways glance.

What happened to her daughter? Nora asked, pained.

She lived, miraculously.

Hold on, Mia said, trying once again to grasp this. You're saying a group of people, a long time ago, way before us, discovered the Resonance—

And have been controlling the World Bank ever since, Shawn said with a smirk, leaning back in his chair, and folding his arms together over his chest.

You can laugh—

And the IMF.

—but they will come for us.

But the Resonance is just a sound, Damian, Mia said. How does that give them—?

That's the secret we're approaching, he said, emphatically.

It's definitely more than just a sound, Leslie said.

Damian gestured to her, acknowledging the support. You have felt its power, he said. I know you have—

Yes, but I'm not ruling the world with it, Mia said.

—and others have too, for a long, long time, and there's a reason, a very good reason the rest of the world doesn't know about this, and that's because it's been kept from us.

I need you to stop this, Howard said, and then pointed to the gun. And I need you to put that away.

Yeah, I can't listen to this, I said. I looked to Kyle and, from the forlorn look on his face, I could tell he felt the same.

You think we're the only people who've ever discovered this? Damian asked me.

Of course not, Jo said, answering for me.

All around the world, Damian said, continuing to look at me, throughout time, people have discovered they can hear it, and tap into it, and each one of them has been kept down, or discredited, or jailed, or burned at the stake. Systematically.

Howard, a large vein now visible in his forehead, pointed to Damian—I am not going to sit here and listen to conspiracy theories about something I have been working years to gain a legitimate and scientific knowledge of.

The conspiracy is what is being done to us, Damian replied. It's only a theory until there's evidence and the evidence is all around us, we are living proof of—

Enough, Howard shouted, startling everyone to silence. That's enough. Now put that away or get out.

Damian looked shocked—Out?

I'm not going to ask you again.

You'd kick me out?

I—

Just like that? Damian asked. This is my family, Howard. I am doing this because you're my family.

I know, Howard said, his conviction wavering.

Emily nodded—We know, hun.

This is about defending what is most precious to us.

Nora leaned forward and touched Damian's hand—Damian, please. Just . . . put it away.

And finally, at Nora's gentle insistence, he relented. He picked the gun up off the coffee table, and locked it back into its holster, concealed from view under his untucked flannel shirt. He then plunked himself back down in his chair.

I can't believe you'd kick me out, he muttered, glancing at Howard.

I-I wouldn't. I'm sorry.

I took a breath and unclenched my fists. I felt a strange mix of anger and protectiveness towards Damian. Perhaps it was the feeling of wanting to protect him from himself.

We are here for each other, Jo said, pouring her voice over the hot coals of the moment. And we love each other. Yes?

Everyone nodded, glancing around the circle.

Let's say it so we remember—We love each other.

We all intoned in unison, after Jo.

And we are working towards something beautiful and difficult and yes, there will be challenges ahead, but we do not need fear and division right now, Jo said.

Shawn removed a Tupperware container from a literary festival tote bag beside him—What we need are some delicious vegan samosas, and thankfully I made twelve.

Everyone laughed, except Damian. Mia clapped appreciatively.

They're not warm, they're cold, but whatever, they're delicious carbs soaked in oil, Shawn said. He opened the lid and set the container off on its journey around the circle.

Is everyone okay? Mia asked. Are we good?

All I'm saying is that they will come for us, Damian said.

And then, with truly cosmic timing, the doorbell rang. Damian gestured to the door, vindicated.

Shawn burst into his inimitable laugh and held up his arms—Well hey Nostradamus!

Ay, dios mio, Nora murmured under her breath.

Howard rose to answer the front door, but Jo stopped him. Everything's fine, he told her.

Love, please, Jo said, imploring Howard to ignore it, but he insisted on checking to see who it was. He crossed to the front door and looked through the peephole. It's a woman, he said. I don't recognize her.

What's she look like? Jo asked, standing a few paces behind him, hugging herself.

She's blond. In her forties.

The doorbell rang again, as Kyle jumped up, crossed to the door, and looked through the peephole himself.

Fuck, he said. It's my mom.

Oh, thank god. Emily laughed in relief. My heart was just—She pounded her fist against her chest.

The doorbell rang again, and Kyle turned to Howard and Jo, panicked—Don't. Please.

She's just going to keep ringing it until someone answers, Jo said.

I know.

None of us want a repeat of last time, Leslie said.

No, my goodness, Nora said.

Emily stood up—I could go out and say something.

No, Kyle said, firmly. She's trying to keep me away, but I can't, this is my—This is where I need to be, with all of you, and she can't accept that. If I go home with her she'll stop me from coming.

Mia reassured him that we wouldn't let that happen.

She'll mess with my head and make me see doctors and I can't, I can't see her right now. Please.

Jo hugged him—Of course, love.

Damian was up now at the living room window, peering out through the curtain. I hate to say it, Claire, he said, but your husband's also out there.

What?

With what looks like your daughter.

My heart sank as the others registered their disbelief. I went to the window, took hold of the curtain, and peeped through it myself. Paul and Ashley were standing having what looked to be an argument beside Paul's car.

They must've drove her here, Kyle said.

I had told Kyle not to give Paul his mother's damn number, and now look. I watched my husband and daughter, their voices mute, and wondered whether they even thought of this as a betrayal. This woman was the reason I didn't have a fucking job, did they not get that? And now they were conspiring with her against me? Classy, guys. Really fucking classy. The doorbell rang again, and Shawn joked that we could turn it into a drinking game.

I really think someone should just tell—Emily started, before looking over at Kyle—sorry, your mom's name?

Brenda.

Tell Brenda that you're happy and safe but you're not coming out.

No, you don't know my mom. That would go down like a ton of shit.

I just wonder—

No, Emily, trust me, she'd go ballistic. It's better just to wait her out.

And then, from the other side of the front door, Brenda began using her voice like a sledgehammer.

Kyle! Open up this goddamn door. I'll be go to hell if you think I'm going to leave here without you. I can wait you out, buddy. I've got all goddamn day. All this time telling me you were at Mark's! How many weeks? I go to his door and he has no idea what I'm talking about. Can you imagine how I felt? And to everyone else in there right now, I'm putting all your asses behind bars. You hear me? Claire Devon, I know you're in there.

I exchanged glances with the others. Shawn donned a comically exaggerated face of panic, like a Munch painting, which cracked me up despite the circumstances. I don't think he realized just how serious the situation was.

I'm speaking to you, Claire. *I am a mother.* Mother to mother, Claire, give me back my son or I swear to God I will destroy you.

Give him back? I was astonished. Woman, you kicked him out!

I turned to Kyle—She kicked you out!

More or less.

More or less?

Not sleeping, not eating, Brenda continued. Calling every one of his friends and banging on their doors and posting messages on Facebook and calling the police and all along you've been keeping him here locked up, hostage. Hey? This is a *hostage taking.* You have kidnapped my boy, an *underaged boy.* I want you to think about how that's going to go down when I haul your asses before a court, yeah?

All the while, I was looking at Kyle trying to decipher what he meant by 'more or less.'

We had a fight and I left, he explained.

You ran away, I said, walking towards him.

I had to.

You told me she kicked you out.

She was trying to stop me from seeing you.

I could have shaken him—You've been lying to her all this time.

It doesn't matter.

Yes it does, actually, I said, livid. Of course it does.

Brenda rang the doorbell again—Kyle? Buddy? Don't do this to me. I love you, buddy, you know that, and you know I don't want you getting mixed up with the wrong kind of people. These people are not good people. They're not normal people—

Shawn snorted—Show me someone who is, lady.

They don't know you, Kyle, Brenda continued, shouting. And they don't have your best interests at heart, okay? They're scared and messed up insecure people who want something from you, okay? You gotta trust me on this, I've been around, I know all about these kinds of people. They seem real nice and sweet and they tell you you're special but they're sick in the head and they drag you down and take and take and take from you, Kyle. Kyle?

I know you can hear me. Come to the window if you can hear me—

All the while, as Brenda monologued to the front door, Kyle remained defiant, telling me he was seventeen, and could leave home if he wanted.

She's your legal guardian, I said fuming, pointing towards the front door.

Doesn't matter, he's over sixteen, Howard said.

We're his guardians too, Damian said.

Yeah, tell that to a court, I replied.

I glared at Kyle and told him he needed to speak to her.

I have nothing to say.

Kyle—

Just then my phone began to vibrate in my pocket. I pulled it out and saw it was Ashley calling. I moved across the living room to a quiet corner to answer it—Ash?

Why haven't you been picking up?

I'm sorry, everything's been so—

I've been telling Dad that he has to stop this but he keeps saying 'They have her son.' And what am I supposed to say to that? How can I argue?

Ash—

No listen, Mom. I need you to listen to me. I told Dad that you guys all just want to be left alone.

Yes.

And he says he has, he left, he left you alone and look where that's gotten us. A child has been kidnapped.

That's—

—bullshit, I know, but what does this look like on the outside? I told him, Dad, they're just listening. That's all they're doing, they're doing their listening thing. And he said, Ash, the curtains are drawn and it's the middle of the day. Can you imagine your mother—? Like, you don't even sleep with the curtains drawn at night! He said you're not yourself, you're not in control. And I said, yeah well neither are you, Dad, and neither is fucking Brenda Francis. He said this wasn't going to be a scene. He promised. We were supposed to have a cup of coffee at her house, to talk to her about the situation and help her find Kyle, that was it, and then she forced us to come over to your place because we thought you two might be there, and then when you weren't—She's had her hand up his ass puppeting him all morning.

I closed my eyes and leaned back against the wall—Put your father on.

Do you love him?

What?

Do you still love him, do you love Dad?

Of course I do.

Then finish this.

Just put him on.

And what about me?

Ash. You know I do.

Then come out. Now, with Kyle. And we can all go home.

I told her I couldn't. She said that, if I didn't, Brenda would call the police.

Ash, I need you to listen to me very carefully, you cannot let Brenda call the police. Do you have any idea what that would mean for me?

She didn't answer.

Do you? Hello?

I'm fucking scared, she said, her voice small and pinched.

Then stop. Then go home.

Me? You're telling me to—You've locked yourself in a house with a bunch of lunatics with the curtains drawn, and you're telling me to stop?

Do not—these people are family to me.

Family? What are you fucking talking about?

You have no idea what we have been through, Ash.

Mom, I'm your family. Dad is your family.

I can't believe you showing up with Brenda, who ruined everything for me, who you, you brought into all of this in the first place with your goddamn texts, do you know how humiliating it is—

Oh wow, yeah, bring that up again.

—to look outside and see you and your father standing out there with her? The betrayal of that? You've thrown me under the bus, Ash.

What are you even fucking—? We love you. And we're fucking scared for you.

You've made this situation so much worse.

You, Mom, *you* made this situation. I mean what is worth this? How can this possibly be worth it?

I have felt it.

Felt what?

I tried to explain the bliss, the purity of experience we had accessed, a wholeness, an interconnectedness surpassing human understanding, beyond flesh, beyond orgasm, beyond spirit.

Orgasm? She balked.

A pleasure beyond the body, Ash. Something so completely unbounded, why're you crying? Don't you hear what I'm saying? We have unlocked the secret of The Hum.

Sex?

What?

Through sex?

No. No, through the sound of the Earth itself.

I can't—Stop. I can't hear this.

And we're at peace.

Mom, listen—

A true liberated peace.

This is killing me, she said, and then screamed into the phone—
You're killing me.

Ashley really laid me on the plinth and ripped out my heart
with that one. Were there any worse words a child could scream at
her mother? I scrunched my face, against tears—Please don't say
that.

If you love me then you'll walk out that fucking door now.

I told her that I couldn't.

Then you don't.

Ash—

You don't.

I love you more than anything in—

No, not enough. Not fucking—

And then the line went dead.

Ash? Ashley?

I crossed the room to the window, and peered out through the
curtains. I could see Ashley's phone smashed on the asphalt by her
feet. She was arguing with Paul once more, and Brenda was walking back over to them across the front yard. I watched for a while
as the three of them conferred. Brenda was incensed, gesticulating
wildly towards the house, and it seemed Paul was doing his best
to de-escalate the situation. Ashley threw up her hands, crossed
around to the passenger side of the car, and got in. I could hear the
muffled slam of her door from inside the house. She sat and waited
with her arms folded, but it didn't look like Brenda or Paul were
prepared to leave anytime soon, least of all Brenda. I turned back
into the room, to the worried and expectant faces of the group, and
told them—I think we might be in this for a while.

And sure enough, within an hour, the police arrived.

17

I NEED TO MAKE CLEAR THAT I NEVER CHOSE THE GROUP over Ashley or Paul. I have found accusations of this nature completely debilitating. I never fail to be amazed by how many opinions strangers or pundits have about the kind of mother I am or was. Literally fuck off. I would have crawled across a desert for Ashley. So why didn't I come running out of the house when she called? Don't think I haven't racked my brain over that same question. The thing is, without the support of the group, I would have quite simply lost my mind. There would have been no one for Ashley to call a mother, or for Paul to call a wife. I also can't overemphasize how responsible I felt for Kyle, who, despite his air of assuredness, was really so vulnerable. I was also operating on months of sleep deprivation at this point and feeling even more light-headed, and almost dissociative since the tunings. When people ask me if I regret that decision, or any decision I made later that night, I tell them that's not a productive question. I can't let myself sink into the mire of that kind of thinking.

By the time night fell, a small clutch of concerned neighbours had gathered, along with at least one local news van. Brenda was still out there with Paul, though I couldn't see Ashley. The police lights strobed through the blinds, bathing the living room in blue and red. At one point, an officer came to the door. Howard and the officer had a brief exchange, which I didn't catch all of, but it seemed to be about Kyle. Howard wouldn't let the officer enter, citing the lack of a warrant, but as Howard said this, the officer tried to force his way inside and Howard had to push the door closed on him. Everyone was shaken, and argued for a while about how to prevent the situation escalating any further.

To calm our nerves, Jo kept the indoor lighting dim and soft and played some ambient world music, the kind you might expect to hear in a yoga class or a spa. She prepared some lentil soup for us, which we slurped from bowls balanced on our laps, while sitting around the living room. Nora sat in an armchair, eyes closed, praying bilingually under her breath. She reminded me of a pigeon perched on a ledge, huddled against the rain. At some point, Damian got up to investigate the backyard, I suppose to assess whether we were being surrounded.

Kyle and I sat together on the couch, a little removed from the others. My stomach was in knots and I was letting out little stress farts, which Kyle had the grace not to remark on. Instead, he asked me how I was holding up. Not so hot, I told him. He said I looked ghostly, and in truth, that's how I felt. Everything felt—thin. It was the only word I could think to describe it. My skin. My breath. My grip on reality.

The Hum feels so intense now, I told him. Ever since the other night, in the park—

What happened the other night was good, he insisted. Please don't regret it.

I told him that I didn't.

It's just that every time we tune, I said, I find it harder and harder to return. Like I feel like if I do it again I might just slip right in, and never come out.

What do you mean 'never come out'?

Just—lost in it forever.

I could tell I was unsettling him, and I felt guilty. In the midst of all this, he didn't need me spiralling out. But ever since the other night, it was as though I had been shifted off my foundations. Maybe we had gone too deep. Or maybe we had done it wrong. We should never have tuned alone.

This is all so fucked, Kyle said, glancing towards the window.

I took hold of his hand, and he gently squeezed it.

You know you could end this right now, I said. If you just walked out that door.

He looked back at me, and searched my face—Yeah, and I would never see you again. They'd never let us.

Maybe that's the sacrifice we have to make, I said, nodding to the others in the room. For them.

He shook his head, not willing to entertain it. I need you with me, he said.

And I need us to leave here, and not in the back of a police car. I'm responsible for you.

We're responsible for each other. We entered this together.

But—

And we either stay together or we leave together, he said.

Without saying it, we both knew that if we left together they would separate us. We existed together only in the time that remained for us in that house. Like a man crushed below a heavy weight, who lives only as long as the weight continues to press down upon him and dies the moment it's removed. I told Kyle that I felt like my life had just totally collapsed in around me, like an addict.

I don't even know what's left if I remove you from it, I said. Or this house. It would just be me alone with The Hum and—

So don't. Don't remove me from it.

The longer we stay in here, the more this is going to build up until it blows. And when it does it'll destroy everything. Not just us.

I know what you two are doing, Howard said, looking over at us. The others in the room fell quiet and turned our way.

What's our strategy here? I asked.

Claire, love, we've been over this, Jo said.

We're a group, and we make plans as a group, Howard replied.

Maybe they just need to see Kyle, I said. Or hear from him.

Jo said that if we stepped out that door, they would separate us and arrest us one by one.

As long as we stay, we hold negotiating power, she said.

What negotiating? I asked. They're asking us to leave and we're not. We have no demands.

We demand to be left in peace, Howard said.

Well clearly that's not a viable position, I replied.

We argued for another few minutes, but to no end. After a pause, Mia asked if I was sure I didn't want something to eat. I told her I couldn't.

It's legit delicious, Jo, Shawn said.

Oh thanks. It's just what I could pull together.

Emily laughed—With three cop cars and a news van outside! I can barely cook when I have Tom's sister and brother over, I get so stressed.

Mia asked Nora if she had had enough to eat and Nora nodded. Nora was holding the tiny gold crucifix at the end of her necklace. Jo asked her if she wanted to go somewhere quieter, to pray or calm herself down, but Nora said no, she was fine, thank you. Just then Damian walked back into the room from the kitchen and began detailing plans for a possible escape route through the backyard.

Howard cut him off—We don't need an escape route.

We damn well might.

What we need is to stay calm.

This is not just gonna be the local police we're dealing with, Howard.

Mia motioned to Damian—Why don't you come sit with me for a bit?

Don't, he snapped. I'm not one of your fucking autistic kids, Mia. Don't use that 'come sit with me' bullshit like I'm one of your kids.

Mia looked taken aback and threw her hands up in mock surrender. But before any of us could respond, a man's voice suddenly boomed over a loudspeaker outside. *Just to reiterate*—The room fell quiet as we all listened. *Our intention is not to use force.*

Their intention, Jo said, drily.

We're not planning to make arrests.

Damian crossed his arms—Right.

We just want to make sure everybody inside's healthy and safe.

How nice of them, Leslie said.

You know, I kind of feel for them, Emily said.

Mia looked at her—The cops?

They're just trying to do their job, Emily said, before turning to Damian. I mean you must empathize a little. You know what it is to serve.

This response is completely disproportionate to the situation, he replied.

There isn't even a situation, I said. It's just a house with people in it.

But no one's telling them that, Emily said. They're imagining a worst-case scenario.

Mia said she agreed with Emily—I think we need to send someone out to be a kind of spokesperson.

No, Howard said. I've told you, they'll rush the door.

It's a crime to harbour a juvenile runaway, Jo interrupted.

But he's not, I said. He's seventeen, he's not a juvenile.

But if they think we're holding him against his will—

I don't want to go with them, Kyle said.

Emily held up her hands to calm him—We know.

They'll never let me see you again, he said. Any of you.

Leslie reassured him that we were not going to let that happen; though I wasn't sure how she could make that promise.

We can't let the situation needlessly escalate either, Emily said.

Mia, having looked something up on her phone, handed it to Jo—Here, look, sixteen without parental consent for leaving home. Yeah? And unless they can prove he's in some sort of bodily danger they have no recourse.

Well that's what they'll try to prove, Jo said, looking up from Mia's phone. That's what they're trying to assess.

I was the one who spoke to the officer, Howard said. Their minds are made up. They will come in here and they will arrest us, and they will take Kyle.

I think we still need some way of communicating with them, Mia said, and Emily nodded emphatically. Silence is way too ominous.

Well we're not sending people out, Leslie said. They'll start peeling us off one by one—

What about a sign in the window, Shawn suggested. We just write on a piece of paper something, like, I don't know, 'Nine of us in here, happy and safe.' Uh. 'Gathering peacefully by choice. Please leave us be.' Or something.

Oh yeah, that'll send them packing, Damian said.

Well it's better than nothing.

Definitely, Emily agreed. Silence is a kind of—

Defiance, Mia said. Like a fuck you.

I'm fine with a sign, Jo said. Howard nodded, and Nora said she thought it was a good idea. Jo looked around the room. Any strong objections? she asked.

No one spoke, so Jo rose from her chair, and left the room to get some sign-making supplies.

And we can keep updating the sign, if we need to, Shawn added.

Leslie said she didn't think anyone should stand in the window with it, for safety reasons.

No, no of course, we'll tape it up, he replied.

What, are you afraid they're going to shoot us or something? Kyle joked, looking at Leslie.

No, I just think the less of our personal images out there, the better.

Fewer, Shawn said.

Sorry?

Fewer personal images. Sorry, I'm a grammar Nazi!

Well maybe you should write the sign, she said, with a little laugh.

Well maybe I will, he replied, imitating her with hilarious accuracy.

Jo walked back into the room holding several sheets of paper, a handful of markers, and some masking tape. All right, so. Let's— She placed the pieces of paper on a large coffee table book about Brutalism. Maybe write on this book so it doesn't mark up the table, she said.

I love this table, Emily said, running her hand across its surface.

Thanks, it's mango wood.

Okay, Shawn said, moving down onto the floor beside the table. Did we like that? 'Nine of us in here, happy and safe. Gathering peacefully by choice. Please leave us be.'

Why do we have to specify the number? Howard asked.

I said that I thought it made us sound like trapped miners.

So does the 'happy and safe,' Jo said, looking at me. Like 'happy and safe and plenty of oxygen.'

Maybe something simpler, Shawn suggested, like 'We are gathering in this private residence—peacefully gathering in this private residence by choice. Please respect our privacy.'

Damian nodded. It's good.

Except that it uses 'private' and 'privacy,' Kyle said. It's just a lot of, you know—

Privates, Shawn said, coyly.

So just drop the first one, Mia said.

'We are peacefully gathering in this residence by choice. Please respect our privacy.'

Great, Howard said. Send it to the printers.

Shawn uncapped a black marker and began to write the sign in clear, bold letters. He misjudged the spacing and had to awkwardly fit the words 'our privacy' into an unplanned-for third line, but it was still legible. He then held up the sign and asked—Who wants to do the honours?

Damian suggested Kyle should. So they know he's safe and—

Happy, Mia said. And has enough oxygen.

And agency, Jo added.

Shawn handed Kyle the sign. Kyle walked over to the window with it, and shimmied in front of the curtains. I could hear muffled exclamations from the crowd gathered outside. He taped the sign up in the window, and then slipped back behind the curtain, into the room—Another news van just pulled up, he said.

Howard's face fell—Are you serious?

KCTV.

Holy shit. Shawn smiled, in disbelief, as if he were already in the future and looking back on a wild anecdote. Damian walked out of the room, grabbed his knapsack from the vestibule, and returned, pulling out his laptop. He set it down on the coffee table and brought up KCTV's broadcast livestream.

I don't want to watch it, Howard said, and Mia agreed.

I kind of do, actually, Shawn said.

Damian held up his hand to quiet the room—I'll keep it on mute.

I can't do this, Nora said.

Jo laid a hand on her thigh—It's awful, isn't it?

I—I have to go, Nora said, rising from her chair. Her hands were trembling.

Go?

I can't stay, I'm sorry.

Jo stood and gently grasped Nora's upper arms—Hold on.

I don't want to do this anymore.

Everything's going to be fine.

I don't want to be part of this, Nora said, stepping away from Jo.

But we made a pact, Jo said.

I know, but I can't. I'm sorry. I can't breathe in here.

Do you want to go into the backyard for a moment? Shawn asked her.

I want to go home, she replied, her distress mounting. I want to see my son. I don't want to be on TV or, or, or in trouble with the police, I don't want it.

Howard rose from his chair—Nora, we need you now. More than ever.

I'm sorry, she said, shaking her head and tearing up.

I don't know what to say, Jo replied. After everything we've shown you. Everything we've been through.

I'm sorry. I love you but I need to go home. I need to see my boy.

So you're just going to walk out, Leslie said, sharply. Into that mob of police and news crews?

I don't have a choice.

Of course you do, Jo replied.

This will go away, they will go, Howard said.

I know, but—

He took a step towards her—You have to be strong, and you have to be patient.

But I can't, I'm not, I'm not strong. I'm scared and I want to leave.

Yes you are, Jo said. I know you are, I've seen it.

My mind's made up, Nora said, summoning what was left of her courage. I'm sorry.

She then turned to the rest of us—I love you all. But I have to go.

She made to exit but Leslie blocked her—Hold on, hold on. That's it?

I will come back.

No, you don't get it, Leslie said, pointing her finger into Nora's chest. If you go, you hurt us all. You make us all vulnerable.

They will try to turn you against us, Jo said.

No, I—

You're stronger than this, Nora.

Leslie brought her face close to Nora's—If you walk out that door, you're not welcome back.

Shawn looked shocked—Les.

That's betrayal, she shot back at him.

Nora's face hardened in defiance—Goodbye, Leslie.

Nora made to sidestep Leslie but Leslie grabbed her, and restrained her as she began to thrash and shout to let her go, before Jo swooped in to help Leslie, telling Nora—Love, you need to gather yourself, okay?

Please, let me go, Nora pleaded, terrified.

Howard reached out to calm her—Nora—

Don't touch me.

We're all in this together, he said. And we're trying to protect you.

Let me go, now. Let *go of me*—she screamed, her face growing red.

Jo now had her in an almost full-body lock—Nora, I need you to focus. All right? I want you to tune with me.

Leslie asked the others for help in calming her. Mia and Damian grabbed hold of Nora's legs to stop her from kicking. Emily hovered close with no real way to add herself to the struggle. Shawn, Kyle, and I stood a few paces back watching, horrified. I knew I should intercede but I was too stunned to know how.

Guys—Shawn shouted, over the melee.

Love, please, Emily cooed, bending down to look Nora in the face. Think of what's at stake. Damian reminded Nora that if she walked outside now, they would arrest her, and try to break her.

Enough! Shawn shouted again, his voice drowned out.

And they're going to turn you on us, Damian continued.

I need you to focus, Jo told Nora, who just kept screaming for them to let her go, her voice growing hoarse. Her brow was sweaty, and her hair dishevelled. I could see Kyle was also in a state of shock, watching all of this unfold.

You're making this worse for yourself, Leslie told her.

Bring her down to the ground, Howard instructed everyone.

Guys, please—Shawn begged. This is crazy.

On the count of three, Howard said.

I finally rallied and managed to shout—Just let her go.

One—

Please!

Two—

Mia suddenly lost her grip, or maybe released it, and Nora wrested free an arm and elbowed Leslie in the stomach, who grunted and doubled over, destabilizing the mass, and Nora tumbled out, her eyes wild with fear, as she gasped for breath. *Dios ten piedad de ti*, she spat at us, before dashing out of the room, tearing open the front door, and running from the house.

Jo pointed frantically at the wide-open door, shouting—Lock it, lock it, lock it!

Damian scrambled to the door, slammed it, and locked it.

That was not okay, Shawn shouted.

It didn't have to be like that, Mia said, shaking her head.

Leslie straightened up, pained and manic. Good fucking riddance, she barked towards the front door.

I looked at Leslie, at this woman I had called a friend for nearly half a year, this woman I had shared some of my most intimate secrets with, and she suddenly seemed like a cruel and desperate stranger with another woman's lipstick smudged across her blouse. She turned to the rest of us—Honestly, I don't even think Nora ever felt it. I think she was faking it the whole time.

And then we noticed, on Damian's laptop screen, the live television feed of Nora pushing past reporters at the end of the driveway. Damian unmuted his computer, and we watched as they descended on her with questions.

Someone has finally emerged from the house. Let's just—ma'am?

How many are in the house?

Ma'am, what's your name?

How many are inside?

Were you a hostage?

Jo exhaled beside me, shaking her head at the screen.

My god, Mia murmured.

What's happening inside? asked one of the reporters. Can you describe the situation?

Are you a member of a sex cult?

Nora looked dazed—What?

Emily looked up from the screen at the rest of us with horror. Did he just say—?

No. No, no, Nora said, shaking her head, and doing her best to push her way through the crush.

Is it a sex cult, ma'am?

Ma'am, who's inside?

Jo just continued to shake her head—Wow.

Did he say a 'sex cult'? Emily asked.

Where the fuck did they get that from? Damian muttered into his fist. Though the moment I heard those two words, I knew exactly who had formulated them, and said them to the press. My heart felt like a time lapse of a rotting orange, mouldering and imploding.

Who are they? asked another reporter.

What does that even mean? Emily asked, searching our faces.

Can you give us names? asked a reporter.

They are my neighbours, Nora said, looking into the camera, her mascara smeared. They are good people.

And so it begins, Howard said, to himself.

As Nora disappeared from frame, a reporter stepped back in front of the camera. So as you just saw, we're still not sure who that woman was, but she seems to be either a member of the Sequoia Crescent Cult, or possibly someone being held hostage by them. What we do know so far is that seventeen-year-old Kyle Francis—at the mention of Kyle's name, his yearbook photo appeared on-screen—a recent graduate of F. G. Saunders High School, is inside the house at this moment, allegedly being held against his will. Also inside the house is his former English teacher Claire Devon—a somewhat blurry close-up of my face in the group photograph of the school's teachers appeared on-screen—who was fired earlier this year after it emerged—

Leslie slammed the laptop shut—I can't.

Thank you, Howard said.

Shawn pointed to Leslie and Jo—That was fucked up.

She betrayed us, Leslie fired back. We're family.

People can come and go as they choose, he said, raising his voice overtop of hers. If someone—

You don't choose your family, Leslie countered. You don't leave your family when the going gets tough.

If they're abusing you?

Abuse? Jo seemed almost impaled by the word. Who was abusing anyone?

I'm just saying—

We shared the most intimate part of ourselves with her.

If someone wants to go—

If someone wants to go they should do it now, Leslie said, pointing at the door, because let me tell you the going's about to get a lot tougher. So bail now if you're going to bail.

She paused dramatically and looked around the room—Anyone?

Jo looked over at me and frowned—Claire, do you have something to say?

I felt like I had stumbled unwittingly into the line of fire—No.

It looks like you do.

I—

Kyle looked at me with concern—Are you okay?

I was confused by their attention, until I realized my mouth was opening and closing, like a fish, and I was shaking, slightly. I suddenly felt like I might collapse. But I told them no, I was fine, really. I just wanted them to stop looking at me.

We're all a little shaken I think, Emily said, trying to dispel the tension.

Howard gestured to the closed laptop—This could undermine everything we've been working for.

Leslie nodded, still fuming—Everything.

They're going to move in, Damian said. There's no way out of it.

Jo said it wasn't helpful to catastrophize.

Howard pointed to the window—Jo, there's a live news broadcast outside our house right now.

Yes, I just watched it, I'm aware.

They're calling us a sex cult.

She raised and dropped her arms—Yup.

I would say this is pretty catastrophic.

What did you expect? she asked, leaning in towards him.

Well—

She turned to the rest of us—What we are doing is historic. Of course there're going to be news cameras. And misinformation, and fear-mongering, and discrediting. We knew that.

But what are we? Emily asked. Really? We can say that we're not this or that, but what are we?

Leslie asked her if it mattered, and Emily said yes, she thought very much. Even just for ourselves.

I'm not sure I feel the need to, Howard said.

Then people will name it for us, they can't help it.

It scares them if they can't, Jo said.

Shawn seemed to consider Emily's point for a moment—We're a—like—

A cell, Damian said.

A what? Mia asked.

You know, like a—

That makes us sound like terrorists, Shawn said.

Leslie said she also didn't feel the need to define what we were.

We're just neighbours, Kyle offered. Like Nora said.

Neighbours who share a gift, Mia added.

A momentary lull fell over the group, and we listened to the din from outside. The hubbub of bodies, amassing. The squawk of walkie-talkies. Cars pulling up, doors opening, slamming. It felt like a siege. Like we should be pouring cauldrons of hot tar from the rooftop, or bracing the front door for a battering ram.

Jo looked around the room at each of us, slowly rose to her feet, and suggested we tune.

Damian looked perplexed—Now?

We need to hold on to why we're doing this.

Howard nodded, and Emily said she thought it was a good idea.

Surrounded by cops? Damian asked.

We need whatever power, and strength, and unity we can draw from it.

Damian removed his handgun and placed it on the coffee table again—Then I'm damn well putting this here.

Howard asked him please not to, but Damian wasn't having it.

Howard, if we're tuning with our eyes closed, surrounded by cops—

Listen—Howard cut in, but Jo placed a hand on his shoulder to tell him to drop it.

We will protect each other, Leslie said.

Damian gestured around the room—Don't think they aren't listening to us, right now.

Well let them, Jo said. We'll listen deeper.

She extended her arms and the group took this as their cue, moving down off their chairs into kneeling positions on the floor. They began to arrange themselves in a circle, when another voice came echoing over the loudspeaker.

Emily?

Emily's hand shot to her mouth.

Can you hear me?

This time it wasn't a police officer—it was Tom.

Oh Jesus, Mia said.

Emily, I'm uh . . . I'm on the road here, outside. If you can hear me, please come to the window.

Leslie looked pointedly at Emily—Don't.

Emily nodded, but I could tell she was wrenched.

Everyone in a circle, Jo said.

I love you, sugar. And I'm scared for you.

Howard implored Emily to ignore him—They're baiting you. You have to be strong.

Please come to the window.

Emily rose from her chair—Maybe I should just—

She was greeted by a chorus of nos from Leslie, Jo, and Damian. She hesitated, and then made for the window, but Damian grabbed her and she yelped, breaking down in tears.

Lash yourselves to the sails, Howard said.

Kyle, kneeling, looked back and noticed that I was still sitting on the couch. He leaned over and, in a whisper, asked if I was okay. I told him that I didn't know if I was ready to tune again. I was worried I wasn't in the right state. But things were happening faster than I could register. The circle was ready and waiting.

You're not in trouble, Em. The police just want to make sure you're okay. We're all worried about you.

Claire, what's wrong? Jo asked me, putting her arm around my shoulders.

I know you can hear me. Please don't—don't do this to me.

I'm worried I'm not strong enough, I told Jo.

Just walk out that door and walk into my arms and I can drive you home, okay?

Strong enough for what? Jo asked.

And we can put all of this behind us.

Strong enough for what, Claire? she asked me again.

Of course you're strong enough, Leslie said from the floor.

What if I never come out? I asked.

Jo looked confused—You mean of the house?

I looked over at Emily. She was composing herself, wiping her eyes dry, and hugging Damian back, thanking him for restraining her. Howard, kneeling alongside Shawn and Mia, gestured over to me—Come on, Claire.

I want you to take a deep breath, okay? Jo said, looking into my eyes. I nodded, and inhaled, like an obedient child. That's it, Jo said. Good. Now, come down onto the floor with us. I think everything will feel clear and centred again once we begin tuning.

Not knowing what other option I had, I slid down off the couch and joined the circle.

Okay, Jo said, looking at each of us. We're all here. We're all present. I know we're all in a very heightened state at the moment, but we can channel that intensity. Okay? I want everyone to focus. With every ounce of energy you have in your bodies. Let every other sound fall away. Welcome The Hum in. Let it penetrate you. Let it fill you.

We closed our eyes and, gradually, The Hum began to emerge from us, moving through us, using our bodies as its conduit.

Let it replace you, Jo said. Atom by atom. Until you are nothing but the frequency of the Earth.

I could see the blue and red strobing light through my eyelids. The room was throbbing. The Hum built in intensity, until the room and our bodies grew hot, until another police officer's voice came over the loudspeaker—*You have five minutes to exit the premises through the front door in a calm and orderly fashion.* And then he repeated himself, his voice crackling through the night. But we could not hear, not above our own raised voices, groaning, wailing, on the verge of becoming and coming apart, fevered and unbounded, thrashing, writhing, possessed, deeper through time, deeper through sound, deeper into flesh, sound into flesh, flesh into light, tearing at myself, tearing through time, tearing our clothes off, knocking over furniture, toppling over tables, lamps, vases—

Claire?

I could hear Jo's voice.

Claire! Kyle shouted, trying to grab at me but I wasn't there, I was shrieking, naked and unfurled into the sound, lashing like a flag on a mast in a hurricane, voices, the voices of the others in alarm—

What's happening?

I don't know.

Oh my god.

And me, my own voice—I can't get ahhhhhhh ugh—

Just—*steady* her.

I'm broken, I heard myself—Broken. Broken.

Broken?

Claire, look at me.

Broken through and it's p-p-p-p-p-p-pouring into my a a a ahhhhhh—

What's—?

Claire, stay with me. Look at me. Look at my eyes. Listen to my voice. Stay in the room.

Have you seen this before?

No, I don't—

What's happening?

Stay with me, Claire. Listen to my voice, hold on to my voice.

Convulsing on the ground now. Paroxysms. Pppppp—

Oh fuck.

Someone do something!

Do what?

Oh my god.

She's having a seizure.

No, she's not.

Maybe she broke through.

Broke through what?

Give me the blanket—Mia's voice.

Blanket?

Just—

Leslie grabbed a blanket from the couch and tossed it to Mia, who wrapped me up in it like a baby, and tried to calm me, shushing and whispering into my ears as I shook, sweating, lolling, lllllahhhhh—

Keep her tongue out of her throat.

It's okay, Mia said. I've got you.

Kyle told them I was afraid I might fall in and never come out.

Fall in?

I've got you, Claire, it's okay, it's—

Butbutbutbut I broke free from Mia's grasp, the blanket, tearing, tearing what was left of my clothes, The Hum tearing through me, flag on a mast, vicious—

Claire—

Somebody—

What's she doing?

She's overheating.

Get her some water.

Why's she making that noise?

Dear god.

Ygghhhh dear god ugh gaaaauuuuuuuuggghhh—

Water!

Shawn ran to the kitchen.

Someone said—Claire, please.

Just grab the jug from the fridge!

Naked. Winds of time, of sound, on the mast. Shawn re-entered at a jog with a jug of water, plastic, see-through, condensation; he handed it to Jo, who poured it over me, just doused me with the ice water.

Holy shit.

Sputtering, gasping. Jo clapped her hands loudly in my face.

Come back to us, Claire!

Ahhhhhhlll of me—in—

Yes.

Come on.

Trying to form words. Making shapes with my lips, tongue—

That's it.

I think she can hear you.

Aahhhhcckk—couldn't do it.

What is it, love?—Emily's voice.

Back up, give her space.

Claire?

K—I said.

It's me. It's Kyle, said Kyle's voice.

K—K—Coming—to—

Come back to me, Claire. Come back. Come back to me.

His hands on my face but I was wailing, embarrassing, why, hands on my face, I, I, I, gotta go gotta get out out of here my skin this room this house this life this sound this sound is too much, all too much, I ran, ran to the front door—Claire! Grab her! Oh fuck fuck fuck—I ran to the front door, unlocked it, and I was out, outside on the front step, the front walk, dazzled by the glare of cameras, police lights, iPhones, gasps, naked, and drenched and shivering from the fridge water, my breasts, my mind, I stumbled a few steps, news cameras, reporters, everyone drawing closer, where's Ashley? I couldn't see through the lights, the crowd, I was shaking, I was the sound. I had become. I opened my mouth. I opened my mouth to speak and I said—There has been a revelation!

And at that moment, Howard and Jo grabbed me from behind, and hauled me backwards, back inside, through the door, and slammed and locked it behind them.

Howard's face in mine—What are you doing?

Claire, are you there?

I was everywhere.

What happened, Claire? Talk to us.

I tried to say more but the words crowded my mouth. Howard took hold of my face by my chin, firm, and gave me a little shake, stop that Jo said, I batted away his hand, and stumbled back, don't touch her, stumbled back and steadied myself. I looked at Jo. And I saw her.

I saw Jo. And I was back.

I was back in the room. I tried to catch my breath. Going to vomit. No. I saw the others. I saw them watching me, afraid. I blinked and I turned to Jo. I turned to Jo and I said—I was you.

I turned to the others and I said—I was all of you. I was the floor. The house. Inside of the refrigerator. The mustard. The eggs. The tree back there, and the worms below, pushing my face through the dirt of, of life of being in the fucking life of it all, my god oh my god, I can't even begin, I didn't begin or end, I had no ending, I was everything—infinite, distant stars, buildings, sky-scrapers and the birds—I clapped—smashing into them.

I turned to Kyle, his face full of fear—You. I was you. Making love to your wife, I was your wife twenty years from now, and your shit in the toilet, your child, your grandchild, jumping into the pool, the water in the pool. There was—I can't even, I don't even know what era I'm talking, am I talking? I guess I am, now. I'm here, back in my—Wait. Did I? Where's Ashley? What time is it? The thing is—there is no thing, everything is the thing, is indistinguishable, just atoms moving, changing places, all of it the same, same thing, and um—the thing, the thing I was going to say, oh I wasn't afraid of death! What is it? It wasn't—death isn't, it doesn't happen, everything just changes places, it's all the same, don't worry about it. Family. Doesn't matter. The people you love. Doesn't really matter either because it's all just, you, me, strang-ers, the bus, it's all just atoms changing places, over time, coming together and apart. Horrible, in some ways, right?

Kyle reached out and touched my shoulder—Claire.

What is a body? What is this? I asked, putting my hands on the coffee table.

It's a table, Kyle replied.

But what is it? I asked, desperate. I was this. Thing. What is sound? Just space in between. I was sound. What is that? A voice? I heard your voice. I heard your voice in time. In space. There was a moment. I wanted to. I thought I was gone. Forever. I thought I was, replaced by sound, rearranged, forever. But okay. I was okay with it. I was not afraid. I heard your voice, and I was not afraid. For the first time.

I looked Kyle in the eyes—I heard your voice. And I knew who I was.

The Hum suddenly spiked, deafening, and the front door blasted open, and in poured officers in tactical gear, three, four, and the crash of the back patio doors being smashed open. Damian dived, grabbed his gun on the coffee table, and raised it. As he did, an officer opened fire, hitting both him and Kyle. They fell to the ground. Like punching bags cut from their chains. All of this in a matter of three seconds, but in slow motion. Shattered glass everywhere, how? Damian, wounded, fired back, hitting the police officer. Two other officers opened fire, striking Damian three times in the chest. All of this in another four seconds. Kyle was not moving. I was on the floor, holding him. Somewhere someone was screaming. I was clinging to Kyle. Warm and wet in my hands. Clinging to him like he was my boy. But he was not clinging back.

18

ONE MID-WINTER DAWN, HE APPEARED ON THE EDGE OF
the clearing. His white-tipped ears twitched and flicked as he
glanced about. Faint wisps of breath curled from his snout in
the cold. He lowered his head and stalked gingerly across the
frost-limned grass to sniff the remains of a collapsed orange tent.
Strewn about nearby were a portable propane stove, and two spent
propane canisters. A sodden blanket. Two ripped pillows disgorg-
ing foam. And what remained of a smashed portable CD player.

19

I GOOGLED:

Can you die from grief?

Can you die from wishing it?

Can you die from a nightmare?

Does crying burn calories?

What happens if you die alone in a house?

How long does it take for a body to smell?

What was the longest time it took to discover the body of a person living alone?

Is time linear?

20

I WASN'T INVITED TO KYLE'S FUNERAL. NOT THAT I EXPECTED
to be. I wasn't invited to Damian's either. Charges were brought
forward but eventually dropped. Brenda threatened a civil suit,
but to this day, nothing has come of it. I spent three weeks in a
mental health unit. Paul visited every day. Ashley went away to
university. Then I was discharged, back into my solitude. Months
slipped by. I stopped tuning. I forgot how to. I wasn't even sure if
it was possible for one person to do so alone. The Hum persisted.
It lost any sense of wonder or joy or meaning for me. It was no
longer a mystery to be approached. It simply became a noise again.
Something to torment my waking hours, hours upon hours which,
for some reason, I had been granted, and a boy I once loved had
been denied. I had a vision of this great ache extending from my
chest in all directions like an invisible parachute, extending even
beyond the walls of my house, like a football field, or an airport
tarmac, just an ever-expanding expanse of sadness.

One winter afternoon I lay on the living room couch, drifting in and out of sleep, with the news playing on the television for a bit of company. I had sworn off the news for a long while. For months, actually. As long as it took for me not to be the news. But that afternoon, as I lay there, I caught fragments of the same local broadcast recycled throughout the day, the leading story of which was about The Hum.

—when, last Thursday, an independent investigation commissioned by the city determined a compressor station along the Phoenix Access pipeline as the source of the mysterious hum disturbing a handful of nearby residents over the past year—

—this morning, after several days of silence, though not the kind residents had been hoping for, Southwestern Gas announced they would be reducing the flow along the pipeline with the hopes of—

—a spokesperson from Southwestern Gas—

—Southwestern Gas confirmed the company increased the flow along the Phoenix Access pipeline as much as thirty percent in the fall of 2018. The company believes this additional pressure may have caused vibrations which—

—migraines, nosebleeds, insomnia—

—a kind of localized mania, leading to the fatal standoff between police and members of the Sequoia Crescent Cult last June—

For days, news anchors, experts, and spokespeople had been peddling a municipal report which attributed The Hum to a natural gas pipeline that ran through the desert some two miles from our neighbourhood. The official story was that Southwestern Gas had increased the flow along the pipeline the previous fall, around the time most of us first began to hear the sound, when the vibration from this increased flow had supposedly caused the foundations of buildings to rattle. All I could do was laugh. Did

they really expect us to believe that everything we had endured—
the headaches, the nosebleeds, the rapture, the raid, the deaths—
was because of a pipeline? Did they really expect me to believe
Kyle was struck by a bullet in his pelvis, and another in his neck,
because of increased pressure along a natural gas pipeline? It was
so achingly banal as to be almost believable. It didn't matter if I
did believe it, or if anyone did, really. I understood the function it
served. Sometimes people need a myth to rally around, especially
after a collective trauma. We were a neighbourhood, and a city, in
need of closure.

Around a quarter past midnight I woke to the sound of Emily's voice on the television. The screen was the only light on in
the house. Emily's face was large, in close-up. The camera cut to a
wider shot, revealing her sitting beside Tom, in the studio. He was
wearing a nicely pressed shirt. There was a daytime view of the
city behind them; it must have been a rerun of an interview from
earlier in the day. I sat upright and watched.

It was like . . . waking up from a nightmare. It felt like I had lost
a year of my life, Emily said.

We were two strangers in the same house, Tom said. Well,
before you started living with your sister, he said, glancing sidelong
at Emily.

Do you still hear the hum? the interviewer asked her. Now that
Southwestern Gas has lowered the pressure?

No, she said, shaking her head. I don't.

Who do you blame for the deaths of Kyle Francis and Damian
Barnes? Do you blame anyone?

I swallowed and closed my eyes, waiting for Emily's reply.
When it didn't come, I opened my eyes again, and saw her staring
down into her lap. Finally, she looked back up at the interviewer,
her eyes glistening. As she opened her mouth, I reached for the
remote and turned off the television.

Months ago, when I was not there, Kyle stepped inside my house, and sat on my bed, and spoke to my daughter, and walked around my bedroom, and fell asleep on the couch in my living room. He had been just one teenage body among dozens that night. And yet, somehow, his scent still lingered. In closets, in cupboards, in the corners of rooms. Sometimes it was enough to make me lean against a countertop and close my eyes. Whenever I drove past the park, I imagined the ruins of his tent hidden somewhere in the brush. I would lie in bed some nights thinking about how easy it would be to get up, put on my shoes, and walk the six blocks through the darkness, through the overgrowth, and to crouch down amongst his things, his old records and books, and whatever remained, but I could never bring myself to do it. It was like a scream at night which no one goes to investigate.

I did stop hearing The Hum eventually, though I was still hearing it days after they had officially decreased the pressure in the pipeline. It stayed with me like a phantom limb—three days, six days, nine days after, albeit fainter and fainter, until eventually, I woke up one morning, and it was gone. I lay in bed, listening to the birds out my window. I focused and strained in the hope of hearing any trace of it in the background, the faintest vibration, but I couldn't. It felt a little disorienting, at first. Like the world was missing the colour yellow, or the taste of salt. There was some register of experience I could no longer access. Though gradually I became accustomed to its absence, as we do with all things we lose.

I started sleeping again. I started setting my alarm in the morning again. I started jogging, and flossing, and checking my emails again. I erased the hour of vile messages from strangers on my voicemail. I started making the bed. I started buying raspberries and tulips. I started listening to podcasts about astronomy, urban planning, the Black Death, the history of medicine, gay conversion therapy, bees, the Harlem Renaissance, paganism, Dolly Parton.

I started making meals with more than three constituent ingre-
dients. I started smiling at my neighbours. I started talking to
Paul—civil and amicable check-ins at first, and then longer and
more involved conversations about current events, our days, about
the ways in which we had hurt one another, and the ways in which
we might find our way back to loving each other in the way we
once had.

And then one morning the doorbell rang. I bolted upright in
bed, and grabbed my phone off the side table—five past nine. Shit.
I pulled on my bathrobe, pushed my hair up into a messy bun, and
dashed downstairs as the doorbell rang again. I opened the door to
find Paul standing there with a box of his things at his feet.

Morning, he said.

Hey. Sorry. My alarm didn't go off.

Don't worry, Ash and I can take care of this round.

I looked out beyond him to the driveway. Ashley was busy
unloading boxes from the trunk of his car. I told him that, if I
jumped in the shower now, I'd be ready for the second load.

You're not having second thoughts, are you? he asked.

What? No, of course not.

You seem subdued.

I'm sorry, I literally just woke up.

He nodded, then picked up his box, and walked into the house.
I admitted to him that I was up late.

Doing what?

I let out a little self-conscious laugh. I uh—finally finished *The
Magic Mountain*, I said.

It took him a moment to register what I'd said, before he
laughed as well.

I know, I said. It took me a while.

Longer than it took to write, probably.

He put the box down by the foot of the staircase.

Well I took a big break from it, I said.

So you thought you'd binge it last night? he asked.

Ashley walked through the front door carrying a large box.

Hey, she said, looking over at me. Sorry I haven't called you back.

She dropped the box with a thud—It's midterms.

I told her that I knew, and not to worry—You're looking good.

Yeah right. Freshman twenty-five.

No.

Whatever, I'm still getting laid, she said, walking into the living room and pulling open the curtains. But Mom, honestly, stop with this Miss Havisham bullshit and open your curtains.

I do! Give me a break, I just woke up!

She disappeared into the kitchen, while Paul leafed through the mail on the dining room table. He held up a stack I had set aside for him—Look, even with the mail redirect.

It's all junk though, I said.

I asked him if he would like some coffee, but he declined—I'd like to just get everything unpacked first.

Ashley walked back into the living room holding a glass of orange juice, and remarked on the lasagne in the fridge.

I made it for tonight, I said. To celebrate.

Aw, she replied mawkishly, but Paul seemed pleased. I asked her if she was planning on staying the night.

I'll see how I feel. I might crash with Yona.

Well I've made up your bed, if you decide to.

All right.

Paul walked back out the door to continue unpacking the car, leaving Ashley and me alone for the first time in months.

I'm glad you've been liking your classes, I said.

A bit less now.

Oh?

She shrugged.

Your art history professor sounds fun.

Yeah, he's okay, she said, nodding, before taking a swig of juice. So, do you still blame yourself?

I was completely caught off guard by her question. What?

About Kyle.

I—Yes. Obviously. Of course I do.

She looked at me for a moment, inscrutably. Well I don't, she said.

Thank you.

But everyone else does.

I swallowed, and nodded.

And so, by extension, everyone blames me, she said. I tried to formulate some words of comfort or consolation, but everything that came to mind felt so profoundly insufficient and trite as to be almost comical. She raised her eyebrows and took another sip of juice, in silent rebuke. Paul returned with a box, thumped it down, and left to retrieve more.

I sometimes wonder what he would be studying now, she said.

I admitted that sometimes I thought the same thing.

English, probably.

I nodded. Probably.

You ever try to talk to him? she asked.

What?

Do you guys ever talk?

No. What do you mean? How would we—?

Well I don't know, you've believed in weirder shit in the past.

No, I said. We don't.

Hmm, she said, and took another sip. Dad told me you don't believe the city's report.

I sighed. She was angling for a fight. I guess I shouldn't have been surprised. She left for university when I was still in hospital. A few emails and a few phone calls weren't going to sweep away

the unexploded land mines. I knew she wanted me to capitu-
late, but I wasn't going to. Ash, what I heard was not a pipeline,
I said.

She slammed her glass down on the coffee table—The whole
fucking world accepts it was but you. Even your old posse. They've
pretty much all given interviews, haven't they? They've all dis-
owned Howard.

Not everyone.

Even Jo.

What else could she do?

What are you even—? Ashley threw her hands up, and landed
them on her head. She then held her head as if it were about to
explode with frustration. Even now, she said. I bet you secretly
think you still hear it.

I don't.

So why can't you just admit it? They increased the pressure on
the pipeline, it caused vibrations, the vibrations caused The Hum.
They decreased the pressure, The Hum went away. I mean what
more do you want, the hand of God to write it in the sky for you?

A pipeline two miles away, I said.

Yes. And they fixed it, she said, eyes widening. They objectively
did, Mom, it's not up for fucking debate.

Okay.

So you either hear it or you don't.

I don't, I told you.

Because they fixed it.

I nodded, noncommittally. Except I could still hear it for days
after they lowered the pressure, I said.

I bet you even still feel bad for Howard, she said.

He's not the villain he's being made out to be.

She ran her hands over her face in frustration—Mom, he brainwashed you and held you hostage.

No one was held hostage.

The nation watched you run out of that house naked and get pulled back inside.

Yes, but—

That Nora woman was tackled to the floor when she tried to escape.

I told Ashley that it was hard for her, or for anyone else who wasn't inside that house, to understand.

This class action lawsuit against Howard, she continued. The only reason all his old students didn't come forward sooner is because they were brainwashed. Just like you. And probably traumatized and terrified.

Ash, listen—

No, you listen, Mom. You had a complete psychotic breakdown. The whole world saw. It was on live television. You're a fucking meme. Tits and vagina and everything. Do you have any idea— Don't even. I—

She took a deep breath, closed her eyes for a long moment, and then looked at me—I would be so furious at you, about what you've done to me, if it wasn't for the fact that mostly I feel sorry for you. You were sick. And you probably still are. A sick—

Ash—

No, shut up and listen to me. Even now, you can't even admit it. You were under insane emotional stress, chronically under-slept for months, susceptible to brainwashing and-and God knows what else. You were not yourself.

Paul entered, dropped another box, glanced up at us, but knew better than to say anything. Ashley watched him walk back out through the door, before saying—He thinks everything can just go back to normal.

Well I hope it can, I said.

Really?

Yes.

She narrowed her eyes—I don't even think you're happy that it's gone.

I told her that of course I was. I have my life back, I said.

What life?

Don't be cruel.

What is it that you want back?

Just—

The quiet?

Yes.

Kyle?

I looked down at the floor.

I don't think you've even accepted that you lost your mind, she said. She then fell quiet, perhaps waiting for me to incriminate myself somehow. What more did she want from me? My name was cleared. Charges were dropped. I had no contact with any of the other Hummers. I was working on my mental health, getting my sleep, taking my medication. Did she want me to beg for forgiveness? To grovel? To eat dust?

I lost everything else, I said.

She nodded, and looked around the living room, as if it were the inside of my mind.

I love you. But I can't help you. She said this like a doctor conveying a fatal prognosis. And I gotta protect myself.

I wanted to hug her, but I couldn't move. I wanted to cry, but I couldn't manage to do that either. I think you should go have your shower, she said.

I brushed my hair out of my eyes and whispered yeah.

I could hear Paul reappearing through the front door, struggling with a large box, but neither Ashley nor I paid him any attention. As she looked at me I wondered—did she not see how far I had come? How hard I had worked to claw my life back? Was she just going to write me off, then, because I wasn't ready to adopt her version of events? I wanted to tell her—I am trying my best, Ash, every single day, to forget what I felt, what I heard, what I experienced, and live a normal life again. As Paul walked back outside, Ashley started for the door as well, but then hesitated. She stood there for a moment, then turned back to me, and gave me a hug. It took me completely by surprise. It was tentative at first, but then strengthened, until she was squeezing me with an almost aching intensity, and I was doing the same. Her hair was in my mouth. I felt the moisture of her face on my neck. The heat of our bodies pressed together. She pulled away and flashed me a look. A look that said—there is love. There is still love. And then she walked out, leaving me alone in the living room.

Paul returned after a minute and dropped another box down in the front hallway.

That's the first carload, he said, straightening up. I'll be back with the rest in forty.

I promised I would be ready to help on his return and tightened the sash around my bathrobe as I crossed towards him.

You better, he said, with mock seriousness. His armpits were damp. I could smell his aftershave.

It's good to have you back, I said.

A slightly wistful look passed over his face. Hopefully, he said.

And then, for some reason, I chose that moment to remind him that I had therapy in the morning. He told me that he already knew that. And we have ours together on Tuesday, he said.

Sorry, I forgot we went over this. I also have an interview with the library on Monday, did I tell you that?

Oh good. No, you didn't.

I told him that I wasn't holding my breath. I suspected too many staff probably knew of me there. But I figured it was good to start getting myself back out there and looking. He suggested we talk more about it after he got back.

For sure, sorry, I said, batting the admin away with my hand.

He smiled at me—Hey, Little Bear.

Hey.

For a moment I wondered if we were going to kiss. Maybe just a peck on the cheek. Or even a hug. But as we stood there in front of each other it became clear that we were not ready for either. We probably wouldn't be for some time.

Okay, he said.

I'll be a whole new me when you get back, I said.

Please don't be, he replied. I smiled. He then turned, and walked out the door. And I watched as he climbed into his car, the car that would soon be our car again, taking us to the supermarket, and appointments, and to visit Ashley on campus. Ashley sat in the front seat, waiting to go. I watched Paul knowing that, good to his word, he would be back in forty minutes with more boxes containing his things, which would soon merge back into the collective holdings of our house, and become indistinguishable again from my things. I watched as they pulled out of the driveway, and drove off down the street, before closing the front door, and returning to the silence of the house. Though of course it was not silence. I could hear the wind rustling the leaves outside. The purr of the refrigerator in the kitchen. The ambient thrum of the air conditioning as it passed through the ducts. My empty stomach made a sound like a motorcycle on the highway at a distance. I should make myself some toast, I thought.

I then remembered, with amusement, the look on Paul's face when I told him that I had finished *The Magic Mountain*, and it occurred to me that I actually had no clear memory of the book's final lines or images, and suspected that I may have fallen asleep before the actual end. I reached into the pocket of my bathrobe, and pulled out my phone. I found *The Magic Mountain* in my audiobooks, and scrolled to the end. I connected the phone to the Bluetooth speaker in the dining room and pressed play.

Adventures of the flesh and in the spirit, while enhancing thy simplicity, granted thee to know in the spirit what in the flesh thou scarcely couldst have done.

The narrator's voice, as familiar to me now as an uncle's voice or an ex-lover's, filled the room. I leaned back against the dining table, and told Google to turn the volume up by two.

Moments there were, when out of death, and the rebellion of the flesh, there came to thee, as thou tookest stock of thyself, a dream of love. Out of this universal feast of death, out of this extremity of fever, kindling the rain-washed evening sky to a fiery glow, may it be that Love one day shall mount? And then, after a dramatic pause, the narrator concluded with *Finis Operis.*

I continued to lean against the table, the lines resounding in my head.

Out of this universal feast of death—may it be that Love one day shall mount?

I knew these words. Perhaps they had entered me after all, as I slept. I imagined, for a moment, Kyle's eyes arriving at those final words, like summiting a mountain, and wondered what had passed through his mind as they did. And then the lines disappeared, the book, the mountain, and I was left with only his eyes. And then those too, I put aside.

Before I make my toast, I will have a shower, I decided. And I will put my hair up in the way Paul likes, and I will get dressed in something nice. Maybe my green turtleneck. As I crossed through the living room, the morning light filled the house and, like a prism, I saw the life I had lived within its walls refracted back to me in a thousand different shades. Ashley will stay for dinner tonight. I felt it in my heart. Tonight I will eat lasagne with my family. And tomorrow, Paul will cook us waffles. We will spread the Sunday paper out over the kitchen table, the radio playing in the kitchen, Ashley on her phone, the three of us sharing space, sharing time.

I reached the staircase, put my hand on the wooden banister, and made it up to the fourth step—when I stopped.

I heard something.

Not the leaves, or the fridge, or the air conditioning, or my stomach. I held my breath and stood very still. I brought my hands slowly to my ears and covered them. I pressed my hands hard against my head, and created a seal with my sweaty palms against the sides of my face, a vacuum of silence—and then lifted them off. It was there. It was not in my head. Much fainter than before, but unmistakable. I gripped the banister. I felt as if my knees might give out. I thought I had made such progress. Maybe I had only willed myself not to hear it. Maybe it was easier to believe it was gone. What if it was there all along, below it all, and never left me? What if it never would?

I began to laugh. Or was I crying? I was overcome—but with what? Relief? Terror? How was it possible I did not know? But I did not. I did not know.

There was so much I never did know.

POSTSCRIPT

I CANNOT SPEAK TO THE SEXUAL ASSAULT ALLEGATIONS
that have been levelled against Howard by several former students
of his at Virginia Tech, in part because, at the time of writing this,
the matter is still before the courts, and also because it feels too
painful for me to wade into. I have chosen, for my own mental
health, not to apprise myself too closely of the details of the case.
I was not aware of these allegations at the time of my association with Howard, as they emerged in the wake of the tragedy
on Sequoia Crescent and the attendant media scrutiny. What I
will say is that it takes immense courage for anyone to step forward with experiences of sexual assault, and I would not want,
for a moment, to dismiss or diminish these women's allegations. I
cannot help but feel an immediate and profound sense of solidar-
ity with them. It is for their sake that I have felt most conflicted
about writing this book, as I would hate to be seen as an apologist
for Howard's previous actions, whatever those might have been.

I have done my very best to represent my experience of events as faithfully as possible, without letting subsequent developments or revelations colour my account. The media's portrayal of Howard as a Svengali ringleader doesn't, for instance, accord with my recollection of events, but then I have been made to second-guess so much of my experience of those months, given the state I was in. Ashley and Paul have suggested that the way I have portrayed Howard and Jo in this book is only evidence of the efficacy of their manipulation of me. If Nora or Emily or Shawn, or any of the other members of our group, wrote their own account of The Hum and Sequoia Crescent, they might have a very different take to offer. I hope, in time, they find the strength and resolve to do so.

My life has returned to some semblance of normalcy. Paul and I have settled back into familiar routines. Ashley is entering her second year of university. I have lost touch with virtually all my friends from before, but I have made a few new ones. I have a steady job that satisfies me. I have grown quite accustomed to this new-found quietude, and the thought of the renewed media interest in, and scrutiny of, my story that this book will prompt has caused me some anxiety. Nevertheless, I feel the potential benefit, to myself and hopefully to others, of telling my story outweighs the drawbacks. Inevitably the question everyone wants to ask me is whether I still hear The Hum. I have found the easiest answer is no.

ACKNOWLEDGEMENTS

The text from Thomas Mann's *The Magic Mountain* is from H. T. Lowe-Porter's 1927 translation, as printed in the 1999 Vintage Classics edition. Simone Weil's quote comes from Arthur Willis's 1952 translation of Weil's *Gravity & Grace*, as printed in the 1997 Bison Books edition.

I would like to express my profound appreciation to Jennifer Lambert and Noelle Zitzer at HarperCollins Canada, and Nicholas Pearson at 4th Estate, for so skilfully midwifing this book into being; to Jane Finigan for seeing potential in me and this story, and pushing me to realize it; to Imogen Sarre and Elinor Burns for their wisdom and steadfastness; to Brian Lobel for his friendship, and for inspiring the character Shawn; to Deborah Pearson for lending this story her voice more than once; to Patrick Eakin Young and Alice Kentridge for providing a home away from home while writing; to Emily McLaughlin and the New Work Department at the National Theatre for nurturing an early version of this story; and to the Canada Council for the Arts for vital support in completing a first draft. I am grateful for all that public arts funding makes possible, and to live in a society in which it exists.

My enduring love and gratitude to my mother and father, my brother, and my grandmother. To my boyo, Alistair. And my extraordinary friends, especially Jennifer Warren, whose voice I hear throughout this novel.

Finally, and above all, I offer my heartfelt thanks to James, for sustaining me through every stage of this book, for reading draft after draft, and proffering so many insights. Thank you for always believing in this story and these characters. This book would not exist without you. And I would not be the writer, nor the person, I am without the years of love, wonder, and adventure we shared.